Jane and the Opera Dancer

Sarah J. Waldock

©Sarah J. Waldock 2019
All rights reserved, no copying of any portion of this book without permission, contact details under author biography.
ISBN 1484071980
ISBN-13 9781484071984

Dedication

Dedicated to Simon my husband for all his help, and to dear Merlin the cat who helped write the first half by rolling on the keyboard a lot, and whom I will never forget.
Many thanks to Adrian Howlett for his excellent help with regards to the history of hothouses and to Colleen who proof read each chapter as I wrote it.

Other books by Sarah Waldock

Sarah writes predominantly Regency Romances:

The Brandon Scandals Series
- The Hasty Proposal
- The Reprobate's Redemption
- The Advertised Bride
- The Wandering Widow
- The Braithwaite Letters
- Heiress in Hiding

The Charity School Series
- Elinor's Endowment
- Ophelia's Opportunity
- Abigail's Adventure
- Marianne's Misanthrope
- Emma's Education/Grace's Gift
- Anne's Achievement
- Daisy's Destiny
- Libby's Luck

Spinoffs:
The Moorwick Tales
- Fantasia on a House Party

Rookwood series
- The Unwilling Viscount
- The Enterprising Emigrée

The Seven Stepsisters series
Elizabeth [WIP]
Diana [WIP]
Minerva[WIP]
Flora [WIP]
Catherine [WIP]
Jane [WIP]
Anne [WIP]

One off Regencies
Vanities and Vexations [Jane Austen sequel]
Cousin Prudence [Jane Austen sequel]
Friends and Fortunes
None so Blind
Belles and Bucks [short stories]

The Georgian Gambles series
The Valiant Viscount [formerly The Pugilist Peer]
Ace of Schemes

Other
William Price and the 'Thrush', naval adventure and Jane Austen tribute
William Price sails North

100 years of Cat Days: 365 anecdotes

Sarah also writes historical mysteries

Regency period 'Jane, Bow Street Consultant 'series, a Jane Austen tribute
- Death of a Fop
- Jane and the Bow Street Runner [3 novellas]
- Jane and the Opera Dancer
- Jane and the Christmas Masquerades [2 novellas]
- Jane and the Hidden Hoard
- Jane and the Burning Question [short stories]
- Jane and the Sins of Society
- Jane and the Actresses
- Jane and the Careless Corpse [WIP]

Spinoffs:
The Armitage Chronicles

'Felicia and Robin' series set in the Renaissance
- Poison for a Poison Tongue
- The Mary Rose Mystery
- Died True Blue
- Frauds, Fools and Fairies
- The Bishop of Brangling
- The Hazard Chase
- Heretics, Hatreds and Histories
- The Midsummer Mysteries
- The Colour of Murder
- Falsehood most Foul
- The Monkshithe Mysteries
- Toll the Dead Man's bells
- Wells, Wool and Wickedness
- The Missing Hostage

Children's stories
  Tabitha Tabs the Farm kitten
  A School for Ordinary Princesses [sequel to Frances Hodgson Burnett's 'A Little Princess.]

The Royal Draxiers series
  Bess and the Dragons
  Bess and the Queen
  Bess and the Succession [wip]
  Bess and the Paying Scholars [wip]
  Bess and the Gunpowder Plot [wip]
  Bess and the Necromancer [wip]

Non-Fiction
  Writing Regency Romances by dice

Fantasy
  Falconburg Divided [book 1 of the Falconburg brothers series]
  Falconburg Rising [book 2 of the Falconburg brothers series, WIP]
  Falconburg Ascendant [book 3 of the Falconburg brothers series, WIP]

Scarlet Pimpernel spinoffs
　　The Redemption of Chauvelin

Other Baroness Orczy spinoffs
　　Lady Molly – Married

Sarah Waldock grew up in Suffolk and still resides there, in charge of a husband, and under the ownership of sundry cats. All Sarah's cats are rescue cats and many of them have special needs. They like to help her write and may be found engaging in such helpful pastimes as turning the screen display upside-down, or typing random messages in kittycode into her computer.

Sarah claims to be an artist who writes. Her degree is in art, and she got her best marks writing essays for it. She writes largely historical novels, in order to retain some hold on sanity in an increasingly insane world. There are some writers who claim to write because they have some control over their fictional worlds, but Sarah admits to being thoroughly bullied by her characters who do their own thing and often refuse to comply with her ideas. It makes life more interesting, and she enjoys the surprises they spring on her. Her characters' surprises are usually less messy [and much less noisy] than the surprises her cats spring.

Sarah has tried most of the crafts and avocations which she mentions in her books, on the principle that it is easier to write about what you know. She does not ride horses, since the Good Lord in his mercy saw fit to invent Gottleib Daimler to save her from that experience; and she has not tried blacksmithing. She would like to wave cheerily at anyone in any security services who wonder about middle aged women who read up about making gunpowder and poisonous plants.

Sarah would like to note that any typos remaining in the text after several betas, an editor and proofreader have been over it are caused by the well-known phenomenon of *cat-induced editing syndrome* from the help engendered by busy little bottoms on the keyboard.

This is her excuse and you are stuck with it.

And yes, there are two more cat bums on the edge of the picture as well as the 4 on her lap/chest

You may find out more about Sarah at her blog site, at:
http://sarahs-history-place.blogspot.co.uk/
Or on Facebook for advance news of writing
https://www.facebook.com/pages/Sarah-J-Waldock-Author/520919511296291

Chapter 1

Caleb Armitage always enjoyed watching his wife nursing her son, his stepson, before they ate their own breakfast in the little parlour that Mr and Mrs Weston had set aside for their use, but he was only paying scant attention this morning since he was frowning over a letter.

"This is the damndest thing," he said.

"What, my dear?" asked Jane, folding her bodice back into place and holding small Joseph up to wind him. "Sir Nathanial Conant wants you to cut short your leave?"

"No, though I should be back to work in the next few days," said Caleb. "No, it's from Chorleigh, Wright and Jekyll – why they feel they have to write to me, as though marriage has robbed you of the ability to manage your own affairs I don't know – but they received an offer to continue to rent the town house for the Little Season and took it upon their silly selves to accept in your name as 'obviously you would want the rents' as though I'm unable to keep you in anything but penury!" he added furiously.

"I think it's time to consider changing our business managers," said Jane. "So what are we to do? Our household is, I'm afraid, too large to consider squeezing into the three rooms of your little house, unless we spend all the rents we have accumulated to purchase somewhere else, either next to it to expand, or somewhere else entirely. We cannot presume on the hospitality of the Westons any longer and our honeymoon at Donwell is over."

"Mrs Armitage, it was a very fine honeymoon indeed," said Caleb, "I believe we became very well acquainted with most of the house and much of the grounds as we explored."

Jane flushed.

"Indeed I think we explored very thoroughly," she said, then became serious. "We shall have to consider deeply what to do; I had hoped to save the rent money but property is always an investment. Call Annie to take Joseph, I pray you, my love; we shall take breakfast and look at the papers and see what property there might be; and we will write to Mr John Knightley and ask him to put us in the way of another firm of solicitors. I find the high handed attitude of Messrs Chorleigh, Wright and Jekyll once again to be beyond the bounds of what is pleasing. And, if you please, Mr Armitage, you have not presented me with a matutinal salute."

Caleb, having called the nursemaid and handed over small Joseph, proceeded to make up for that with a thorough kissing that necessitated a slight delay to taking breakfast as both parties were somewhat mussed from the experience.

Jane turned to her own correspondence over breakfast and broke the wafer on a missive written with a feminine hand. She quickly scanned it for a signature.

"Oh, this is from Nessie – Agnes Fanshawe. She was at school with me, when Colonel Campbell so kindly paid for my education. She's a poor relation too, the last time I heard from her, she wrote that her cousin had offered her a position as a companion to his betrothed wife," she hesitated, "and a very hard position it was too, for she wrote that her Cousin Henry had determined to marry an Opera Dancer no less, and wanted her made into a lady."

Caleb whistled.

"Reckon she'd have her work cut out there, Jane-girl! What's wrong, she wants to run away and considers you a safe haven?"

"I don't know yet," said Jane, "the wretched woman has crossed and re-crossed her page and her hand is so agitated she might as well be writing that she needs safe haven indeed – yes, I fear Nessie is the sort to presume on an acquaintance to ask that sort of favour – or whether she reports that she has married a mulatto Pope. No, that cannot be it. Ah, I have it! it's not mulatto, it's murder. Some one has murdered Popham – her cousin Henry I believe – and she wants us to go immediately and do something about it."

"Strewth!" said Caleb. "Untangle a bit more, Jane-girl, and maybe it isn't murder any more than mulatto; but if it is I'll write to Sir Nathanial and ask if I can be officially assigned. I should think that asking you to help constitutes calling in Bow Street."

"It does," said Jane, "really, though quite willing to lean on others, Nessie is quite astute when she puts her mind to it. She has already written to 'whom it may concern' at Bow Street to ask that her friend's clever husband should be assigned… now how is it that she has heard of you?" Jane frowned at the closely-written crossed sheet. "Ah, I see, she spent some time as a companion to Julia Redmayne who wrote to her all about what happened in Yorkshire, silly indiscreet creature that she is, and Nessie put two and two together. It is to be hoped that the letter she has sent to Bow Street will be read by Sir Nathanial, who will at least have some inkling who might be meant by 'my friend Jane Fairfax's husband'. How lowering for you, my dear, merely to be my *caro sposo* as you might say," she chuckled at him.

Caleb grimaced.

"I pray you not to recall to mind that besom, Jane-of-my-heart or I may find pressing duties elsewhere!" he said. Jane leaned over to kiss him.

"I would do almost anything to avoid turning into Augusta Elton," she said. "Well if we are to stay with Nessie and investigate her murder it means we will not have to worry for a while at least about presuming on the hospitality of the Westons; if Nessie wants our aid she must deal with having our nursery as well and our staff, for I will not leave my babies and Simmy."

Caleb grinned.

"I wonder if she will think the cure worse than the sickness?" he said.

"Caleb, my love, surely you do not regret taking on a ready made family?" Jane fluttered her eyelashes at him.

Caleb picked her up and sat her on his lap.

"The ready made family, no. Sometimes I feel right slumguzzled by the appurtenances of a lady's children though – I never expected to have servants, Jane-girl, and I fear to be looked on as a posturing fool for travelling with so many."

Jane laughed.

"Three maids, a governess, your man, and a tutor for our son are not what most households would consider many, my love. Even Isabella Knightley, who prides herself on her frugality, descends upon Hartfield with no less than half a dozen nursery maids and her own maid to boot. John Knightley, like his brother, does very well without a man, but then Fowler is more your assistant than your man. It would be an imposition if we took your three villainous ex soldiers along."

Caleb laughed.

"Well they are happily employed still in uncovering a smuggling ring somewhere in rural Essex, the last I heard" he said. "Gabriel petitioned me to retain their services a while longer; Sir Nathanial is paying for them, so it's no skin off his nose and helpful to have extra men. Now what are we likely to need for this unlikely murder?"

Jane rose from the pleasantly distracting perch on her husband's knee and sat down again to peruse the letter with great care.

"Very well, as far as I can unravel this, Nessie and the Opera Dancer – who rejoices under the unlikely name of Floradora d'Ambrose and, according to Nessie, has letters from a friend written to her as a more believable Jemima Harris – were invited to a long weekend house party by Floradora's intended, Mr Henry

Popham, cousin to Nessie by some degree, and whom he asked to be the hostess in lieu of anyone more suitable. Lovely man, if he put it that way, he almost deserves to be murdered," she added.

"Would you choose Agnes Fanshawe to be a hostess?" asked Caleb.

"No, but there was no need to put it that way, if put it that way he did; which I have no reason to doubt, since Nessie holds – or held – him in some fearful awe for making her feel so much below him as to be insignificant."

"A proud man? one wonders that he would deign to marry an opera dancer then," said Caleb.

"Yes, it does seem strange," said Jane, "however, he appears to have been quite besotted by her. It seems as though he has done some financial backing of plays, Nessie says something about another backer being invited too. As well as sundry of Mr Popham's nephews, nieces or cousins. It was by way of a time to introduce his intended to the family, and no mention to be made of Flora's – Nessie calls her Flora – origins. So apparently the houseparty also includes Mr Popham's sister, her spouse and offspring, and a couple of cousins as well as this other man who knows Flora. It's a little difficult to read; Nessie has cried liberally onto the paper smudging it, really I cannot feel that she was fond enough of so proud a cousin to have such an outbreak of sensibility!"

Caleb held out a hand and Jane passed the letter over.

"I'd say myself," he opined, "her tears were more over the distinct disharmony of the household and their reactions to the news that the man they all appear to have expectations from was to be getting married. There's a garbled reference to twins and 'baiting Beau Popham' and complaints from Popham's sister that she should have been hostess; which leads to the thought that this was not a very pleasant house party at all."

Jane sighed.

"And to think I thought the Redmayne house party singularly fraught with friction!" she said. "Must it always be so with wealthy men who have not got clear heirs?"

"Considering what cases of sudden death I have seen, there need not be much wealth at all and there can be friction and jealousy even with a clear heir," said Caleb dryly.

"Ah well, at least I do not enter the situation with close friends; for I felt it incumbent upon me to support the Redmayne sisters as I felt such rapport with dear Euphelia," said Jane. "Nessie and I were never close, though she writes with the sort of cloying affection that would seem to suggest we went about with arms around each others' waists. It was an affection she was wont to assume when she was unable to return an essay in French and needed help," she added thoughtfully.

Caleb laughed.

"I wager it put you off helping her more than it encouraged you!" he said.

"Well, yes; but one couldn't help being sorry for her," said Jane. "If she had been pretty, her air of helplessness might have attracted some chivalrous male willing to immolate himself on the altar of fluttering butterfly airs and cherish her until he got bored enough to take a mistress."

"I wince," said Caleb. "Is she truly that hopeless?"

"No; but she does a very good impression of it," said Jane. "It got her out of all kinds of trouble at school. I – I wouldn't say she was precisely duplicitous but at times it came close. She learned not to play off her airs on me so we shall get a relatively straight story from her. One does wonder what sort of woman Mr Popham's sister must be though, if Nessie is by comparison a better hostess."

"Well no doubt we shall find out when we get to…" Caleb glanced back at the missive, "…Amberfield

Abbey. Impressive address; I wonder what his ancestor did for Henry VIII."

"Mr Knightley always claims that his ancestor was a pirate-in-chief in the king's fleet to get Donwell," laughed Jane, "which somehow I doubt. More than likely it was
bought and paid for ; and possibly not at the time of the dissolution. However, that is not to the point. Merely that we shall arrive too late to view the body and will have to work entirely with hearsay evidence."

"Be good experience for young Henry Redmayne then to review the same," said Caleb. "I doubt he's going to want to be left out; and he was a good helpmate before. Well, at least Miss Fanshawe has kept her head enough to tell us that he was stabbed in the neck with an ornamental dagger, a page separator which he also used to open letters with and that 'Flora had only added to the horror of the situation by reverting to Shakespeare'. I wonder just what Miss Fanshawe meant by that?"

"I suspect, since there is a superstition that you should neither quote from, nor directly mention, 'Macbeth' – the euphemism is to call it 'The Scottish Play' – that the silly wench said 'who would have thought the old man to have had so much blood in him', the comment by Lady Macbeth about King Duncan," said Jane, dryly.

"Well being an opera dancer I expect she's familiar with a lot of the plays," said Caleb, "it's one of the few I know! Tactless remark to make about her betrothed though."

"Judging from what Nessie has said, I suspect she took the chance to have a comfortable and easy life without anticipating reciprocating her lover's passions," said Jane, "and jumped at the chance to be a wife not a mistress."

"I won't say you're wrong, Jane girl," said Caleb, "and more we can find out when we arrive."

Chapter 2

Amberfield Abbey was a large and imposing building that owed little beyond its name to any monastic community, and Henry Redmayne remarked cynically to Caleb, Jane and Simmy that even the picturesque ruins in the grounds would likely be found to be no more than a folly built as a garden adjunct. Since there also appeared to be a 'rustic' bridge going nowhere and a Greek temple by the lake this seemed only too likely a prospect.

"Palladian, built in the last quarter century or I miss my guess," said Caleb of the house, "well I suppose one might expect modern conveniences if one might not have the pleasure of medieval ghosts."

"They might yet walk, disturbed by the destruction of their home by rude builders," said Simmy with relish.

"In my experience," said Jane serenely, "ghosts are the product of an over-active imagination and partaking of cheese and wine too late in the evening."

"Oh all the spirits come out of a bottle you mean, Jane!" said Henry gaily; he had taken to calling Jane and Caleb by their first names at their request; he being, as Jane said, quite one of the family and willing for Simmy to be informal with him.

Simmy laughed and Caleb and Jane chuckled.

"Rather harmless ghosts than phantom armies and dutch courage to attack them," said Caleb, dryly. "I saw a group of the South Essex find a tun of best brandy and we of the First Foot had to tackle them bodily, they were all for going and putting paid to Bonaparte himself whom they swore was in the local church. First time, I wager, that bunch of rogues were ever set to go willingly to church! They were more inclined to the prayer 'let someone else be paying' and the litany 'mine's another, luv'."

"The Duke of Wellington had a few things to say

about his infamous army, I believe," said Henry. "The 'scum of the earth, enlisted for drink' weren't they in his estimation?"

"Some of them most certainly," said Caleb. "Personally I enlisted for regular food, and plenty others did too, but we had some poor characters I have to say."

"Tut, sir, and you the byblow of the Duke of York!" laughed Henry.

Caleb chuckled.

"Oh you heard that pure invention of Fowler's did you?" he said. "Mentioning that my mother was unwed in one breath and that royal dukes father plenty of side issues in the next and unable to be brought to book for lying! It was for that Elton woman's benefit of course; I would that you will forget it!"

"Not so, Caleb, my friend!" said Henry, merrily. "Who knows who might speak out for a man rumoured to have royal blood that would be but rude to a Bow Street Runner that they think beneath them? I was ready to be, until I got the measure of what a man you are; and I count myself a remarkably intelligent man and good at judging another, that I was ready to call you 'sir' from the first!"

"You forgot to say 'modest'," said Jane mildly.

"You won't get the better of Ma Jane in a word contest, Henry!" declared Simmy.

Henry cuffed him gently.

"Crowing over your dominie really is not the done thing, old man," he said.

The coach drew up at the front steps at this moment, the second coach with servants, luggage and the two younger children stopping a little way behind. Caleb sprang out to hand Jane down and lend assistance to her maid Ella, who had sat quietly in the corner sniffing in occasional disapproval at Henry's banter. Henry lifted Simmy down, careful of his game leg.

"I wonder if there's any fish in the lake?" said Simmy.

Henry sighed.

"I fancy, old man, you and I will have to go on wondering" he said. "Strictly work; when it isn't work for your pa, it will have to be declensions as it won't be long before I'm due back in Oxford and I shan't be likely to see you before Easter; the old man will want me over for Christmas, you know, with Richard dead."

"Oh well, you can invite us too," said Simmy.

"*Simmy!*" said Caleb, awfully. "That is the worst of bad manners, to invite yourself!"

"Doesn't stop a lot of the gentry doing it though," said Henry Redmayne, cheerfully. "Well, have to see about that! Come on; we appear to have to run the gauntlet of oppressive looking servants!"

Simmy pulled himself up; he had nothing to be ashamed of in his appearance, dressed in immaculate pantaloons and the cropped jacket of a youth he was every inch a young gentleman. Henry too was glad that he had abandoned the careless dress he had affected to irritate his brother, and had sought to emulate the quiet elegance that owed nothing to the extremes of fashion of either Corinthian or Exquisite, preferring that favoured by the likes of the Honourable Clement Featherstone, Mr. Knightley of Highbury, and Caleb Armitage himself. Caleb was dressed for travelling in his black Bath-coating coat by Scott, the mark of a military man. Purchasing coats from such a source was expensive; but in the long run an economy to be certain of long wearing and comfortable yet stylish clothing.

Jane felt quite secure in her own stylish costume. Her gown was of white jaconet muslin with a high Elizabethan collar and trimmed at the hem with a flounce and the latest in Spanish puffs. Over it she wore a lavender velvet spencer, plain but beautifully cut, modestly trimmed with Buckinghamshire lace, which also lined her fine bonnet trimmed with lavender ribbons and delicately shaded ostrich feathers. The butler who opened the door bowed.

"Madam will be Miss Fanshawe's friend and her, er, family no doubt?" he murmured, only an infinitesimal pause as he took in the extra people.

"Indeed: Mr. and Mrs Caleb Armitage and family," said Jane, firmly, inclining her head. "Miss Fanshawe has informed you then that she called for our support and aid; pray conduct me to her right away. I am sure Fowler will be able to see that our household is duly disposed with least inconvenience to the running of the house; my husband's man and comptroller of our household," she explained.

Fowler and the butler here would be likely to find themselves in some kind of rivalry as was common amongst servants; they might as well get over staring suspiciously at each other as soon as possible.

As Jane swept within a small, rather dumpy figure came running down the grand staircase.

"Jane! My *dear* Jane!" she cried, holding out her arms.

"I should watch your step if I were you, Nessie," said Jane, mildly, "as your shawl is trailing rather. Two sudden deaths in the household would try the nerves of the most patient of servants."

Agnes Fanshawe came to a halt and made a moue.

"Jane, you are so detestably *practical*!" she declared.

"Indeed; I rather thought that was why you wanted me to come, and to bring Bow Street's finest to uncover the murderer of your cousin Henry," said Jane calmly, "allow me to introduce my husband, Caleb Armitage; his son, my stepson, Simon Armitage; my daughter Frances and my son Joseph. Mr. Henry Redmayne, Simon's tutor during his holidays from Oxford and friend of the family, Miss Adcock our family governess. I trust you did not expect me to abandon my children to answer so peremptory a summons?"

"I – er, no, no, of course not!" Nessie Fanshawe took refuge in fluttering her hands distractedly. It was a well practised gesture, and Caleb, seeing it for the first time, saw quite what Jane meant about the affectations of helplessness. It would have been more effective from a young woman of more ethereal figure and he firmly banished thoughts of a quotation from 'Hamlet'. He also hid a grin – an expression banned to him now as ill bred – as he watched his wife effortlessly take charge of situation, hostess and house in one short conversation. Miss Fanshawe went on, "Jane, dearest, Mr Armitage, er…Simon, pray come and meet some of the guests!"

"I'd rather have a straight story from you about exactly what is going on, unmarred by the tear blots that smudged your letter, Nessie dear," said Jane, "but I suppose in courtesy I can hardly avoid meeting your guests right away."

Caleb hid another smile as Jane's use of the word 'dear' put him strongly in mind of the way she spoke to little Frances, who had learned that she had a will of her own at some ten months old and was inclined to try to exercise it.

"Oh! Well I suppose they will not think it odd if I take you to see your bedrooms and see you settled in" Nessie fluttered a little more. "I – I am not sure where to place your dear children and their er, staff" she added helplessly.

"Never fear, Miss Fanshawe, Addy and I will confer with the housekeeper and come up with something adequate!" declared Henry Redmayne with a bow. "I'm happy to share a room with Simmy if there's a shortage; we're each as boring as the other on the subject of fishing!"

"Oh there are plenty of rooms – it's a great rattling mausoleum of a place!" said Nessie quickly. "But they are mostly under Holland covers."

"Oh my servants and Addy will happily assist your housekeeper," said Jane. "Simmy and Henry, you had better come with us, the women will not want you underfoot while they see to finding you rooms."

"Yes ma," said Simmy.

"Ita, Mater Jana," said Henry solemnly.

Jane gave him a Look and he twinkled unrepentantly.

Jane and Caleb exchanged a look however as Nessie Fanshawe inclined her head politely to Simmy's bow; she might be a bit helpless but she had not turned a hair at his twisted features, withered arm and limp. What she thought of him was unfathomable; Nessie Fanshawe was a lady.

"There's not really a lot to tell," sighed Nessie as Ella bustled around in Jane's room and Fowler did likewise in the adjoining room that was Caleb's, the communicating door open between them. "Did – did you wish to come to my sitting room?" Nessie cast a quick glance at the servants.

"Fowler and Ella assist us by speaking with the servants; they have a need to know what is being investigated," said Jane, firmly.

"Oh! I – well, I don't know how these investigations are conducted," said Nessie, "So obviously I… dear Jane, surely you are not yourself employed by Bow Street?"

"Oh not at all," said Jane, "I am by way of being a consultant, as an avocation, and to help my husband. He is employed in the more delicate cases requiring a gentleman."

"Invalided as I was out of the army, and my father unwilling to bear a hand I required some gainful employment," murmured Caleb, "and serving my country as an officer of the law rather than in the army seemed a suitable solution. I don't , of course, use my military rank."

"Oh, er, no, of course" said Nessie.

"All the royal dukes are too hard up to pursue their duties by any offspring they have at the moment" said Henry, brightly, with an innocent look at the fulminating glare Caleb gave him.

"*Oh*!" said Nessie. "Oh I *see*! Of course, Mr Armitage, very embarrassing for you, very brave of you to take what some folk might consider a *demeaning* occupation."

"I don't," said Caleb, "I consider it a fine opportunity to pursue justice without having studied law the way young Henry here is doing. And I'd be much obliged, Miss Fanshawe, if we could get down to facts to give some idea of one principle of law I do know well, which is to say *cui bono*."

"That's 'Who benefits'" said Simmy. "I'm going to study law too."

"Er, splendid!" said Nessie. "Well, the facts are quite simple; we all arrived at various times over the Friday afternoon and evening, and Cousin Henry introduced Flora as his intended bride; she has done very well, Jane, she would pass as a lady in most particulars, you know! Mrs Kemp – Cousin Henry's sister – was inclined to take umbrage at not having been invited to be the hostess, and her husband, the Reverend Kemp almost found out about Flora, when he chided her for quoting from plays lest anyone think she might be an actress, but Mr Morton took exception to his canting, Mr Morton is a wealthy man, a cit, I'm afraid, but a friend of Cousin Henry, they've both backed plays you know! And Flora is really an actress, she just took on the job as opera dancer when there were no parts for her. Picking up the role of a lady came to her very well indeed! It was all very uncomfortable because Gabriel and Michael Kemp – they are twins – were trying to bait the Beau, that's Daventry Popham, and their sister was trying to make them stop, but she's younger than they are, and Luke Popham – he's another cousin, like Daventry Popham is, wasn't helping because he despises dandies or exquisites or whatever Beau Popham is.

Anyway, everyone went to bed, and there was a lot more peace at breakfast because Flora and Mrs Kemp and the Beau took theirs in their rooms; but Cousin Henry was pretty furious about something he'd got in the post. He went into his study and I know he wrote a letter to his solicitor because I heard him roaring for a boy to ride with it into London. If he is coming, he should arrive today; how fortunate it is that you were staying only a few hours ride away, dear Jane! And he sent a servant for Flora; she said when she came out that they had been discussing settlements, but I fear that Cousin Henry assuaged his temper by *misbehaving* a bit with her, and I feel guilty, for I am her chaperone; but she said nothing *untoward* took place, at least she seemed a bit uncomfortable when I first asked her and almost *snapped* at me, dear Jane! To ask what I meant, and then when I asked bluntly if we were likely to have to bring the wedding forward in case she was with child she laughed and said no. But she had taken off her spencer and had crumpled it most awfully and her overskirt was all tucked up too, and I told her quite sharply to go to her room and make herself decent, because a lady she did not look at all. And then when Cousin Henry did not come to luncheon, Glossop went to see why, and there he was, dead."

"In his chair?" asked Caleb.

"Yes indeed; and that knife through his throat and the window curtains blowing. It *could* have been a prowler, but I didn't think Cousin Henry would still be sitting in his chair if any stranger had come in, do you?"

"Now *that* observation, Miss Fanshawe, is the thought of a clever woman," said Caleb. "I salute your shrewdness."

Chapter 3

"I do believe, Jane-girl, your friend could out-talk Aunt Hetty," said Caleb, humorously.

"That's why I've never found Aunt Hetty as much of a gabster as some people do," said Jane, "being used to Nessie, Aunt Hetty is comparatively restful as well as being anything but helpless. Nessie *is* shrewd, in some respects, but she doesn't know what to do with her observations."

"Most people don't," said Caleb, "and that's the point of having trained officers of the law, and I'd like to see a lot more training too. She did the right thing, however, calling for someone who can take her inferences further. I suppose you asked her to go down to alert her other guests to our presence so she could spread Henry's spurious tales to them."

"As Henry said, it doesn't hurt to have people falling over themselves to co-operate with someone who might have influence if not wealth," said Jane, cynically.

"And doubtless you'd like Mr Fowler and me to find out what we can from the servants?" said Ella. "So far as I can gather, that silly little maid, Peggy, who showed me where to come being as full of gossip as an egg is of meat, a dresser is someone they are not used to; so I can overawe most of them. Miss Fanshawe doesn't even have a personal maid, she and Miss d'Ambrose made do with a single maid of all work in the little house where they were living, and left her on board wages for the house party. Peggy let me know the staff just despise her for dressing herself, and Miss d'Ambrose too, whom they apostrophise as 'jumped up'.

"Hah, I wonder what they'll think of me," said Caleb.

"With all due respect, Mr Caleb," said Fowler, "they will be unable to tell you were not born a gentleman.

You have the manner perfectly; if I may say so, because you have the beautiful manners your excellent mother taught you that transcend class."

"She had been a maid in a well-off household until the master got her into trouble with my eldest sister," said Caleb, "then my da took her and my sister on, but where we lived marriage was a luxury; which is how come you and Henry can get away with your taradiddles, my lad. My da was a good hard working man; he taught me how to shift, until the influenza took him. Well, shall we go forth and attempt to beard these lions by becoming a den of Daniels?"

A maid was waiting to lead Caleb, Jane, Henry and Simmy down to a salon, a nursery having been established hastily across the passage from Jane's and Caleb's rooms and Henry and Simmy each in their own rooms next to it, and Miss Adcock in the dressing room of the room adjudged suitable for a nursery. It might not be ideal, but at least they were all close by.

There was no further conversation while they were conducted downstairs and the butler was waiting to announce them.

Various curious eyes turned upon them as they entered and were announced.

Of the men, the obvious exquisite, with the wasp waist to his mulberry coloured coat, pale lemon inexpressibles and shirt points so high that he had to turn his whole body to change the direction of his gaze was presumably Beau Popham; and Simmy earned a poke from Henry for murmuring that his breeks were so tight they might popham out. The Beau did not have quite the muscles for skin tight breeches, and the envious look he cast at Caleb's well muscled thighs would have made Fowler's cup run over. At the other end of the spectrum of dandyism was the other Popham,

Luke, who was dressed with some aspirations to the Corinthian, though Caleb noted with some satisfaction that the man's tasselled Hessians were no shinier than his own. There appeared to be some competition between Luke Popham and Daventry Popham regarding the height of their neckties. Luke Popham favoured the uncomfortably formal intricacies of the Oriental, and the Beau had an outrageously huge Waterfall. As well as the uncomfortable Trone d'Amour Caleb had learned to tie for his wedding – and promptly forgot – he had learned to tie the Mathematical, whose height might be adjusted to the tastes of the wearer, and the cool and comfortable Maharatta. Today he wore the Mathematical and Henry emulated him. Much might be told of a man by his choice of tie; and how well he achieved it.

As for the two youngest men present, who presented identical faces if not identical sartorial aspirations, it was plain that one was attempting to copy Luke Popham as far as was possible, in his choice of quiet colours and a badly tied Oriental; and the other was as careless of dress as had Henry been, save that he had made some effort with his neckcloth with the easy to tie Horse-Collar knot. There was some suggestion of the Byronesque about his efforts though he clearly did not dare wear any loosely knotted scarf or open collar to emulate that romantic gentleman.

The oldest gentleman made no pretensions towards cravat tying, being blessed with a lack of choice in the matter for the wearing of a clerical dog-collar; and the final member of the gentlemen present wore a purple kerchief loosely knotted with the eccentric choice of black velvet jacket, lavender smallclothes and a waistcoat of royal purple lavishly embroidered with silver. He also wore his hair long and caught back with a velvet ribbon at the nape of his neck though he was no older than forty, Jane thought; and that his coat was cut in the new style of frock coat meant that he might, at first glance, almost be mistaken for a footman in elaborate livery. His rings, fobs and ornate quizzing glass removed that impression quite rapidly, especially as he was eyeing up Jane with that item, his eye grotesquely enlarged through it. Jane resisted the urge she always felt when being quizzed to pull a grotesque face; and quickly checked that Simmy was not succumbing to a similar urge. As Henry had him by the ear, he had presumably been checked in such a desire. Jane relaxed. She knew there was nothing in her own fashionable appearance that would be found wanting in any of the quizzing glasses that had appeared in the hands of those who considered themselves arbiters of fashion, from the top of the frivolous beribboned cap she had changed into when she removed her bonnet to the toes of her silken slippers.

The eyes of the three women were on her also; grudging acceptance that this was a lady from the oldest, frank admiration from the youngest, who looked enough like the twins to be the sister who tried to pour oil on troubled waters, and an expression between approval for her sartorial choice and angry envy from the third, quite exotic looking young woman, who had to be Floradora d'Amrose, *alias* Jemima Harris.

Jane knew that she and Caleb had to seize the initiative or become merely guests whose motives in investigating might be questioned; but Caleb, used to bearding potential suspects in their own environment, was before her.

He made a courtly leg – Mr Weston and Mr Knightley had added to Fowler's coaching – and smiled.

"Good afternoon, ladies and gentlemen. You are doubtless aware that Miss Fanshawe wrote both to my charming wife, a friend of hers, and to my superior in Bow Street, Sir Nathanial Conant, requesting discreet and expeditious aid in clearing up this tragedy. I am sure you will all do your utmost to aid me in this quest."

Jane made a mental note to tell him how much she

enjoyed the word 'expeditious'.

Beau Popham spoke up, or perhaps it would be more accurate to say, drawled,

"My dear fellow, why *should* you be so sure we will all do our utmost to aid you? I would have thought it was in the interests of whoever killed Uncle Henry to do everything to the contrary."

Caleb inclined his head.

"Oh, quite so, Mr Popham; but then, I shall be able to make a note of anyone who is less than helpful and consider it a point in their disfavour towards being crossed off my list of suspects as innocent."

Beau Popham gave a slow hand clap.

"Bravo; placing us in a position where we are suspect merely for having scruples about talking to the likes of Bow Street Runners. When, by the way, did they start recruiting gentlemen to so sordid a business?"

"When it became apparent that gentlemen could be as capable of sordid crimes as any other man, Mr Popham," said Caleb, "to preserve the sensibilities of the ladies unwittingly associating with the same, of course."

"Of course," said Beau Popham. "I will co-operate; your tongue is worthy of fencing with and I think your brain able enough to forestall me if I amuse myself at poor Uncle Henry's obsequies' expense by playing games. At least the process should not be boring."

"I'd have said, myself, that the process was briefly a fraction more exciting than Mr Henry Popham bargained for," said Caleb dryly.

The Beau laughed a sardonic laugh.

"Oh very nicely put, Mr Armitage," he said.

"Strictly speaking," Luke Popham spoke up, "the Beau should not refer to Cousin Henry as 'Uncle'; he and I are but cousins, though we bear the family name and his true nephews and nieces do not. You should understand the ramifications of the family, Mr Armitage, since it will show you who has more motive to kill Cousin Henry. Being the spoilt child of his favourite cousin, Daventry stands, for example, to gain more than I, who have I dare say but little interest in his will."

"I think you are out of line, Luke!" it was the Reverend Egbert Kemp who spoke up. "It is preposterous that Miss Fanshawe should take it upon herself to call in Bow Street to harass bereaved relatives when it is perfectly plain that poor Henry was done to death by a house breaker!"

"Phlegmatic, even lethargic, man this Henry Popham then, Reverend?" asked Caleb.

"I – no, not at all! why ever would you suggest such a thing?" cried the Reverend.

"Well, sir, you imply that he was too lethargic to get up in surprise, even if not in outrage, when someone entered his study through the French window," said Caleb. "I admit that as yet I have but heard a description of the room – I shall look at it for myself presently – but it seems to me that a man who is hale enough to be contemplating matrimony with a young lady would be unlikely to remain seated at his desk when a stranger entered, though he might well do so for a relative."

The reverend gaped.

"An excellent point," said Beau Popham, "you are right of course; he would not have bothered to rise for any of us, even his female relatives. He would have been on his feet in an instant roaring in outrage if a stranger or one of the servants had strolled coolly in through the window; and they would have had to cross the room to his desk too."

Caleb bowed.

"This point did not escape Miss Fanshawe, which is why she sent for the husband of an old schoolfriend who might be expected to utilise tact and discretion," he said. "She is to be congratulated for her sense, *and* in this case well directed sensibility."

It had not escaped Caleb's notice that both the Reverend and his colourless little wife had been directing distinctly frosty glances at Nessie. Nessie flushed slightly and looked pleased at this encomium.

"By Jupiter, sir, you mean it was one of us in this very room? That's something out of the common way!" said the would-be Corinthian twin, enthusiastically.

"And you would be one of the Masters Kemp?" said Caleb. "I fancy your Uncle Henry was less enthusiastic than you appear to be."

The youth flushed.

"Well – it's not as though we knew him very well," he muttered, "he sent us money occasionally but he rarely had us to stay because he couldn't stand Papa telling him how he ought to live his life and he doesn't like sickly women," he glanced at his mother. "I'm Michael; my brother Gabriel over there."

His father was glaring at him and he pretended not to notice.

"I see," said Caleb, "a pair of singularly angelic names which do not appear to match the countenances."

That elicited a couple of identical boyish grins though Gabriel Kemp's smile quickly disappeared to return to its Byronesquely brooding expression.

"I did not think that it was a housebreaker, though I would have cited the fact that there were also a sufficiency of small valuables in Uncle Henry's study that any self-respecting house breaker would have surely taken to sell," said Beau Popham, "not least the expensive Sevres snuffbox on the table beside him and his gold watch, chain and fobs and a selection of rings. Any man who is not too nice to stick a knife in a man is unlikely to be too nice to rifle his body. And by the way, Luke, I have been calling Uncle Henry 'Uncle' since my mother insisted upon it when I was in short coats and Uncle Henry no older than we are. I am closer to him than you more because I took an interest in his avocation of the theatre than because he fagged for m'father at Harrow. Come, Mr Armitage; I will show you the study to permit the outbreak of outrage amongst the assembled company."

Chapter 4

By mutual consent, Jane remained to listen to the outbreak of outrage while the Beau led Caleb off to the scene of the murder. The body would almost certainly have been removed, but Jane felt that she had had a sufficiency of scenes of murder when there was her most able husband to read the clews that she need not.

"So, Mrs Armitage, pray tell us how you have become involved in – murder investigation," said Mrs Kemp in a failing tone. The implied spiteful criticism was clear enough even though it might not be something on which the woman might be called.

"Why it is simple enough," said Jane, "my first husband was murdered when he was unwise and naïve enough to fall in with bad company. I wished to help uncover the identity of those who had caused his untimely demise, and found during my assistance of the officer assigned to the case that it was possible to consider remarriage. Mr Armitage is an excellent step father to my children. Naturally I do my best to do as well by *his* son" and she smiled at Simmy.

Simmy, nothing loath to play games, came over to her and leaned against her like the picturesque and unlikely looking cherubic youngsters to be found in fashion journals that depicted youthful garb alongside adult fashion.

"Oh dear me! Hartshorn if you please!" cried Mrs Kemp. "That child's face – surely it is not a natural physiognomy but a grimace he is pulling?"

"Here, Nessie, didn't you say that making personal remarks was unladylike?" demanded the exotic Flora.

"I believe I did pass such a comment," said Nessie, hiding her delight that someone else had made the comment about Mrs Kemp's rudeness. "But you should be less censorious, Flora dear, of a woman who has reached an age when all things might be more forgiveable; you must be aware that the aged have as little tact as children."

"Does that mean I can comment too, Ma?" Simmy asked Jane.

"No. Gentlemen of any age employ tact," said Jane. "Mrs Kemp is suffering from the loss of a brother. It would be most unkind for a young gentleman to take any notice of her little lapses in courtesy. Bereavement permits greater licence."

Simmy bestowed a beautiful bow on Mrs Kemp.

"I am most sympathetic for your loss, madam," he said.

"Nothing wrong with the brat's airs and graces," said the eccentrically clad gentleman. "I'm Abel Morton, Mrs Armitage, I know we haven't been introduced but I'm happy to do the necessary myself. What occurred to the poor lad?"

"Alas, it was a defect of birth; we have not found a surgeon who can agree as to the cause save that most declare it was probably what also cost his mother her life," said Jane. "However a well built up shoe means that Simmy – really he is too old to be Simmy now – has no trouble getting around."

"I do pray he is not retarded!" declared Mrs Kemp "I could not bear to look on a face drooling in idiocy as well as so hideously twisted!"

"Madam, the boy is remarkably clever and well ahead of many of his age in Latin, and taking well to starting on Greek too!" said Henry, hotly.

"Ooh! My Angel-boys, my smelling salts!" cried Mrs Kemp.

The twins looked acutely uncomfortable at this appellation and their sister, Emma, Jane recalled she was named, silently searched her mother's reticule to pass her the vinaigrette. She was taking in every detail before speaking out, Jane thought; and gave Jane a deprecating smile.

"Well, Armitage cannot help having a son with such

deformities, clever or not, but it's too much to expect my wife to have to look at him!" declared the Reverend Kemp.

"Cicero would explain that attitude *damnant quod non intellegunt*," said Henry coldly. "Pray translate, Simmy."

"*Damnant*, they condemn, *quod*, what, *non intellegunt*, they do not understand, that one is nice and easy," said Simmy. "I like Cicero, he understood people pretty well and didn't like them much because he knew so much about them."

"Exactly," said Henry. "*Inhumanitas omni aetate molesta est* as he also said; 'inhumanity is problem in all generations', and whilst one might have expected better from a man of the cloth I suppose the shepherd of the flock might take *O, praeclarum custodem, ovium lupum!* as appropriate under the circumstances."

"'What a good protector of the sheep is the wolf'," said Jane. "A little beyond Simmy as yet, Henry" she added as the reverend spluttered slightly at being called a wolf.

"I figured out *lupum* because of the werewolf story we read," said Simmy, cheerfully.

"I don't want to know," said Jane, hurriedly. "Mrs Kemp, I have disarranged my household for *your* convenience to help my friend Nessie so that the murderer of *your* brother might be uncovered. I have refrained from making personal remarks about either of your sons, who might benefit from it as their appearances could be rectified with some care and may be held to be faults of their own not accident of birth. I pray you do me the courtesy of refraining from further personal remarks about my son, even if they stem from a not unnatural jealousy that I am more greatly blessed than you are."

"You tell the old cat" said Flora, reverting to type, to a hastily murmured,

"*Really* Flora dear," from Nessie.

Mrs Kemp proceeded to have hysterics and the girl Emma plied the vinaigrette with the vigorous hand of one used to such tantrums.

"Well I may as well start asking a few pertinent questions," said Jane, "and Henry, I *pray* you not further exercise your clever tongue on those incapable of competing in the same field; before you move into the realms of Horace."

"As you command, Ma'am," said Henry, bowing his head.

Simmy was heard by Jane to murmur *sotto voce* to Henry that he wished he might only have a quizzing glass to depress the pretensions of the one who had rooms to let in her garret. Henry took advantage of attention being diverted to the moaning woman to cuff him and lend him his own quizzing glass.

Nobody might take exception, after all, at young Mr Simon Armitage peering through a quizzing glass after the manner in which Mr Morton was already doing through his.

One did, of course.

"Now look here, you young Jackanapes!" shouted Gabriel Kemp, leaping between his mother and Simmy "That's insolence!"

"Oh?" said Simmy. "Why shout at me then and not at Mr Morton? Is it because I'm smaller than you and crippled so you think you could take me on?"

"He has a point, you Bartholomew Baby," said Henry, "after all, Simon did not *ask* your mother to start insulting him; and you know, you should drop her a hint that insulting her betters when they are young might just be recalled when he comes of age and has influence."

Gabriel went white, recalling the rumour Miss Fanshawe had innocently repeated about Mr Armitage. Jane sighed. Really, it was too bad that people were so ill bred that they could not resist making a song and dance about Simmy's odd appearance unless they thought he outranked them socially. She hated unpleasantness; but she had not been about to let that horrible woman pass hurtful remarks without making a stand for Simmy, even though disguising it initially as sympathy; perhaps she should not have made barbed comments about the sartorial aspirations of the twins but enough had been enough.

"I think," said Jane, coldly, "There has been enough of this ridiculous furore. If anyone is so ill-bred as to feel a need to enact a Cheltenham tragedy over my son's appearance, I fear that such persons are to be pitied their inability to behave with decency in polite company. However my husband and I have a task in hand, and I assure you that the vulgarity of some of the potential suspects will not weigh in our minds as it is evidence that we weigh not personal feelings. Reverend Kemp, I suggest you remove your wife until she is able to act with the becoming decorum incumbent upon the wife of a man of the cloth."

Jane's icy dignity found the reverend gentleman meekly coaxing his hysterical wife upstairs where she might indulge her hysterics to her heart's content or, as Henry muttered for Jane's ear only, not, as she might not enjoy them so well without an audience.

"Thinks she owns the place she does, just because her brother was master here," said Flora. Jane sighed. The voice was beautifully modulated but the sentiments expressed and the manner in which they were expressed might as well have been in the strident tones of Covent Garden. However if Mrs Kemp were in the habit of taking ill over everything and using it as an excuse to make discourteous criticism, Flora had some excuse.

"One thing I need to know, is whether anyone else went to see Mr Popham that morning as well as Miss d'Ambrose," said Jane. "If anyone went to his study we can perhaps obtain a better idea of the time of death – ah, and here is Mr Daventry Popham who might also answer the same question," she added, as the door opened and Caleb and the Beau walked back in.

"I went to see him almost immediately after breakfast; the window was not open then" said Michael Kemp reluctantly. "I – I was heading for the stables, and – and I thought it worth while asking for a loan, as he'd been pretty scathing about the set of my jacket," he added resentfully.

Caleb surveyed him.

"Aye, lad, it's worth saving up for the best tailor you can afford," he said. "It doesn't need to be Scott or Weston so long as he knows what he's doing."

"Personally I favour Nugee," murmured the Beau.

"Well to each their own," said Caleb equably. "I prefer Scott but then I'm a military sort of man. Was he amenable to be touched? And did you go by door or window?"

Michael flushed.

"I knocked on the window as it was closed," he said. "He opened it, and asked what I wanted. I told him I was a little short and he damned me to hell and asked if I thought that this was a – a house party or a sponging-house party. He – he said he was sick of people hanging on his sleeve and told me to, er, go about my business, then he slammed the window and snibbed it."

"He snibbed it? you're certain?" asked Jane, intently.

Michael stared.

"Yes," he said, slowly. "I'm certain. That – that means it definitely was someone from inside, doesn't it? and who came through the door?"

"Not necessarily," said Caleb. "You knocked and he opened for you. Someone else might have knocked likewise, and Mr Popham felt secure enough to sit himself down again after letting them in. Someone who was not trying to touch him for some blunt, perhaps – or someone he had asked to come and see him, whom he was expecting, and did not want to be in the throes of an argument with a young relative, and that made him shall we say *blunt* with your request. If I may be pardoned the pun" he added.

"I say, might it have been a tenant, or a neighbour rather than one of us?" asked Gabriel Kemp, interested despite himself.

"I'm not about to rule that out, though generally speaking someone only kills for gain; and unless there is found to be a clause in Mr Popham's will, or he is found to have been threatening eviction or prosecution of any of his tenants or neighbours, his close family do look most likely," said Caleb. "Henry, lad, you and Simmy might ride round the estate and find what terms the deceased stood on with his tenants and neighbours. And don't bore them with Cicero, there's a good lad."

Henry grinned.

"Jane already told me off for considering descending to Horace," he said. "We can do that readily; come, Simmy! Let's go find the Bailiff, who can give us some pointers about who to seek out."

Simmy trotted off happily at Henry's heels, happy to have a useful task to perform for Caleb.

"Mr Armitage!" said Abel Morton. "If you feel that it's family and neighbours as is likely to be the culprits, you won't, I'm sure, have any objection to letting me leave? Only I am wishful to return to town."

Caleb regarded him thoughtfully.

"Being by way of a partner to Mr Popham in his backing of plays I'm not too sure about that," he said, "but if I speak privately with you after dinner as one of the first, assuming nothing arises that means I wish to ask you to stay, there is no reason you cannot leave first thing in the morning."

Abel Morton bowed; with that he had to be content.

"Excuse me, Mr Armitage, but do you really think a young girl like me might be a suspect at all?" asked Emma Kemp. "For someone of Royal Blood, treating the ladies as suspects is not very chivalric nor courteous."

"It was neither chivalry nor courtesy that put a stiletto through the jugular of Mr Popham either" said Caleb "and unlike a stabbing in chest or back, which requires considerable force, I do not rule out the possibility that a woman might have done this. However, you are not high on my list, so I will speak with you this evening too – obviously in my wife's presence – and hope to eliminate you. And I pray you, cease this silly talk about royal blood," he added.

Emma Kemp gave him a knowing smile and inclined her head at his becoming modesty.

Caleb was glad he had sent Henry away. He was itching to tell that young man what he thought of schemes to increase his consequence! And it might not be a good idea to do so....

"While I think of it, you should know that I've locked the study up," he informed the company, "and pasted a strip of paper over the door too, with my seal upon it in case anyone finds another key. I've only had a chance at a cursory search but I want Mr Popham's solicitor present before I do a proper search. Anyone who wishes to tell me anything about any visit to him during the morning would be better to speak up in case any sign of their presence is subsequently found and naturally fosters suspicion."

That he might deduce who had visited the study by finding clews was met with stunned silence!

Chapter 5

"So, did anyone else go to see Mr Popham?" asked Caleb "it's a good general question to start with. If we can trace who saw him when it will make finding out when he died much easier; and if we know when exactly he died, we may be able to determine who can vouch for whom at various times during the morning."

Luke Popham gave a scornful laugh.

"That might be difficult, as generally speaking we avoided each other. I for one evaded the cub," he nodded at Michael, "whom I saw follow me out. I had my groom take my horse out and tether it in the paddock and swear blind to the boy he hadn't taken note which way I'd gone; so when the cub went off hell bent for leather to try to find me on a ride he thought I'd favour it was easy to stroll out from the tack room and ride off in another direction. Being saddled with a brat who apes one's style badly is too tedious for me," he added, "the unconscionable time he took following me however is now explained by an attempt to cut a wheedle with Cousin Henry."

Michael was scarlet with mortification.

Gabriel surprised Luke by speaking up.

"You have no call to speak like that, Cousin Luke – and swearing in front of ladies too – because you were young once and doubtless admired and copied someone. I shall be glad if my twin loses his admiration for you over that piece of unkindness; I – I'd rather he admired the Beau!" he added. "At least he's civil and puts up with us teasing him."

"One was young once," murmured the Beau.

"Go to the devil you ill-dressed brat, you are even more of an embarrassment to be related to than your twin!" snarled Luke.

"Mr Popham," said Caleb, "you are asking to have me invite you outside to show you the horse trough if you cannot moderate your language in front of my wife, whatever custom you and your cousin might have held about such language in front of the ladies – and children," he nodded at Emma, " – in his house."

Luke stared; took in the size of Caleb's hands, and the development of his muscles and the smooth way he had risen to confront him.

"I apologise," he said. "It's enough to make a saint swear! Being under suspicion like this, even those of us who had few, if any, expectations, especially since Cousin Henry was getting married! If anyone was likely to gain it would be the harpy from Hampstead who was likely to benefit from his will – and a clever piece she is to entrap him into a betrothal, for I've my own suspicions about Miss d'Ambrose."

Jane laid a hand on the arm of Flora as the young woman seemed likely to launch herself on Luke Popham. Jane sighed. Poor Nessie! She had taught the girl how to achieve the right tones, how to move, how to serve tea, no doubt, and make the right gestures; but the girl Flora was quite plainly playing a part as a lady, not becoming one in the same way that Caleb had become every inch a gentleman. Her every instinct was similar to that of Dorothy, to whom Jane had taught enough to permit her to support the position of a milliner's apprentice, and who was doing quite well. Dorothy was a clever girl who had shaken off her past to some extent; and Flora might be clever, but Nessie had concentrated too hard on the appurtenances of what made a lady rather than encouraging Flora to learn by precept and example.

"What, I pray, is wrong with Hampstead?" asked Nessie with some asperity. "We have a nice little house there, convenient for the city if need arises and such pretty countryside!"

"And out of the way while you train Cousin Henry's light o' love to pass herself off as good enough for the family," said Luke.

"*Cousin Luke!*" cried Nessie. "Cousin Henry would not have asked me to be Flora's chaperone if there had been anything improper in his conduct towards her; you put me to blush speaking of such things in front of a child like Emma and my dear friend Jane!"

"You observe the rough and ready manners and speech of the Corinthian, my dear Agnes," said Beau Popham, waving a languid hand. "I think we are all aware that Miss d'Ambrose has risen from a position somewhat lower than aspirant bride of Amberfield Abbey, but I for one am, I hope, charitable enough to assume that she has not, at least risen from the horizontal."

"What did he just say?" demanded Flora opening enormous pansy eyes wide in confusion.

"He said that he thought you have learned to support the position of a lady from a birth of humble origins but that he did not suggest that you had ever been a Cyprian," said Jane.

"And you talk to me about the words I use?" demanded Luke of Caleb.

"Better euphemism than some she might have used to translate your cousin to that ninnyhammer," said Caleb. "Jane-girl, I know you've heard it in the line of my duty, but it ain't a word to use in polite company."

"No, my dear; I know," said Jane, "but I fancied it was one that Emma might not have heard and her ears are too young for frank discussions without some circumlocution."

Luke gave a shout of laughter.

"I wager you'd not turn a hair if someone called her a Prime Dell," he said.

"On the contrary, Mr Popham, I would consider the use of such vulgar canting terms by a gentleman to be quite out of line in a salon in mixed company," said Jane, "and had we been provided with tea I must needs have upset the urn of hot water over your to force you to withdraw."

"Virago, ain't she?" said Luke to Caleb.

"I like her that way," said Caleb.

"What is a Prime Dell?" asked Emma.

"Something any decent mother would wish her daughter to have no knowledge about and a term I would spank my own daughter for using," said Jane. "I have heard some insalubrious language as an unfortunate consequence of my husband's calling; but not usually from the mouths of those who call themselves gentlemen, and never in the salon of a respectable residence. Your cousin, I fear, gives every impression of having sailed the Marshalsea for his command of such words."

"Bravo!" murmured the Beau.

"A hit! A very palpable hit!" declared Mr Morton who had been almost forgotten.

"That's Hamlet that is," declared Flora.

"Well, my dear Flora – dear me, I believe I quote a song," said the Beau, " – Luke appears to be suffering the slings and arrows of outrageous Armitage. And correct me if I am wrong, but I hear Glossop's too, too solid flesh approaching to apprise us that it is dinner time."

"Goodness, Mr Popham, that's all bits from Hamlet too!" said Flora, in some admiration,

"The play's the thing," murmured Jane.

"Papa will not permit us to read Shakespeare's plays," said Emma "He says that playgoing is lewd and wicked. I'm not precisely sure what lewd is, but if a fine lady like Mrs Armitage sees no harm in it, I think papa must be wrong."

"Your father, my chick, is a narrow-minded old fool, which was why Uncle Henry would not tolerate him here if he did not have to do so," said the Beau, "which as I recall was more or less what Michael said when he first mentioned that the advent of the Kemps at Amberfield was an unusual occurrence."

"Leave the child alone, Beau," said Jane firmly,

"give her a few years to find her feet before you strop your tongue on her."

"Actually I was trying to enlighten her so she was aware of why her parents were not considered especially desirable house guests," said the Beau. "She seems a pleasant enough child despite their efforts."

"Sensible governess," said Michael, by way of explanation. "We've never had much to do with our parents until we got older. We boys get to go to school too of course so we get a bit of exposure to the outside world, though Gabe doesn't dare wear his Petershams or even wear a loose bow about his neck, never mind go without a cravat at all!"

"Well at dinner, I should certainly think not," said Jane firmly. "It's a question of politeness to others; who would wish to see the workings of the throat as a man eats? It is not called Adam's apple for nothing as it is far more prominent on a man. Besides, watching its gyrations would surely make a woman laugh at a man, and that is not conducive to good relations."

Gabriel Kemp's thought processes were quite apparent as his eyes widened in horror at the idea of being laughed at by women just for keeping his throat on display when eating. This was an horrifying thing for him to contemplate; and Jane suspected that there would be no more protests about wearing a proper cravat from that quarter.

Mrs Kemp did not join the company for dinner, though a substantial tray was ordered for her by her husband. Of those seven deadly sins he eschewed, gluttony apparently did not feature as he looked upon the viands laid out with an eager expression.

The board that was laid was certainly fine enough; Mr Henry Popham's cook was to be congratulated in not succumbing to any of the temperaments supposedly attributable to the best chefs. A choice of larks breaded and browned or lobster were served with shallots; they and carrot soup with parsley were removed with a goose, well stuffed with sausage meat, a haricot of mutton, davenport fowls and raised pies, with cabbage, creamed turnips, spinach and roasted parsnips and onions as side dishes throughout. The dessert was sumptuous too, chocolate creams in fluted glasses – expensive and not easy to make, Jane knew! – served with ratafia biscuits and a selection of comfits and fruit. Simmy did almost as much justice to the spread as the Reverend Kemp; but he might claim excuse of the appetite of a growing boy.

Conversation was quite desultory and stayed away from such details as murder; Reverend Kemp asked Nessie several questions about the orangery which were sufficiently didactic in tone that he might as well, Simmy confided to Henry, have been preaching a sermon on the subject. It may be said that Henry, hardly more than a schoolboy himself, countered,

"Blessed are the orange-growers for they shall be full of juice."

The private conversation went steadily downhill from there and Jane devoutly hoped that with her beside Simmy, and Caleb on the other side of Henry, nobody else heard a very warped version of the beatitudes. However if they did, at least this was a family she would never have to see again; and Reverend Kemp had rather brought it upon himself. She brought it to a close when the conceit of a pineapple was served with dessert and Simmy declared,

"Blessed are the pineapples for they shall never pine for apples, unlike Adam and Eve."

"Enough," said Jane.

Both young people subsided.

The tone of voice was one which was familiar to both.

As the ladies prepared to withdraw, Caleb rose.

"I pray you will not linger long over the brandy,

gentlemen; my wife will speak privily with each of the ladies while we pass it around, and then it will be my turn to speak to such of you as I may manage in an evening. This may be all as we have dined not much later than country hours; so I will see Mr Morton first, Mr Gabriel and Mr Michael next, in no particular order, they being young enough to wish to seek their beds at a reasonable hour, Mr Kemp after as an older man will also not wish to be long out of his bed, and the Messers Popham may draw straws to see who goes first. I trust this will be an arrangement that is to your satisfaction" he added, in a tone which said quite plainly that if it was not to their satisfaction, this was a matter of complete indifference to him.

There was a long and speaking silence.

"Ladies!" said Jane, brightly.

The three ladies present followed her meekly.

Chapter 6

"Very well, I would like to get on with this somewhat distasteful business," said Jane. "I have had a brief word with Nessie; I may want to talk to you again, Nessie, but it seems ludicrous that you would call for aid from Bow Street if you were in any wise involved in killing your cousin, since the housebreaker theory advanced by the Reverend Kemp might be let stand."

Agnes Fanshawe gave a little shriek of horror.

"Jane, surely you would not for a minute consider that I – *I* – might have anything to do with murdering poor Cousin Henry?"

Jane regarded her gravely.

"It is the task of the investigator to consider every possibility, however unlikely," she said. "I cannot see much in the way of motive as it stands; but I have to exercise my imagination and consider how much motive you might have if your cousin considered that you were not doing well enough in helping Miss d'Ambrose and considered dispensing with your employment; or worse if he thought you had introduced her to someone who proved to be a seducer, or other such possible, albeit highly improbable, situations."

"Mrs Armitage, you haven't half got a wild imagination, you ought to be writing plays, you reely should," declared Flora, her modulated tones slipping slightly.

Jane smiled.

"One needs a fairly, er, wild imagination at times to get inside the thoughts of wrongdoers," she said. "Nessie, do stop looking at me as though I have two heads; I outline only wild conjecture of what might have set you and your cousin at loggerheads, I do not say that for one moment I believe such a farrago of nonsense. You've too much good sense to introduce questionable men to your household and I am sure that you will succeed well enough with Miss d'Ambrose given a bit more time, though now the reason is a little superfluous."

"I thought she had succeeded?" demanded Flora, belligerently.

Jane smiled.

"The voice is right. The mannerisms are over-rehearsed and the action a trifle wooden and contrived as yet, if I may couch it in the terms of a critic."

Flora scowled.

"Oh dear, and I thought it was going so well!" said Nessie, actually wringing her hands.

"Nessie, it is going very well," said Jane. "I fear however more time is needed."

"Well if I don't have to impress any of Henry's swell friends, I can live quiet like, Ness, with you as my companion on whatever he has left me," said Flora. "Were you going to talk to us separate, Mrs A?"

"SeparateLY" corrected Jane, absently. "And please do not call me Mrs A. My name is Mrs Armitage. I wish to speak with Emma first so she may retire at will to bed, and too have an unpleasant experience quickly over. Come child; we will go into the music room that I noticed adjacent to this room, I had the chance to order a fire lit in there before we sat down to dinner so it should not be cold."

Emma followed her obediently, and Jane shut the door firmly.

"She eavesdrops, you know, like a servant," said Emma.

"She? She is the cat's mother you know," said Jane. Emma flushed.

"Flora. I don't think she's from a very nice family, Mrs Armitage," she added.

"I see," said Jane. "Flora has been, however, attempting to learn to fit in with her betrothed's family and it is well to give her the credit for trying. She will have trouble listening at this door, however, which is why I chose this room to conduct interviews; the doors are covered in green baize in order that the rest of the house need not be disturbed if anyone is playing the harpsichord in here, or any other instrument. It is a common enough arrangement. Let us, however, leave Flora aside, and talk about you."

Emma gave a nervous giggle.

"I didn't kill him," she said, "I – I don't think I could kill anyone; I can't even watch when mama drowns kittens."

"That's her job is it?" asked Jane. It was unfortunate that bessie cats always found a tom who hadn't been gelded; and not all the kittens could be kept, but the destroying of the kittens was heartrending and not for the faint hearted, and threw another light on the supposed sensibilities of Mrs Kemp.

"Yes; papa will have nothing to do with Jezebel and her kittens," said Emma. Jane reflected that it was just like a man of Kemp's stamp that he would expect the mice to be kept down and would yet manage to give a disparaging name and doubtless moralise on the proclivities of the unfortunate cat, forgetting that her nature was but instinct and thus part of God's design. He would be the first to complain if his communion bread and the surplices stored in chests were subject to the depredations of rodent teeth, no doubt. It was doubly interesting that he would not take responsibility for the culling of the unfortunate kittens but that Mrs Kemp was quite capable of doing what she saw as her duty, and meant therefore that killing in defence of her family might not be beyond her at all. Jane made a mental note that Mrs Kemp would bear being questioned too.

"Your mother called the twins her 'Angel Boys'; does she like to have pet names for you all?" she asked.

"Well not me," said Emma, "she tells the story of how when they were born they put her in mind of a painting she had seen somewhere with putti and declared that they were her Angel-Boys at that moment and insisted on calling them for the two Archangels whose names are definitely mentioned and are not considered in the least to be suspect or spurious. Papa complains about folklore from the Apocrypha, but if they were written at the same time, who was it decided what was Apocryphal and was it more in the nature of what they could fit in to print than what was a valid story? I hope you don't mind me asking you your thoughts on this, because I could not ask papa or mama, papa would be very angry because it is questioning the Bible, and mama would tell me not to worry my head about things that are the province of scholars. I don't want to be a scholar or a bluestocking, in fact I'd like to be frivolous and one day to wear a gown with a décolletage, but I want to know."

Jane, granddaughter of a clergyman and considering herself quite a bluestocking, had to think very fast.

"I think that what may or may not have been left out was the choice of mortal men, who can be fallible," she said. "However they did their best to choose the stories they felt would best illustrate the love and power of God. There are those people who consider the Apocrypha valid or they would not have been preserved. The Good Lord gave us brains to use, and questioning is a part of that use, though you will not find many men who will agree that this applies to women, bluestockings or otherwise."

"Your husband likes you to be clever," said Emma.

"Yes; and you may be lucky to find a young man who likes to hear your thoughts and to debate with you rather than telling you what to think," said Jane. "However, this gets us no further forward in the matter of my investigations. Did you go at all to the study?"

"No, I would not have dared!" said Emma, frankly. "Uncle Henry was in a towering bad mood, anyone should have been able to tell, even my idiot brother Michael, from the moment he opened his mail. He left breakfast quite abruptly. I went to find my embroidery so I might be seen to be usefully employed if mama wondered why I was idling and not running errands for her."

Jane was coming to the conclusion that if she had disliked Mrs Kemp before she was disliking her even more.

"And did anyone see you at your embroidery through the morning?" she asked.

"Only Cousin Nessie, who was engaged in copying a piece of music from *La Belle Assemblée* to play as a duet with Flora," said Emma, "she was as cross as crabs because it needed simplifying for Flora's part and it took a lot of concentration. Then she went to find Flora and I think they had a few words because Cousin Nessie sounded upset, and Flora spoke sharply, but I did not hear what they said, and I was very good and did not purposely listen either," she added with naïve honesty. "Then Cousin Nessie came back, all of a swither, shaking her head. Flora joined us about half an hour later and demanded Cousin Nessie come to help her with the flowers. I'd run my needle into my finger and Flora was very decent about it, and showed me how to soak my embroidery in a little salt water to take the blood out."

"Your mother has not taught you how to do that for – well, each month?" Jane was astonished. Emma shook her head.

"She leaves that to the servants," she said.

If Jane's opinion of Mrs Kemp had been low before, it dropped dramatically at this point. Emma declared that she had gone to watch the other women arrange the flowers for the day and had kept herself thus occupied until luncheon; at which point the discovery had been made. Jane dismissed the girl and called for Flora.

Flora flung herself onto a chair in the music room.

Jane noticed that she had one kind of behaviour and movement in front of men, another for women.

"You know, Miss d'Ambrose," said Jane, "adopting the languor of Cleopatra for men and reverting to Kate for women is a decidedly unladylike way to go on. There are those ladies whose poses change subtly when men are in the room, but the contrast is so marked for you, I would advise you to choose one role or the other, and not try to play both at once. There are plenty of men who admire a woman who is vigorous and knows her own mind, you do not need to cast yourself as a siren if it is uncomfortable."

"Lud, I've done it so long, it is second nature!" confessed Flora. "See here, Mrs A-rmitage, you know all about my background, I understand?"

"In broad, yes; Nessie wrote to me when your betrothed proposed the task to her, to ask for my advice. I told her that in my experience, ladies and gentlemen were made so by their ability to behave with courtesy at all times and to anyone, and that learning manners of speech and habits of etiquette are but appurtenances that may come with practice."

"I know a lot of gents as have no manners at all," said Flora.

"Then they betray their rearing," said Jane, "and are treated as gentlemen by other true gentlemen as a courtesy to their birth and family and are doubtless the objects of unkind stories in clubs. You have found it easier to find a protector by the languorous airs you play for the men?"

A look of fear and anger came into the pansy brown eyes.

"And who says I have had protectors?" demanded Flora.

"I beg your pardon if the assumption was inaccurate" said Jane. "It is of no moment to me; a girl without family is in a nasty situation and must make what living she can as best she might. The opportunity

for marriage was, I am sure, a welcome way out of a hard way of life, whether acting, dancing or any other activity, and I cannot blame you for taking it, even if you were no more than passing
fond of Mr Popham. Your grief does not seem profound enough, nor have you taken refuge in silence to hide deeper feelings, and I cannot see any evidence that you are entirely prostrated with sorrow at his demise."

"Well, I was fond of him, see, Mrs Armitage but like you say, I didn't love him. He was my way out and I'd do what it took to make him happy, like you say," said Flora. "Mind, I wager you'd not turn a hair if I was a street dell!"

"No, why should I?" said Jane. "You have managed to achieve a lot; I would hope that the family would see to arranging a pension for you even if there is nothing in the will granting you provision, and if not, the settlement Nessie wrote to me that you were to receive will be sufficient to set up a nice shop and employ a girl as a modiste or milliner with the ability to speak nicely to customers; not as pleasant a position as lady of this house but in the situation of the worst coming to pass it will at least be a good living."

"Well, Mrs Armitage, I know Henry had sent for his solicitor to change his will, and I've seen it too, so I won't be having to bow and scrape to swell morts in a rag shop," said Flora.

"Is that what you were discussing the morning he died – dear me, yesterday?" asked Jane.

"Yes," said Flora quickly. "Well, I saw the will then. We – we discussed other things. I expect Nessie told you I was a trifle mussed," she added.

"Do you feel he had recovered his good humour then by such means?" asked Jane.

"Well, put it this way, he wasn't shouting no more" said Flora.

There was a knock at the door and Glossop came in.

"Excuse me, Mrs Armitage, Mr Popham's solicitor

is here. What should I do?"

"Have the housekeeper prepare him a room, ply him with brandy in the library where there is a fire and offer him a light supper" said Jane. "My husband or I will
speak with him presently, but he will wish to recover from his journey."

Glossop bowed.

"Very good, ma'am," he said. Flora was gazing at Jane with envy.

"And that's what makes you a lady and why I can't learn," she said bitterly. "You know right away what to do; and I wouldn't."

"Why, Miss d'Ambrose, it is very simple," said Jane, "he is a man who has travelled far in the cold on urgent business; what he needs is to have his comforts seen to. Let us join the others and I will go and apprise the solicitor of the situation."

Chapter 7

Jane tripped into the library where the spare, soberly-clad, middle-aged man was sitting with a glass of brandy. He looked at her and frowned.

"You need not think that fashionable clothes will take me in, young woman; I am not disposed to be fooled by you at all, however besotted Henry may be," he said.

Jane raised an eyebrow.

"Are you by some chance assuming me to be Flora d'Ambrose *alias* Jemima Harris?" she said coolly.

He stared.

"Well if you are not, who the d-deuce are you, madam? I know every member of Henry's family so don't try to tell me you're a long lost cousin!"

"Frankly, sir, I should not wish to be related to any of the Pophams or Kemps," said Jane frostily. "I am Mrs Jane Armitage; I was at school with Agnes Fanshawe and she asked me to come to lend my support to her, and to bring my husband for his professional abilities in this sorry situation."

"Sorry situation! Well that's one way of putting it, what I want to know is, where's Henry and why am I talking to you?"

"I'd have said haranguing me might have been a better descriptive as you are not permitting me to provide any explanation," said Jane with her sweetest smile. "Doubtless this is why you are a solicitor and unable to conduct a fair cross examination at the bar. Perhaps I might resume my explanation?"

He scowled.

"I'd rather wait and hear it from Henry," he said.

"You'll be waiting a long time then," said Jane, tartly, starting to become irritated.

"What do you mean?" he demanded.

"He's dead," said Jane.

47

"What? Why wasn't I told?" he leaped to his feet.

"I have been trying, but as you opened the conversation with an ill-informed barrage of insult, the normal courtesies and amenities were rather circumvented," said Jane. "After he wrote to you, he was murdered; and Nessie – Miss Fanshawe – called on my aid and my husband's services."

"And what services does he provide that are not in my purview? And you speak lightly of murder – hearsay of course!" cried the solicitor.

"My husband is an officer at Bow Street, sent by Sir Nathanial Conant to deal with such cases as require a gentleman's touch," said Jane, "and I assist him by questioning the ladies. You are doubtless expert in civil law, my husband specialises in criminal law. And though the fact of Mr Popham's murder may be hearsay, there are a sufficiency of witnesses who saw the dagger in his neck, and indeed the body with the appropriate perforation to adequately attest to it as a fact. I trust I have your attention now," said Jane.

The solicitor's face had drained.

"Stabbed! I – I thought that it might be a melodramatic claim about poisoning by That Young Person if – if something untoward had happened. I – Henry dead! Murdered! Why, now I shall never know what it was that he wrote to me about!"

Jane's heart sank.

"He did not apprise you of the reason he was reported to be much angered at breakfast?" she asked.

"No, not at all; he wrote that he had discovered something that showed he needed to consider deeply the disposition of his finances and begged me to attend him in all haste to discuss what might be done. I am quite mystified," declared the solicitor.

"Well then, there is little that can be done," said Jane, "my husband made a cursory search of the man's study for any letter which angered him – it is conjecture only, but he became agitated over the arrival of the post, and is presumed to have been angered by some correspondence he received – but there was nothing apparent, and Caleb has locked the study and placed a strip of paper sealed upon the door to await your arrival to go through Mr Popham's papers."

The solicitor brightened.

"Very proper sentiments; far beyond what I would normally expect of Bow Street!" he said. "I had not heard that there were gentlemen associated with the Runners other than the magistrates themselves. Most heartening!"

"There is such a thing as professional courtesy," said Jane, promptly placing the onus on him to be professionally courteous to Caleb. "I do not believe I caught your name, sir, and I should hate to be caught out when introducing you to my husband. I trust, by the way the brandy is to your liking? I left the vintage to Glossop's discretion when I suggested you might be in need, I have no knowledge of Mr Popham's cellar."

"Oh, quite! Quite! My name is Avery – Lionel Avery," the solicitor was warming to Jane, who was all that a lady should be, and with an excellent grasp both of language and the important things of life. It might be said that Jane did not reciprocate this warmth; but the family solicitor would be a useful ally. She rang the bell and when a footman entered in response asked him to bring Mr Armitage to the library when the gentlemen had finished with the port. The footman bowed and left, and in short order Caleb walked into the room as Jane was explaining patiently how a man does not let strangers enter his study, cross the room and stab him without making some movement to deny them such an action.

"You'll be Mr Avery," said Caleb, "Glossop waited until the port had passed round several times before he thought to mention your arrival. The younger gentlemen are no good to any man for questioning, and that fellow Kemp is no good to any man for anything but he was like that before he touched the port. Will it disturb you to search the study tonight? I'd hate there to be a clew that a mysterious fire destroyed or something of that nature."

Avery permitted himself a thin smile at Caleb's description of the Reverend Kemp; and Jane was proud that her husband had probably extracted from Glossop what the solicitor's feelings on his client's family members might be.

"After a good brandy and some refreshments I consider myself fortified enough to look at the study," Avery declared. "For what are we looking in particular? Ah, some correspondence that may throw light on why I was summoned, yes?"

"Indeed," said Caleb.

"And the will," said Jane. "Miss d'Ambrose told me she had seen the will yesterday morning when she was speaking to Mr Popham and that it was in her favour. If the will is missing it would indicate that somebody had destroyed it for their own purposes."

"That's interesting, Jane-girl," approved Caleb.

"He made no mention of having signed it when he wrote," said Avery, "though if he were agitated he might have neglected to mention it. I sent it to him just a few days ago for final approval, and to sign in front of witnesses. I rather understood he had expected his brother-in-law to be one of the signators; and perhaps Miss Fanshawe, who was not mentioned in the will but for whom he set aside a small annuity."

"Oh I am glad of that," said Jane, "Nessie is a tiresome creature in large doses and if she has an annuity she will not be dependent on not irritating anyone she might end up as companion to."

"I understood she was your friend" said Avery.

"Yes; and I'd go out of my way for her," said Jane, "But live with her I could not. Though she might suit someone *deaf* I suppose," she added. Avery gave a bark of laughter.

"The woman's tongue is hung in the middle," he said, "babbles like a brook with as much purpose."

"Oh I think if you listen instead of letting the brook drown you, you'd find Nessie has mostly very good purpose," said Jane, "she's shrewd enough. And clever enough to let most people think she's stupid. She's probably doing a very good job of leading the conversation of the other men round to what they decided not to tell my husband."

"Well now!" said Mr Avery, interested. "Maybe I should get to know her better."

Jane hid a little smile. Avery had appreciated her own wit, but would be more comfortable with a woman who knew how to hide her intelligence; and he would make a very good husband for her friend who would not then be cast in relative penury on a small competence.

Caleb unsealed the study door having called for candles, and the redoubtable Fowler. Henry presented himself, and brought Simmy's apologies.

"I packed the cub off to bed," he explained. "You'll want our report on whether we found anything yet; the answer is negative, but we do have a list of people from the bailiff to visit. The grooms saw no strange gentlemen hanging around, for if there was anyone who came from outside, we thought it unlikely that they be any but gentlemen, or Mr Popham would not be so relaxed. And no hints brought suggestion that any female was hanging about. We decided that a female need not be a lady for a man to treat her with a relaxed indifference."

"Well done," said Caleb. "I doubt your enquiries tomorrow will yield much either; but it is important to cover the ground. Mr Avery, the theory was postulated that a tenant or neighbour might have knocked on the window and been someone that Mr Popham would feel at ease to sit back in his chair to speak to the same."

"Quite so, quite so!" Avery nodded eagerly. "And

who is,er, Simmy?"

"My son" said Caleb. "Like Henry here, who is his tutor between terms, he has aspirations to enter the law. Henry has urges for the bar, but Simmy considers that a solicitor has more opportunities for legal larceny."

Avery looked at him uncertainly; but Caleb had a perfectly straight face. The solicitor decided he must have misheard, or else the law officer used his words inappropriately. Henry was chuckling quietly to himself.

"As if he weren't bad enough, you must needs encourage him," sighed Jane. "Be concerned that the boy might want to enter Parliament!"

"Now, now, Jane-girl there's no call to accuse the boy of immorality!" said Caleb.

Mr Avery gave up.

This banter was beyond him.

It did not take much searching to find the will; Caleb decided to make that the first task and look through the correspondence second.

"It is not signed," said Mr Avery in satisfaction, "she evidently lied to you, Mrs Armitage."

"Maybe not intentionally," said Jane. "A will for a wealthy man is a complex and ornate thing. Flora is, I am afraid, a rather vulgar piece and ill educated, and still sufficiently close to a rather unfortunate situation to be somewhat venal in her outlook. I fancy she might look at that part of the will she considered important, to wit, that portion relating personally to her, and did not check to the end of the will. If when she spoke with Mr Popham he indicated this as his intentions she might not be aware of the legal implications. This will then is not legally proved; is there a previous one?"

"Yes indeed," said Mr Avery. "I have all Mr Popham's legal documents with me – so ill-formed and angry a letter gave me no indication what I might need,

so I have brought all the paperwork pertaining to the estate, settlements, tenancy agreements and the last Will and
Testament itself in case he wanted to check previous clauses if he was considering re-writing his will yet again. There being legacies to most of his relatives, if he was angry over some irregularity on the part of one of them, cutting them out of his will or reducing their legacy would be something that should be considered."

"Tell me, Mr Avery," said Caleb, "to whom does the bulk of the estate accrue if the previous will were to be enacted?"

"Not if, my dear fellow, it will be," said Avery. "It goes in the main to Mr Daventry Popham with, as I recall, a rider that he was the most convivial of all Mr Popham's relatives despite his execrable taste in clothes, and the hopes added that he would not spend the greater part of the income from it in dressing to be even more ridiculous than he already is. Sometimes when clients insist on precise wording of clauses it can be very entertaining, dear me, very entertaining indeed."

"I can imagine so," said Caleb. "Well, I did glance at such letters as are here; and I have to say that there is more than one that might suggest a distinct lack of confidence placed in any of a selection of his relatives. Shall we go through them?"

Chapter 8

Mr Avery sat at the desk and reluctantly drew a pair of spectacles out of his pocket to balance on his nose.

"I need them to decipher some of the more execrable handwriting some people have," he said, sounding defensive.

"I can read them out if you prefer, sir," said Caleb, "I'm quite good at deciphering handwriting; I generally untangle the reports of my less literate colleagues for Sir Nathanial."

"And if they all write as badly as Gabe Stogumber, that is quite a feat," said Jane, who had seen that officer's correspondence with Caleb.

"Lud, Jane-girl, Gabe is literate by comparison with some of our lads," said Caleb. "Laborious business, writing, when you ain't used to it. While you're there, however, Mr Avery, you'll see how it is that no villain could easily sneak in those big windows, even if they were open to start off with."

"No, quite," said Mr Avery.

"Nessie's astuteness in noticing that is the reason we were called in," murmured Jane. "I should tell you that the Reverend Kemp was for the theory that an outsider had done it."

"Well Kemp is a fool as well as a mealy-mouthed canting hypocrite," said Avery.

"Come, sir, I'm sure he also has his bad points!" said Henry. Avery stared, then realised that he was being teased, and laughed.

"Also has his bad points! Very good, my boy, very good! How I would like to suggest it is evidence that Kemp covers up that he performed the murder – but alas! I fear him to be guilty of nothing more than narrow-minded stupidity. He faints at the sight of blood, you know; a nose bleed, a cut finger, it is all the same. He is most decidedly in the camp that denies transubstantiation, you know; he could never take Communion if he believed that the wine truly turned into the Blood of Christ."

"I suppose some people are just afflicted with that particular sensibility," said Jane. "Unfortunate in a parson; how does he deal with the dying who are coughing up blood?"

"Sends a locum," said Avery. "Aye, extraordinary, ain't it? sort of thing you'd expect of the Beau, if you thought he followed the ways of exquisites in those ridiculous novels girls like to read, but he's stout enough. Strips his natty coat and waistcoat to assist the horse doctor in the birthing of a foal if you can imagine."

"Throws a new light on the Beau," said Jane. "His conversation is stimulating enough, if somewhat inclined to the cynical. Is that too why Mr Popham liked him, his practical streak?"

"That and other matters," said Mr Avery. "You see as well as Henry being a friend of the Beau's father, whatever deprecating comments the Beau makes to the contrary, it transpired subsequently that they both had a tendre for the same girl. The Beau's father won her hand, and Henry has always been devoted to the interests of her son. I'm given to understand that there is something about this Miss, er, d'Ambrose that reminded him of his boyhood infatuations."

"The Beau does have a pair of dark brown eyes of similar shade to Flora," said Jane. "If they are inherited from his mother, it explains rather better why an otherwise hard-headed and proud man like Henry Popham should lose his head over a ..." she took a breath, "over a young lady who does not, to all appearances, have much in the way to recommend her beyond a well developed figure and an ability to remember lines. I do try not to dislike her," she added.

"You dislike her? Caleb raised an eyebrow. "You were all that was compassionate over the girl Dolly."

"Dolly was broken hearted over Frank's death," said Jane, "and she's a good kind girl who cares about people, and merely had an unfortunate profession. Flora is altogether too calculating for me to take her in any wise to my heart."

"Fair enough," said Caleb, "however, on with the task in hand. There are five letters here; two are but bills for certain expenses one might expect to occur in any gentleman's establishment, the monthly reckoning from the cobbler for the shoes of the servants, made or repaired, including a new heel to the boot of the groom Jem Hackett, and the other is from the doctor for the setting and treatment of the broken ankle of the groom Jem Hackett. Sounds like he was kicked by a horse."

"He was, Caleb," said Henry. "Simmy and I heard the story while we were looking for other clews; the ill-natured bay of Mr Luke Popham, and never a red ribband in the tail at all."

"Careless," said Caleb, "that puts a slightly different complexion on these ordinary looking bills, Mr Popham might have been less than happy that his young cousin's carelessness cost him the services of a groom for a month and the unnecessary expense of a doctor's bill and cobbling. Though he must have been expecting these bills; not the sort of thing to drive him into a rage."

"The amount might have reminded him how angry he was," said Jane, "and fired a slightly intemperate nature."

"I grant that," said Caleb.

"What then are the other letters?" asked Avery.

"The first one is from the leader of a company of actors" said Caleb. He cleared his throat and read,

"*Dear Mr Popham,*

It is with deepest regret that I write to you, since the monies you and Mr Morton have provided have been insufficient to date to be able to put on the play 'The Rivals' by Sheridan as stipulated in our contract. Whilst you have provided all that you had pledged,

Mr Morton has so far only provided a proportion of the promised sum,, and all that has been given has so far has been spent on costumes, scenery, licences to perform &ct &ct and there is a deficit for such things as the hiring of a venue. As you and Mr Morton made a verbal undertaking to be each other's guarantors I find I must ask you for a round sum of some fifty guineas which will cover all remaining necessary expenses.

I trust I find you well, your most obedient...'. Oh, all the proper usage," said Caleb.

"Well! I should think any man might feel unhappy that his partner in a venture had left him to find the rhino to the tune of a couple of ponies," said Henry.

"I would be inclined to agree," said Caleb.

"Henry Popham, being fond of playgoing, the more perhaps because it offended his brother-in-law, was accustomed to spend large sums to finance plays being performed," said Mr Avery. "However, it is a large sum to find when another has promised to pay. I do not know the specifics of the arrangements Henry was wont to make with Mr Morton; only that it was Mr Morton, who also at times likes to direct plays, who intended introducing Miss d'Ambrose onto the cast and thereby introduced her to Henry. As a long time friend as well as his solicitor, naturally I expostulated when Henry proposed making this girl his wife if she could learn to support the role of a lady. I am, I have to say, somewhat prejudiced against Mr Morton for introducing her to him."

"The witness has declared an interest in the case, m'lud," said Henry Redmayne.

"Idiot boy," said Jane affectionately. He bowed floridly.

"I have noticed that barristers like to playact and flourish quite as much as any actor," Caleb remarked to Mr Avery. The solicitor gave a thin smile.

"The main difference between the professions lies in the fees; for posturing at the bar telling an improbably dramatic farrago of nonsense, a competent attorney at law may command a salary considerably in excess of that the fellow who postures on the boards telling an improbably dramatic farrago of nonsense" he said.

Henry chuckled unrepentantly.

"Your point, I believe, sir," he conceded.

Mr Avery preened slightly. Jane reflected that it was a little unbecoming for a man of middle years to be so inordinately proud of scoring a verbal point against a youth not into his twenties, but it had been a nicely put verbal play. Henry certainly appreciated it, and Jane felt certain that the phrase would be heard at Oxford in the next week or so when he returned.

"The next letter, if you please, my dear?" asked Jane.

"Certainly. The hand is irascible… a moment… ah, yes, I have the habit of his heavy downward strokes now" said Caleb. "I see a man with gout and a red nose being the author of this, very peppery. It runs,

'My very good sir,

It is my understanding that you hold as your gift the living of the Parish of St Michael and all the Angels, Amberfield, where one might find that loathly and miserable discredit to his cloth, one Egbert Kemp'. Well the writer appears to know Reverend Kemp fairly well," added Caleb as an aside. "Sorry… *'the aforesaid Kemp should be cast out and unfrocked as a damned disgrace, sir, and as a poltroon, a fool, an imbecile, lacking in any common graces and unable to take a fence without looking like a sack of turnips into the bargain'.* I wonder if that's the real offence? Ah no, we're coming to it. *'he has no care for his parishioners, sir, and refuses to visit them, declaring that all illness is caused by sin and a lack of faith and exhorting any unfortunate sufferers to renounce their sin and pray. What kind of man is that, sir, I ask you, to have care of a Parish which includes a charitable institution for those bereft of limb in the service of their country?*

Does the madman believe that repenting of doing their duty to the King, God bless him, will bring back limbs carried away by artillery or shot? I demand that you do something about this state of affairs, your most ob't &ct Colonel Murray Wilson.' Which seems a fair demand to me if he's telling it as it is. Would that enrage Mr Popham?" Caleb asked Avery.

"Dear me, Egbert Kemp is getting worse," said Mr Avery. "I doubt however that it would enrage Henry; nor even surprise him particularly. Colonel Wilson is a neighbour and a patron of the hospital he refers to. It employs the men as best they might making simple furniture to sell. What Wilson fails to understand is that it is very hard for a man to throw his sister's husband out of the living, however much he might detest him, and the more because he dislikes his sister too."

Caleb nodded.

"That he would go out of his way to accommodate her because he will not be unfair," he said. "The third is quite straightforward. It reads '*deer Mister Popham, yor nevvy have been around my house and have had his way wiv my dorter Sukey and now she is wiv child. Wot are you going to do about this? Abram Reed*'. Poor man. I should have thought Michael and Gabriel were a little young to be chasing petticoats but I suppose they are old enough to have the urges, and trammelled enough by their father."

"I suspect it might equally be the Beau or Luke Popham," said Jane, "Mr Reed is not, perhaps, cognisant with the family ramifications and therefore he, and indeed his daughter, might believe either of them to be Mr Henry Popham's nephew too."

"That *is* a good point, Mrs Armitage," said Avery, "and Henry would have been angry if any of those four young men had been seducing any of his tenants. Bawdiness and licentiousness in plays he was quite happy with; indeed he said it was a way that mankind might let out the beast within by enjoying the baser side of himself vicariously. Outside plays he was generally rather stiff-rumped. Which is another reason I was so amazed at the way he was so readily besotted by this Opera Dancer."

"I understand she took up dancing when there was no acting work," said Jane. "She told Nessie how she had been a nice girl in a good establishment and had been asked to drink with a client, and when she woke up her clothes were disarranged. I don't say it isn't true, and she holds to the story that she has never, er, danced horizontally, but I don't actually believe her. I fancy Mr Popham wanted to believe her."

"Alas, I fear you are correct," sighed Mr Avery. "So it seems likely this last letter was the one to enrage poor Henry. And one of the young men killed him to prevent him forcing the young man to marry this Sukey – as well he might have done to teach him a lesson!"

"I had been wondering if there was yet another letter since there are signs of a document having been burned in the grate," said Jane.

Chapter 9

Caleb turned to stare at the grate.

"You're right, Jane-girl," he said, "well spotted in this uncertain candlelight; I am glad I didn't order a fire lit or that might have been destroyed utterly. Whoever did it was evidently in a hurry; there is the remains of a fire into which it was thrust, it being a cold day. *Bless* Nessie for having the study locked and no servants permitted to disturb it; that woman has the makings of a fine legal mind."

"Dear me, yes, I appear to have quite underestimated her in dismissing her in my mind as a poor little dab of a thing who talks too much," said Mr Avery.

Jane permitted herself a small smile of satisfaction. Caleb could not know her hopes for Nessie, but how fortuitous that he had said just the right thing. Mr Avery was not precisely love's dream, but Jane had every expectation that he would be a kindly husband and when a woman was some years advanced above twenty she could not really hope to be fortunate enough to find true love. Finding Caleb had been like something out of a novel, save that in a novel he really would have been the child of someone eminent and would be finally acknowledged as the true and legitimate heir; but she had only found happiness because of being prepared to defy convention and marry out of her class. Nessie would never do so, and would be shocked that Jane had done so, if she ever found out the truth. Emma Knightley had not been very happy about it, that great stickler for what was right and proper, and had not Mr Knightley spoken to her about what a fine man Caleb was, Jane knew she would have lost Emma's friendship. Caleb's put-down of Mrs Elton had not harmed his case either in Emma's eyes!

Caleb noticed Jane's smile and his lips twitched.

Jane was playing games, was she? Well Nessie Fanshawe could go further and do worse, and Avery likewise.

"Henry, lad," said Caleb, "you're the most lithe of us and with the best eyesight; can you, with a quizzing glass make out what is said on that half burned fragment?"

"I'll try, Caleb," said Henry, dubiously, "but would it not be easier to lift it?"

"Observe if you will," said Caleb, "how there are some words apparent on the charred portion, white on grey. Lifting the unburned fragment would make what is on *that* easier to see, I grant you; but the charred section would crumble to dust."

"Oh, I understand," said Henry. "So it needs to be read, each of us look at it, and a copy made and we sign it as a true copy of what was there?"

"That would be the sensible course to preserve it as evidence," said Mr Avery, "and the unburned corner then appended to the document."

"Very well" said Henry, easing himself down to lie full length on his front on the floor by the grate. "will someone write what I can see? And I say, Caleb, if you move those candles and use *your* quizzing glass to focus the light I wager – yes, like that" as Caleb moved to use the lens to increase the light. Henry gave a grunt of satisfaction. "Excellent, quite clear to see if not to understand. I think it's the right hand edge near the bottom and fortunately neither crossed nor recrossed. There's 'r-a-l-d-a' at the top of the fragment, the next line is 'elf ridiculous' the next line 'thoroughly' and the next 's-s-e-d garters' – I think that's garters, I apologise for an indelicate word, Jane – and the bottom is moderately clear, 'will tell you all about it later'."

"And the signature?" asked Caleb.

"You will not believe the ill luck," said Henry in disgust. "It curls back through the bars of the grate and is burned off. Have you written that down?"

"I have made a transcription by the lines as you have read them," said Mr Avery. "By your leave I will verify them; I believe knowing what I look for I will follow the transcript."

"And then I'll hold the glass to direct light for you, sir," said Henry to Caleb. "A court of law will not pay special attention to Jane's testimony, more's the pity, because her *mens* is more *sana* than most men."

"The writing however might be worth me observing," said Jane; and as the men moved out of the way for her she perused the fragment and added, "I would suggest this is the writing of a young person or someone not very well educated; it has a roundness to it that suggests someone for whom letter writing is not a skill to consider especially facile."

Henry laughed.

"That would cover most of the chaps at Oxford," he said.

"Possibly, in terms of felicity of style and frequency of correspondence to home, save when pecuniary embarrassments demand!" said Jane. "However I suspect that years of working under the dominie will have honed their hand to something mature, if not wholly legible."

"Unfortunately, only too true," said Henry, "most of the chaps do tend to write 'dearest mother, I hope you are well, can you persuade father to let me have a draught on the bank please' sort of letters."

"You, at least, have more grace than that, lad," said Caleb, "and I should think your father is proud of you."

"He is pleased that I can help with the fees by tutoring Simmy," said Henry. "I fancy it will be a while before he can adjust to me being his only son though," he sighed heavily. "Still he appreciates that there was no scandal – and that you have not formed a distaste for the family for my brother's disgraceful behaviour towards Jane," he inclined his head to Jane and Caleb found himself reliving the awful moment when Jane had fallen and gone prematurely into labour. However, she had survived and Richard's actions were no fault of young Henry!

"Nothing to do with you – and if he was a little spoilt, I fancy he had a bad twist to his character that was not entirely down to any spoiling, or you would be as bad, my boy," said Caleb.

"It was his expectations of Uncle Joseph," sighed Henry. "A friend of his was left very well off by an uncle, and Richard persuaded himself the same would happen to him. He always had an inflated idea of himself. However, that is in the past; will we speak further to anyone tonight?"

"I think not," said Caleb, "though it will be courteous to tell them so."

They withdrew to the salon where those who had been at dinner were still waiting. The twins appeared to have largely recovered from their over-indulgence, though Mr Morton was complaining of a headache.

"Considering how badly that candle is guttering and casting such a flickering light about the room I am surprised everyone has not got a headache," said Jane, tartly, entering the room to see the flame growing and shrinking and casting monstrous nightmare shadows over the largely numb company, perhaps too insensate from being treated as suspects to have the initiative to snuff it. Emma had not withdrawn to her bed, but was asleep in a chair, Nessie sat hunched over the fire, more conscious of its flames than the candle, Flora was lounging languorously at the men, not helped by the leaping flame that cast in cruel relief her rather bony face, and Jane had an absurd desire to cast them as the three witches from Macbeth. The Beau was also dozing, and Luke was regaling the Reverend and his sons with an unlikely sounding story about how a friend of his had outsmarted a would-be crooked horse trader.

At Jane's words, Michael leaped up and blew the candle out with more vigour than good sense, and the hot wax sprayed across the flock wallpaper to a cry of dismay from Nessie, who leaped to her feet.

"Michael, you might have used the snuffer!" she cried. "It's what it is there for!"

"It did spread rather, didn't it?" said Michael ruefully.

"I'm sure Nessie will permit you to make amends by lifting each wax spot with a hot knife in the morning, and taking out the candle grease with a ball of two day old bread," said Jane. She had no idea if Nessie knew how to deal with such a problem, but by explaining it to Michael she might hint if Nessie had received a less practical upbringing than Jane had from Miss Bates! As Nessie cast her a grateful look, Jane was glad to have spoken.

"It's a good illustration of murder, really," said Caleb. "A single, thoughtless, violent action has unforeseen and far spreading consequences, and brings misery for others in its wake. And ultimately the most misery to the culprit."

"I wager you have no idea who did it," sneered Luke.

"Not yet," said Caleb. "There has not been the time to look at, sift and weigh evidence. However that too must wait, studying the documents in the study has taken sufficient time that it would be unkind to keep you any longer this evening to question. Tomorrow is another day."

"And you have seen the will and *know* I am Mistress of Amberfield, haven't you, whatever anyone might say?" demanded Flora.

"I will not believe that Cousin Henry made a will in that female's favour!" Luke almost spat.

"He had it drawn up," said Caleb.

"You see?" said Flora, gloating.

Caleb bowed to her.

"From your point of view, Miss d'Ambrose," he said, "It is an unfortunate fact that Mr Henry Popham had not signed that will. The will you saw is invalid; and the only legal will is his previous one, which Mr Avery here has with him. It will be read tomorrow. Mr Avery has commended the will to my care to place somewhere very safe," he added. Avery started to open his mouth to say something, changed his mind, and nodded.

"Quite so, quite so," he said. "May I, er, express my condolences to all the family; such a shock! Carried off in his prime, I must say, to arrive and learn of this shocking murder has quite unmanned me. I will read the will on the morrow. And now I bid you good night," he added.

It was a hasty retreat to escape from the loud sobbing and hysterics in which Flora was now indulging, declaring that someone had conspired against her to prevent 'dear Henry' from providing for his own heart's love and bride in all but name. The Armitage ménage was glad to leave her to it. She was just running up the octave accusing the Beau and Luke and Mr Kemp of preventing Henry Popham from making legal his heart's desire and demanding that they should accede to a dead man's wishes and agree to abide by the unsigned will.

Whether it was the Beau's slow hand clap or Luke's snort of derision or the reverend quoting the psalms about those that storeth up riches for themselves and knowing not who would gather them, Flora was in full blown sobbing hysterics that woke Emma up with a start as the solicitor and the Armitage party withdrew out of earshot.

"I – er, I had better give you my bag and all the papers in sooth," said Mr Avery to Caleb. "Is there somewhere they can be locked safely away?"

"Oh I shall do better than that," said Caleb. "I shall give them to my man, Fowler, a man of infinite resource and sagacity, who will find a place so devious to hide them, even Jane and I would have trouble finding them.

Good man Fowler; trust him absolutely."

Avery nodded.

"Always good when a man can trust his man absolutely," he said. "I wish I had my clerk with me; he acts as my man when we are staying with clients, but I little thought to be gone for long! Have you any idea who might have done this?"

"Oh I have plenty of ideas who *might* have done it," said Caleb, "which is a whole different thing to knowing or even having a shrewd idea. Early days; questioning of everyone and considering those letters will bring answers I am sure."

Chapter 10

"Are you too tired to give me the thoughts of the maids while you see me to bed, Ella?" asked Jane. Ella smiled her prim smile.

"Mrs Jane, I'm never too tired to do what I can to help; and moreover I fancy you've had more to do than have I, for you look burnt to a socket."

"Or even done to a cow's thumb," said Jane.

"Mrs Jane, you never learned such vulgarities from my lips!" said Ella, disapprovingly. Jane laughed.

"I honestly cannot recall where I heard that," she said. "It is picturesque in a way, is it not?"

"It is not what *I* consider picturesque, Mrs Jane," said Ella repressively. Jane laughed.

"We shall agree to differ, Ella," she said, "I find the rich use of the language by every layer of society quite fascinating; from the *flash whids* of the criminal classes up to the circumlocution with classical allusion of the highest. This perhaps is why I am so fond of word play in charades."

"Hmm, and these charades nothing but an opportunity for young men to make suggestion of improper comments if you ask *me,*" said Ella. "Were you wanting to play with words, Mrs Jane, or hear mine?"

"I want to hear yours, Ella; I beg your pardon" said Jane.

"Well now, the housekeeper is efficient enough but you would not believe the amount she can gossip! Enough to curl your hair, Mrs Jane! She moans about Miss Fanshawe's organising of the house but she had to admit that Miss Fanshawe does know what she is doing, it was fitting in around Miss d'Ambrose as what she resents, and so do the maids – they all think she's nothing but a jumped-up miss who is no better than she ought to be. They consider her vulgar and say that when she laughs she *shows her gums,*" declared Ella awfully, "I couldn't help but be reminded of that girl Dolly."

"Dolly worked hard enough to better herself," said Jane, mildly.

"Oh I don't say she didn't; but the words I've heard, Dolly would have been more welcome as a wife to Mr Popham, being at least a good natured girl and willing to learn, and not a lazy little piece, which by all accounts Miss d'Ambrose is, ready to lie abed until all hours if permitted, and wants to be waited on hand and foot; and the maids resent that in someone they don't see as any better than themselves. And she's one as will hand out slaps and throws things if she's displeased and has no respect; why even the morning he died, when he sent to ask her to attend upon him she said 'oh good G-d, what does Mal-vo-leo want now' in a cross tone. There! I don't know what a malvoleo is but it sounded spiteful as well as her naughty blaspheming."

"It is a Shakespearian reference," said Jane, smiling to herself at Ella's disparaging sniff. "Malvoleo was steward to Olivia, and was a pompous fool who was gulled into believing that his Lady loved him. I must say it's not an entirely apposite choice since it was Mr Popham who was the one of higher class, not Flora; I suppose the comparison is to a stiff-necked, proud man whose infatuation makes a fool of him."

"And that," said Ella, "is the general view of the household – that she was leading him around by the nose!"

"Poor Flora – Nessie has tried, but I fancy the fault is more in the pupil than in the teacher," said Jane. "Flora seems to have impressed no-one with her assumed arrogance to ape, so unsuccessfully, the ways of a great lady."

"The servants always know the origins of anyone spurious," said Ella, smugly.

"Really?" said Jane. "What do they say of Mr Armitage then?"

Ella flushed.

"How you do take me up, so, madam!" she said, firmly making it clear that she was punishing Jane by being formal. "Mr Armitage is an exceptional man; and besides, That Man Fowler is so good at dropping sly hints that they are all convinced they've 'just heard somewhere' about how he's the son of the Duke of York, a war hero who charged into a breach at the head of a forlorn hope group and was made a colonel on the spot by the Duke of Wellington himself being only a major before."

"Dear Lord!" said Jane, faintly. "The story grows in the telling! What is Fowler thinking of?"

"Oh that wasn't Fowler, Mrs Jane dearie!" said Ella, forgetting that she was at outs with Jane. "All that war hero embellishment was by the footman Mr Caleb gave a burst of barrack-room invective to for eavesdropping. He reckoned nobody short of a major could have that command of language."

Jane sat back and laughed weakly.

"They say nothing travels faster than rumour!" she said. "Tell me, Ella, did you discover anything from the maids about whether any of the young gentlemen here have libertine propensities?"

"Mrs Jane, what do you take me for?" demanded Ella.

"I am sorry to offend you, Ella," said Jane, a little perplexed.

"I am indeed offended that you should think I would fail to find out anything so basic!" said Ella. "The one who pinches the – the hindside of the maids and puts his arm about their waists and tries to kiss them is Mr Luke; though Mr Michael has tried to copy him, he had his face slapped by the girl in question and he begged her pardon. Mr Popham did not permit liberties with his maids though, you may be sure of that! and when Mr Luke kissed Ruth – she's a chambermaid – she went straight to the Master, and complained, and Mr Luke was told that he had better watch his step. This was some time ago, not during this visit," she added.

"Excellent work, I thank you," said Jane. Ella hesitated.

"The staff are concerned about who will inherit," she said. "If it is to be Miss d'Ambrose, I fancy most will prefer to seek other situations. She had told the girl who dresses her that she was in the will," she added.

"Miss d'Ambrose was labouring under a misapprehension," said Jane. "The will that names her chief legatee is unsigned. You may pass that on. I believe the house goes to Mr Daventry Popham but I am not sure."

"That will be a relief; and that it's not Mr Luke too," said Ella. "No woman would let her daughters come here if Mr Luke were the squire. Mr Caleb is waiting to come in, so I expect he will have a full report from That Fowler," she added, and glided out.

Caleb kissed his wife.

This being a pleasant occupation it took some considerable time; then he asked,

"Does she really dislike Fowler as much as she seems to?"

Jane chuckled.

"Oh I think it is but a matter of form," she said. "I have learned a lot from her intelligencing," and she proceeded to fill him in.

"Ella is very good," said Caleb, "Fowler covered similar ground concerning the gentlemen; the twins are held to be pleasant enough and are generally spoken of as 'young limbs' more after the fashion of schoolboys than as of young men. They are not really seen as anything but boys by the staff. The Beau is laughed at but in what appears a kindly manner, he is held to be a man to go to in trouble, he helped a footman to confess to breaking a valuable vase and pleaded his cause not to lose his place. However, there is a lot of ill feeling about Mr Luke's propensities, but not as much as the ill feeling concerning the Reverend Kemp's larcenous tendencies."

"He has larcenous tendencies? The old hypocrite!" said Jane, shocked.

"Yes, he is rather, isn't he?" said Caleb cheerfully. "Apparently he doesn't consider it theft to hie himself down to the cellars and help himself to bottles of brandy; considers it the just due of a guest to be given the best by his brother-in-law, even when that means secreting several bottles to take home with him. Apparently last time he also managed to make off with a firkin of crayfish and whole loaf of sugar."

"My goodness!" said Jane. "I, er, hate to cast aspersions, but it would be convenient to blame one known to appropriate brandy for the peculations of others?"

"No, it seems that he was seen and was quite blatant about it," said Caleb dryly, "and it too late to tell the master because he left while Popham was out riding. I'd say that argued something of a guilty conscience, but he's brazen enough before the servants. Glossop calls him 'The Gannet from Thanet' as apparently he hales from eastern Kent. It's usually the brandy though. Not that the origins of that brandy would bear close investigation; I've every suspicion it was 'run', but that's not in my brief for the time being. I'll drop a word to the Beau to be a little more careful about where he gets his liquor."

"It might be purchased legally now we are at peace with France," said Jane.

"It might, but it isn't," said Caleb. "Glossop, in waxing hot to Fowler about the depredations of Kemp, let slip that he even descended on the cellar where are kept those bottles that swam over. I'm sure you're aware of the euphemistic term for meeting smuggling vessels being 'bottle fishing'".

"I had not heard it; but one learns something new every day," said Jane. "Well, that is neither here nor there as things stand."

"I don't know about you, Jane-girl, but I'm too tired to stand," said Caleb, yawning.

"Yes, so am I," said Jane, "I will have to ponder on all that Ella has said later; I'm sure I haven't taken in everything. Any more from Fowler? If you repeat it, at least you won't forget it even if we miss anything of significance until we go over it again."

"Only that the servants despise Mr Morton too, as a vulgar fellow but concede that at least he's good for some reasonable vails," said Caleb. "His clothes are odd but very expensive; unless he's punting on the River Tick and expects hourly to be dunned by the bums he's a warm enough man. I wonder why he didn't cough up the rhino for his part of the agreement over the play?"

"Perhaps I should quote from *The Rivals,*" said Jane, with a twinkle in her eye, "'We will not anticipate the past; so mind, young people, our retrospection will be all to the future' which I shall interpret as saying we can ask him tomorrow."

"I've never seen it," said Caleb.

"Frank took me when we were first married; before things became so sour," said Jane, "however I would prefer to see it with you; Sheridan has a way with words you would appreciate more than Frank was able to do."

"At the moment the only words I would appreciate, my dear, are 'pray snuff the candle and come to bed'," said Caleb ruefully. "Mrs Armitage, I am too tired to speak, but I believe I am not too tired for matters arising from our marriage vows."

"Mr Armitage, I pray you, douse the candle and repair to bed to further those very matters," said Jane, gravely.

Caleb, notwithstanding his alleged tiredness, took the precaution of wedging the handle of the door onto the landing with a convenient chair; any trying to come in by the other door would have to come past Fowler, sleeping in Caleb's dressing room, and Fowler was armed.

There was, after all, a murderer in the house; and Caleb did not intend the matters arising with his wife to be in any wise discommoded by the same.

Chapter 11

Breakfast was not well attended. Nessie, the Beau, and the twins were there but otherwise it appeared that people preferred to take their breakfast in their rooms or were rising late; Luke Popham had apparently ridden down to the nearest inn to breakfast where he wouldn't, in his own words, reported by Fowler, have to peer at the faces of damned interlopers. Both the Reverend and Mrs Kemp breakfasted in their rooms, which as Henry said cheerfully was probably down to feeling fragile in the case of the reverend and wanting to be thought to be fragile in another sense by his wife.

"Why is he feeling fragile?" demanded Simmy, who never neglected breakfast. Simmy, in point of fact, was on his second breakfast, having wheedled the cook when he first got up, and having won the heart of that peppery individual by praising the dressing of the previous night's goose, was rewarded with slices of some of the left over raised pie and the intelligence that the remains of the goose, larks and Davenport fowl would appear on the dinner table as a fricassee of fowl and such late green peas as the gardener had managed to nurture.

"He drank too much and unwisely," said Henry, in answer to Simmy's query, not being one to believe in telling children convenient fibs, "so his delicacy this morning is his own fault. If I didn't rather like Gabriel and Michael," he nodded to them, "I might suggest we sang loudly to cheer him up, but I don't intend to disrespect them."

"You know we have to stand by our father, Redmayne," said Gabriel.

"And mother," added Michael.

"Of course you do," said Henry, "which gives me the more respect for you; and for that I hope it doesn't turn out to be either of them as killed Mr Popham."

"They couldn't!" declared Gabriel "Papa would

never kill anyone; he passes out at the sight of blood and besides it breaks the fourth commandment!"

"He's good at breaking the sixth to make off with Uncle Henry's brandy," said Beau.

"Common knowledge is it?" said Caleb. "Then the motive of being afraid of being revealed as a thief does rather evaporate."

Michael paled.

"He said it was a gift!" he said. "Do you accuse my father of lying as well as of theft?"

Caleb snorted.

"I accuse your father of having a sufficiently active imagination and elastic interpretation of the laws of hospitality – we won't go as far as the law of the land or the Ten Commandments just now – that he could believe that his peculations were of the nature of gifts owed to him. I fear his grip on reality is more of an issue than his grip on morality."

Michael and Gabriel exchanged a look of dismay. They did not seem entirely surprised, however.

"Is this the usual complement of visitors to attend breakfast, Nessie?" asked Jane.

Agnes Fanshawe shook her head.

"No; usually Cousin Luke would join us, the Reverend Kemp and Emma, and Mr Morton had tended to do so. Flora likes to rise later and take a cup of chocolate and some thin bread and butter, usually right before most of us are ready to take luncheon. The men don't always attend luncheon, of course, having breakfasted heartily."

The Beau was busy discussing a full platter of beef, pickles, bread and butter, fried kidneys and kedgeree to illustrate her point.

"You don't fear losing your figure, Mr Popham?" said Jane. "You do not fit the paradigm of an exquisite as portrayed in a novel, I have to say."

"Fortunately, my dear Mrs Armitage I seem not to accumulate *avoir dupois* in the least and may eat as I please; which being so I please myself and eat as I will," said the Beau. "I personally see no reason that a fashionable man should not also indulge in early rising in the country; I am no sportsman and I would hate above all things indulging in such vigorous, er, entertainment as boxing, but I think I am no fribble to be reduced to fainting and tears at the idea of facing a hearty breakfast. You, a fashionable young lady, also do not shrink from breaking your fast well enough!"

Jane laughed. She had helped herself freely to buttered eggs, toasted bread and gammon as well as bread and butter and raspberry jam because she had found that a good breakfast set her up well for the day.

"Oh I do not shrink from breakfast, Mr Popham; my apologies for being led astray by novels and the cartoons of such as Gillray and Cruikshank," she said.

"I don't say they haven't got it right in a lot of cases," said the Beau, "but then, I like to be unique rather than being bound to the paradigm. And I like the style of clothes I choose because they are clothes that make an effort to be decorative, rather than be the drab clothes of a Corinthian, whose main aim appears to be to ape a coachman. I have no desire to ape a coachman; I am a gentleman and I don't mind who knows that."

"It is not to ape coachmen but to show a gentleman who is a sportsman and capable of dealing with his own nags and carriages!" shouted Michael.

"Please, Michael! I am not deaf!" said the Beau. "It looks much like the costume of the coachman to me, with the insistence upon the many capes on a drab driving coat, but if there is some subtle distinction then I confess myself unable to see it; outside of the quality of the fabric meaning that a Corinthian might be capable of fettling his own prads and carriages but is unlikely to risk his fine clothing to do so. I concede that you might be able to tell the difference, just pray do not screech in my ear over breakfast. That *does* turn my stomach."

"Paltry fellow," muttered Michael.

"He has a point," said Gabriel.

His twin glared at him.

"As for *your* sorry get up…." Michael began, only to be interrupted by Jane.

"I do trust that you young gentlemen are not about to bicker in so puerile a fashion as to make me wonder if you are indeed any older than my son," she said.

They gave her identical hurt looks.

"Mrs Armitage, it should be plain that we are some half dozen years older than Simmy!" said Gabriel.

"You mistake me," said Jane, "since I referred not to my stepson but to my son Joseph, who, as a baby, screams when he does not have his own way. "

The Kemp boys lapsed into offended silence.

The Beau rose, bowed to Jane, and sat back down to his meal.

Mr Morton appeared in the door of the dining room.

"Not too late for breakfast am I?" he said. "I fancy I may have drunk a touch too much port last night."

"You're not the only one," said the Beau.

"Well, I have to say, with this terrible murder, it is a rather nerve-wracking thing to happen, then being under investigation from Bow Street, however considerate and discreet the officer and his good lady; I should think it would drive a Methodee to drink too much," said Mr Morton.

"Unlikely; they don't drink at all," said the Beau. "Can't say I agree with the stand but I see why they make it; drinking too much is a blight upon the lives of the poor, you know, hardly any better than Hogarth's day when he drew his famous 'Gin Lane' and 'Beer Street' pictures. Drinking doesn't make any man happy but it does taste good and at least a rich man may drink his fill as he can purchase a better quality of misery."

"Philosophy so early in the morning?" said Morton, helping himself to toast and jam.

"Not so much philosophy as following through the train of thought you brought up," said the Beau.

"Demme, if I wouldn't rather have a Methodist in St Michael's than Kemp, who manages to combine the worst features of a squarson with some of the more erratic puritans one read about in history."

"What's a squarson, Mr Popham?" asked Simmy. "I never heard that word."

"Well, lad, it's a parson who tries to act like the local squire, hunting, shooting and generally being more concerned with the figure he cuts as a gentleman than the souls of his parishioners," explained the Beau, shifting round to face Simmy, his high shirt points being enough to keep the boy from his view if he did not move.

"Oh, like Mr Elton would like to be if only he had the bottom to hunt," said Simmy.

Jane's exclamation,

"*Simmy!*" was unfortunately coincident with Caleb's shout of laughter.

"Conflict of discipline?" asked the Beau, affably.

"More a case of trying to teach the scrapegrace when and where to express his opinions," said Caleb, ruefully. "I should not have laughed; such thoughts, Simon my lad, are best not expressed in public. Especially as Mr Elton would not have the bottom to call you out on them" he added.

"Rather bad form to mock the afflicted, old man," added Henry, "after all, Mr Elton suffers from being married to Mrs Elton; you should show Christian charity towards him."

"Prig," said Simmy, amicably.

"So, what's the order of today?" asked Mr Morton.

"Questioning people one by one," said Caleb. "There are a number of matters arising from the correspondence which Mr Popham received on the morning he was killed; and a number of factors within them that might have made him particularly angry with more than one of those people assembled here."

"Oh, then that lets me out," said Mr Morton, in

relief. "I've never done anything to annoy Henry; good friends we are!"

"Mr Morton, perhaps you should think about the state of your finances before you say that," said Caleb.

"The state – Mr Armitage, I fear I fail to understand you at all!" said Mr Morton. "There is nothing whatsoever wrong with the state of my finances, whoever says that there might be is a liar!"

"Indeed?" said Caleb. "Then you feel you might have agreed to back a play put on by a fraud?"

Morton frowned in incomprehension.

"Mr Armitage, you speak in riddles."

"Perhaps we should wait and pursue this in private after you have finished eating," said Caleb. "I would not wish to embarrass any man in public."

"You really do speak in riddles!" declared Morton. "I know no fraudulent men, and I have done nothing that I am ashamed to speak about in any company; well perhaps a few minor peccadilloes hardly worthy noticing that I might be a little loath to speak of in front of a real clergyman worthy of the name…er, meaning no offence, you boys."

"We've heard worse," said Michael, gloomily.

"Well in that case, and if you are as transparent as you claim, Mr Morton, perhaps you would care to explain why Mr Popham had a letter from the man who is to put on '*The Rivals*' by Richard Brinsley Sheridan, asking him, as your guarantor, to provide the fifty guinea deficit from your share of the backing."

Mr Morton went pale and his mouth dropped open.

"One moment" he said and ran out of the room.

"Do you think he's shabbed off?" asked Simmy.

"*Abiit, excessit, evasit erupit*" murmured Henry.

"Mr Redmayne, I pray you, not Cicero at the breakfast table," said the Beau.

"He had not the manner of a man fleeing but of one struck with thought," said Jane, "the more marked because of its scarcity I fancy."

"We need the fair Flora to put us right but I believe it's *'Troilus and Cressida'* that had the line 'The most unkindest cut of all'," said the Beau, unashamedly mopping his plate with a piece of bread and butter.

"Well, if you don't need Simmy and me, since finance isn't our strongest suit, we'll be off with the list the bailiff gave us," said Henry.

"One moment," said Caleb, and murmured in Henry's ear. The young man nodded.

"I'll confirm it is as you thought," he said. "It sounds believable. Come Simmy – work for your pa awaits, no gentle dalliance with classical nymphs today!"

Simmy made a sound of disgust at the idea of dallying with classical nymphs and went out happily with Henry.

"You've a good lad, there," said the Beau, "cheeky as they make them but with a good core of obedience and duty. Pity too many people will judge him on his looks."

"Then at the bar they'll underestimate him," said Caleb. "Ah!"

Mr Morton, flushed and embarrassed looking, swept back into the room brandishing a piece of paper.

Chapter 12

"Look! I had never posted it!" cried Mr Morton. "It was still in the pocket of my carriage coat, I had merely forgotten to post it! I will never tease Flora – Miss d'Ambrose I mean – again for her habit of leaving her correspondence lying on the hallway table in the hopes her maid will remember to post it, for I have been even worse, I put the thing in my pocket, meaning to drop it off at the Post Office as it was only a local letter inside London, but I remember, I was thinking about my wardrobe and what I should need to pack for this weekend, it quite took up my thoughts, and I walked right past the receiving office and home again! And so I came away with it in my pocket!"

"And what, precisely, is this letter?" asked Caleb.

"Eh? Did I not say?" said Morton.

"No, sir; you failed to explain in any way why it should be of any significance," said Caleb.

"Well, then I'll tell you; aye, show you too, as it's a little behind the times," said Mr Morton, "and I shall take the wretched thing personally to deliver. It's a draft on my bank to the tune of fifty guineas to cover what I owed; I had provided some of what I promised in advance but I know these people, the world of the theatre can be very profligate, and if they have the money all at once in their hands, they will spend it! so this was what I held back to be sure they would have enough to hire a venue. My goodness! I trust this will not mean more delays? I had hoped to drive back to London as soon as possible, Mr Armitage."

Caleb nodded.

"Mr Morton, if you will permit me a glance at that draft and permit me to note the name of your bank in my Occurrence Book, you may leave as soon as is convenient," he said, "I really do not think you have anything to do with this; and a man with a reputable bank can always be found should I need to clarify any evidence with you."

Mr Morton seized his hand and shook it, then proceeded to open the sealed letter and show Caleb the bank draft and covering letter. Caleb made a few notes and wished Mr Morton well.

Having an excitable man who was not part of the family sent on his way would make life a little less hectic.

Mr Avery arrived looking a lot less tired and appeared to be ready to get down to business.

"My thanks, Armitage, for the loan of your man to bring me breakfast and shave me" he said. "I should like to get on and read the will as soon as possible; all the members of the family will need to be present of course."

"That could be the sort of mission that we need the Duke of Wellington to organise," said Caleb dryly. "As far as I am aware, Mr Luke Popham is breakfasting in the nearest inn, and nobody else is yet abroad. I am given to understand that Miss d'Ambrose rarely rises before eleven, which she declares early and was put out to be called to see Mr Popham more than an hour earlier than that on the morning of his death."

"Well I don't see why I should have to wait upon the dilatory habits of those of the household who cannot manage to be up by quite half past nine," said Mr Avery, irritably.

"Quite so, sir," said Caleb.

"Well then, it is an easy enough matter," said Jane, crisply. "The servants shall be sent to those persons not yet abroad, and a boy despatched from the stables to go in search of Mr Luke Popham with a message that the will is to be read in the library at ten of the clock, and any who are not attendant upon that reading may be held to have no interest in it whatsoever."

"Bravo, Mrs Armitage; but better to make it half past the hour of ten," said the Beau, "to have to dress even in an hour is a distressingly short time; consider the sensibilities of those involved!"

"I was considering the sensibilities of Mr Avery and of my husband and myself," said Jane tartly, "and as I can manage to dress in no more than twenty minutes including a thorough wash, I fail to see why others should be unable to do so."

The Beau shuddered.

"Too unkind!" he declared. "Really, Mrs Armitage, you are a goddess amongst women to be so rapid in both ablutions and costuming! I fear I might swoon at the thought!"

"Mr Popham, you can dress quite as rapidly, I wager, if you have to," said Jane, "you may choose to enact the ways of a feeble creature but you have claimed to be unique."

"A conundrum of etiquette," murmured the Beau. "Does one take exception at being called feeble or accept the compliment upon one's uniqueness? Dear me, I fear I am at a loss for words!"

"No such luck," said Michael. "Papa and mama will manage it, Mrs Armitage, and so will Emma. Shall I go and tell them?"

"If you please," said Jane. "You had better set the hour at half past ten; it may take as long to find Mr Luke Popham."

"Unless he has drunk too much and breaks his neck on the way back by riding his ill-natured bay too hard," said Michael, viciously, plainly still unforgiving about Luke's disparaging remarks of the day before.

"No such luck," said Gabriel echoing his brother's early words.

"Gentlemen!" Mr Avery was shocked. "This is your cousin that you are speaking about!"

"I don't think our best friends would call us a close and loving family," said Michael, bitterly, "certainly someone did not feel any compunction in doing Uncle Henry to death; which is hardly the act of a loving relative, and though I don't pretend to have felt enough for Uncle Henry to shed many tears, I'd like to know who did it, and if it was a member of the family, I should have said Cousin Luke was more likely than anyone else."

"An interesting accusation, you cub," Luke Popham strolled into the room, still clad in the buckskins he had worn for his morning's ride. "I believe I feel the urge to take you outside and give you the thrashing that you deserve that your father has obviously neglected to bestow upon you."

He made as though to seize Michael's arm, but Caleb moved with the speed that always still astounded Jane to stand between them.

"I believe you will not do so, Mr Popham," said Caleb, pleasantly.

"And can you tell me why not?" said Luke Popham, silkily.

"Because in the absence of the boy's father I would be forced to knock you down if you tried," said Caleb. "Assault upon a minor – I couldn't let that pass."

"I wonder if you could knock me down?" mused Luke Popham.

"Yes," said Caleb, simply. "I may be big, Mr Popham, but it doesn't mean I don't have science. And since I've survived more people who wanted to knock me down than you have tied cravats, you do not want to make me wrathful."

"I wonder if you know how many cravats I need each morning" said Luke.

"Oh you strike me as a fairly efficient man; I doubt you need more than a dozen" said Caleb, who was wont to wax irritable if he needed more than one attempt.

"Ah, you flatter me; but you have at least an appreciation of the art," said Luke. "How many cravats do you spoil each day, Mr Armitage?"

"I haven't the time to waste on such effete shenanigans; I keep to a simple style I can tie in less than three attempts and if I am hamfisted I wear a Belcher scarf," said Caleb, "I have my duty to do; if you'd served your country against Napoleon you might have understood the word."

"I believe we are reproved, dear coz" said the Beau. "Effete shenanigans! He has not, at least, called you feeble, Luke. There are, Mr Armitage, more ways of serving one's country than charging into breaches as forlorn hopes, you know."

"I've never been a part of a forlorn hope so if you heard that idiotic fable, I pray you forget it," said Caleb. "Though I was at Corunna, it's where I picked up the slight limp. I take it you were engaged in other service?"

"*How* you do focus on things and take one up" murmured the Beau. "I have a facility with languages; did a little translation for some people. Nothing too arduous, I assure you."

"We were glad of those who gained us intelligence," said Caleb, nodding to him. "I apologise; I became irritated. It was uncalled for to take umbrage at the foolishness of the insignificant."

Luke Popham looked ugly.

"Do you call me insignificant?" he demanded.

"Frankly? Yes," said Caleb. "I am an officer of the law and beyond the ways in which your life is significant in my investigations, I have no interest in you whatsoever. However, I *am* interested in the ways in which your testimony will affect my investigations so I would suggest that you hold yourself in readiness to be questioned after the reading of the will; I have a number of very pertinent questions to put to you, my lad."

"Anyone would think you suspect me of killing poor cousin Henry!" cried Luke.

"Since you've got the best clutch of motives so far, perhaps that should not surprise you" said Caleb, grimly. "We will examine them in detail later. In the mean time, I suggest you might want to wash, even if changing in a reasonable time is beyond your powers, since the ladies will not wish to smell the stables while listening to the will being read."

"The will is being read? Why was I not told?" Luke scowled again.

"Because you didn't give anyone a chance when you started on that foolish boy and his hasty words," said Jane. "And caused all present to think shame on a grown man for taking such violent a stand against a boy of – what, sixteen? – for speaking a little intemperately after you had trampled on his hero-worship. Murder brings out the worst in people very often, but I pray you, do show that your worst is just a little better than that of the highwayman who tried to threaten me in my husband's last case."

"Why Jane! You must have been terrified!" cried Nessie. "What did you *DO*?"

"Do? I shot him of course," said Jane. "Nessie, dear, I do wish you will tell Miss d'Ambrose to hurry herself; I understand you are the only person who can handle her with tact. She will not like it if I have to come and fetch her."

"I wager she would not" said the Beau, looking upon Jane with renewed respect. "Shot him, by Jove! Mr Armitage, I am not sure whether to congratulate you on your remarkably capable wife or commiserate you upon the same!"

"Oh the congratulations are in order," said Caleb. "Shall we go through to the library and make ourselves comfortable? Those who are late comers must perforce then take the extremely decorative and highly uncomfortable chairs with the striped satin seats that try to precipitate one onto the floor."

"Ah, yes, Uncle Henry was sadly deceived in the purchase of those," said the Beau. "I believe I warned him that they were not all they appeared; but when Uncle Henry set his heart on something, alas, his normally shrewd mind was inclined to perceive only a roseate image of the truth."

Caleb and Jane both shot him a sharp glance.

"How much did you find out about Jemima Harris?" asked Jane, bluntly.

The Beau elevated his eyebrows.

"Ah, you know about her real name?" he said. "I believe I found out most things. Uncle Henry, however, was of the opinion that she was a poor girl wronged. I'm not saying there haven't been those that are, but all I discovered was very much to the contrary. If she was ready to be a faithful wife to him, however, I would not in any way have intervened; it was his life to lead, not mine. And I perceived a certain look not unlike my poor mother which doubtless led to his infatuation. Yes, I know – knew – most of Uncle Henry's secrets" he added. "Because he trusted me, though; not because I went looking. There is a deal of difference."

"There is, sir; there is" said Caleb. "And I am hoping you do not turn out to have killed him, for I am afraid I like you more than I thought I should. If you did, I would urge you to tell me so in short order, in the hopes that there might be some mitigation. If I have to find out, I will be less lenient."

"I did not kill him," said the Beau, "my cousin's innuendoes about my expectations despite, I am angry that he has been killed. Not sorrowful; not yet. I do not permit myself that luxury. But I want to see his murderer caught and brought to justice."

"I have not yet failed," said Caleb.

"Then I place my trust in your abilities," said the Beau, inclining his corseted body stiffly in a bow.

Chapter 13

The library was an even more austere room in daylight, the heavy drapes at the long windows on one side of it tied back to let in the morning light. The view was out onto the sculpted park and led cunningly through artfully placed bushes across the lake to the classical folly. The new, overstuffed chairs were perhaps a sour note in the room but they were in the latest and most fashionable style. Jane eschewed them and settled in a rather old armchair turned towards the fireplace. The fire was a little sluggish as yet and Jane was glad of the cashmere shawl she had brought down to wrap around herself. Its bright, jewel-like colours, too, were most reminiscent of the warmth of its exotic origins, a wedding present from Caleb's sister who had married a man in the Honourable East India company, and for whom such shawls were not such over-priced luxuries as they were in the home market. Indeed, Caleb's brother-in-law, John Perrin, did a little business on his own account, which was permitted as perquisites, in sending such shawls for sale on the merchantmen that he docketed in Calcutta. Jane was happy to be tucked almost out of sight of the family, able to listen to what they said.

Caleb took a seat on a stool behind a projecting book case; he too wished to be forgotten. Mr Avery took a seat at the head of the large library desk and waited for the family to file in and seat themselves. The Beau pulled up a buttoned leather chair and absently arranged other chairs more or less facing the desk. The twins piled onto a chaise longue and waved to their sister to join them as she came uncertainly into the library; then Luke Popham came in, smelling more of soap than of the stables, having too compromised by changing into trousers and pumps and changing his coat. He kept the waistcoat that was, Caleb noted cynically, not quite able to be identified as the famous Four-Horse Club livery of blue with wide yellow stripes, being blue with yellow stripes piqued at the edges and with a couple of fine white lines within the yellow to give the impression of association with those famous whips at first glance but was not close enough for any true member to really call him on.

The Reverend and Mrs Kemp entered next, the reverend's eyes a little bloodshot, and Mrs Kemp looking warily about.

"That boy won't be here, will he?" she asked.

"Which boy, Hester?" said Mr Avery.

"That ugly little monkey of a boy who's supposed to be the son of that Bow Street Runner," said Mrs Kemp.

"Oh, young Simon! Delightful boy, what little I saw of him," said Mr Avery. "The lad came to see me this morning before I left my room; was interested to know if I had any knowledge of tenancy disputes or law suits with neighbours to help his father out. Very keen on his studies but I'd not be surprised to find him as much a young demon of mischief as Michael and Gabriel."

"*Lionel!*" cried Mrs Kemp, "how can you stand there and suggest for one moment that My Angel Boys are – are young demons of mischief? And if you think That Boy is likely to be stealing while we are all engaged in here…"

"Hesther, before you go any further, let me remind you that there are laws about slander; and slandering the son of an officer of the law is likely to get you a civil suit that will have you living on bread and scrape for the foreseeable future," said Mr Avery. "To leap from a young demon of mischief – as anyone who knows them and has suffered their practical jokes knows fine well Michael and Gabriel to be, it's not a year since they filled my umbrella with peas so that I was showered with them when I opened it, to start accusing a young man of unimpeachable character of theft based on some incomprehensible prejudice is quite untenable. You are making yourself a figure of fun. And if you show such antipathy to the child, I would not be surprised if you found frogs in your overshoes or something similar."

"I doubt that," put in the Beau, "I have every reason to suppose that our young Cicero has too much respect for frogs to submit them to that sort of ordeal."

Avery gave him an uncertain look and Mrs Kemp dissolved into sobs. Her offspring cringed together on the chaise longue.

"Really, Hesther, I can't see why the brat should be expected to be at the reading of the will; it's a family affair," said the Reverend Kemp, testily, "I wish you will keep your voice down; my head aches badly this morning, I fancy Henry's port was corked."

"I fancy it's more likely the result of a man so greedy for more he helped himself to the lees after Mr Armitage was called away and another decanter wasn't called for," said the Beau.

Kemp gave him a fulminating glare.

Luke Popham laughed.

"Well I'm not often in agreement with you, Daventry, but on this occasion I fancy that I am. Devil take it, where's that blasted female?"

He sat back in his chair whistling loudly the air of the birdcatcher's song from Mozart's '*The Magic Flute*' until Kemp grimacing in pain struggled to his feet.

"You – you *ATHEIST!*" he cried.

"Desist, Luke" said Avery. "I'm sure I am not feeling much edified by your demonstration of a stable boy's skills; do try to remember that you were born a gentleman."

Sullenly, Luke stopped whistling.

Into the rather strained silence, Flora erupted, looking stormy. Nessie fussed in on her heels.

"I don't see why I've been dragged down at this ungodly hour of the morning when I was lied to and misled about the will," flounced Flora, flinging herself onto one of the fashionable chairs, and promptly holding her tongue as she fought not to be precipitated in an undignified fashion from its shiny and unwelcoming caress.

"Blasphemy!" managed the reverend.

"Miss d'Ambrose, apart from your most intemperate language which must offend the sensibilities of any lady or gentleman, it is almost eleven of the clock, and I and the rest of the family have been waiting on *your* convenience, since it would be discourteous to leave you out of the reading of the will," said Avery, "you are rather presumptuous in behaving so and I request that you sit quietly, or else if you reject the courtesy of my invitation you may withdraw."

"Oh as I've had to get up, I might as well stay," said Flora, sulkily.

"Stand not upon the order of your staying," said the Beau, ironically.

Flora gave a little shriek.

"Mr Popham! You should not quote from *that play*! It is bad luck!"

"I didn't quote from Macbeth, my dear Floradora; I misquoted," drawled Daventry Popham, "and I do not scruple to name it either. A pity, my dear, that you were not more nice yourself about quoting from it when you spoke the words of Lady Macbeth upon seeing Uncle Henry's bloodstained corpse."

Flora was ashen.

"No! it is from 'Lear'!"

"No, my dear; it is Lady Macbeth who wonders that the old man should have so much blood in him," said the Beau, spitefully.

Flora promptly had hysterics.

"*Now* look what you have done, Cousin Daventry!" said Nessie, crossly, reaching for the vase of rather scraggy chrysanthemums on the mantelpiece, removing the flowers, and dashing the water from the vase in

Flora's face.

"You are quite the spoilsport, Cousin Agnes; just as it was starting to become interesting," said the Beau.

"Daventry! Miss d'Ambrose! Really, this will is not going to be read at all if you will not all cease from behaviour that would shame a group of children!" declared Mr Avery.

"I rather fancy that Mrs Armitage would manage a suitably scathing put-down to us all if you care to ask her, Lionel," said the Beau.

"I do not; I am capable of holding my own and if any do not care to listen I will read the will anyway and if you are too busy impressing yourself with your own clever wit to hear what I have to say, it will be no fault of mine!" said Mr Avery. He settled his spectacles on his nose and unfolded parchment.

The Beau settled down with a look of spurious interest. Flora subsided into quiet sobs.

Mr Avery cleared his throat, and produced the will.

"May I just say that this is not the most recent will; the most recent, however, had not been signed. It would have made Miss d'Ambrose the principle legatee. For this reason she has, I feel, some right to hear the previous dispositions of Henry Popham's property. She is well provided for with a settlement and Henry's death does not alter that; nor the fact that he has already arranged with me an annuity for his cousin, Agnes Fanshawe, and the ownership of the house in Hampstead for her kindness to his intended" he paused.

"Oh! How *kind* of Cousin Henry!" Nessie flushed and looked pleased.

"That Mrs Armitage female says you didn't succeed though," said Flora maliciously, "she's not entitled to it, Mr Green-Bag because apparently she didn't make me enough of a lady."

Mr Avery glared severely over his spectacles.

"The annuity," he said, "was for her kindness to you and her efforts. There is no stipulation concerning success or failure in her venture; indeed I would consider the venture doomed as one cannot make a silk purse from a sow's ear. I suggest you keep mumchance, Miss d'Ambrose or I may have to ask you to leave. For Henry's sake I am making every effort towards you; but you make it very difficult; very difficult indeed."

Flora achieved a flounce which was in danger of making her silk gown slide her off the slippery chair.

"The reason for providing an annuity for Miss Fanshawe," explained Mr Avery, taking off his glasses and polishing them vigorously, "was because he wished her to be one of the signators of the will that was not signed; and it is not customary for those who will receive legacies to be signators. She receives no legacy under this earlier will, since at the time, Henry Popham was scarcely aware of her existence and only became so when he was in need of a chaperone for his chosen bride."

Flora's head came up sharply as a thought struck her.

"If he expressed an intention of leaving it to me, and spoke about it to you and your clerk, that's an intent declared before witnesses; surely that counts as an oral will?" she demanded.

Mr Avery smiled a wintery smile.

"Whilst I believe such things are accepted as valid amongst the illiterate classes, where there is but little to leave, it is not strictly speaking legal. You have your settlement, Miss d'Ambrose; you may be fortunate in having impressed the heir sufficiently to permit you more. That will be a matter for discussion later."

"Whichever of us it is, I'd advise against having anything more to do with the jade," said Luke.

"Oh Cousin Luke! I know she is not very ladylike, but truly, she is trying very hard!" said Nessie.

"Trying, in any case," said Luke.

"Cousin Nessie, had Miss d'Ambrose made some effort to become part of the family instead of making it clear that she expected to be mistress of the house and ban us from it as she chose, she might perhaps have been more likely to have been the recipient of kindly charity despite her origins," said the Beau. "Don't start screeching – Jemima – I would not have cavilled at your past if I thought you would do well by Uncle Henry. Can we move on? It will be luncheon before we're done here otherwise."

"Certainly" said Mr Avery. He went on,

"'*This being my last will and testament, being in sound mind and spirit*' there being a few legacies to servants which I will skip as minor bequests" he added "'*To the hospital for crippled soldiers in the village of Amberfield, I leave the sum of three thousand pounds which I would have left to my brother-in-law had he been a more convivial person and had he not already managed to steal quite easily that sum from the pilfering of my cellars*' you said something, Mr Kemp?"

"Preposterous!" spluttered the reverend.

"Indeed, such a level of peculation is quite preposterous," agreed Avery. "Where was I? ah yes. '*to my sister, my advice that she should try a new hat from time to time, if not to make her more becoming, which would be beyond any milliner, then at least to provide some work for some poor girl; and an annuity of four guineas a year for the same, to be revoked if it is not spent on hats.*'"

"My brother is ridiculous to insert such a clause!" declared Mrs Kemp.

"I did urge him to be a little more generous," said Mr Avery "No woman could possibly purchase a decent bonnet for under six guineas; but he was adamant. Let me go on: '*to each of my nephews, two thousand pounds to be held in funds until they reach the age of twenty five, or by discretion by my executor if they should marry before this. Three thousand pounds to my niece Emma, who will require the extra to overcome the disadvantage of her parents, also to be held in funds until she is twenty five and released at the discretion of the executor if she is able to have a Season."*

Emma sighed; and murmured to her brothers,

"Not much chance of that!"

Mr Avery went on,

"*'To my cousin Luke, who is a poltroon, I leave two thousand pounds for the sake of his father, who was a decent man, on the proviso that he is not found to have caused the pregnancy of any of my staff or tenants, in which case the money shall be forfeited and two hundred pounds to go to any such infant or infants and the residue, if there is any, to an orphan asylum of the choice of my executor.'*" He looked hard at Luke who shrugged. "Well," said Avery, "this is what Henry wanted written. And now, we come to the heir and residual legatee."

Chapter 14

"What's this about an executor? He was stabbed, not executed!" declared Flora.

Mr Avery took off his spectacles and regarded her with some irritation.

"An executor executes the will and testament; which is to say, is in charge of seeing that the legacies are duly provided to those supposed to get them and any other bequests made by the testator – the one who has made the will," he explained.

"Well how am I to know that?" asked Flora, sulkily.

"You could have worked it out by the context in the same way that I did" said Emma "And you could have asked Cousin Agnes later so as not to look a fool in front of everyone, the same as I was intending to do."

"Emma dear, speaking out in that bold way is so unladylike," said Mrs Kemp.

"I'm sorry, mother," said Emma.

Jane pitied the poor girl; well a lot could happen in three years. Perhaps with Mr Avery's connivance – and she had stopped disliking him now, especially in light of his praise of Simmy – if she and Caleb were back in the town house, she, Jane, might bring Emma out in three or four years time when the child was old enough.

Mr Avery resumed his spectacles and picked up the will.

"I doubt that there are any surprises to be found here" he said. "*'to my cousin, Mr Daventry Popham. being the most convivial of all my relatives despite his execrable taste in clothes, I leave my house, the home farm and income thereof, and any residue once the other bequests have been made, in the hopes that he will not spend the greater part of the income in dressing to be even more ridiculous than he already is.'* And that, ladies and gentlemen is the will in its entirety."

The Beau was smiling ruefully.

"How like Uncle Henry to have made observations like that. Dear me, I fear that sartorially speaking, we have never agreed; if only he had been more observant of high fashion and wore his shirt points higher and starched it would have been quite impossible for anyone to have stabbed him in that fashion. I had never thought of my taste to be equally a form of armour before but I will certainly never eschew my high collars and a well starched cravat. I confess it is not a surprise as I have always understood myself to be the heir, though I am a little surprised that Luke and the twins were left relatively little. However, the twins at least I invite to treat my house as a second home, I wish I could say that I felt as hospitable towards my dear cousin Luke. You see," he gave an apologetic smile, "it is so very hard to like someone who has tried to suggest to Mr Armitage that I killed my uncle for the inheritance and who is damnably rude without having Michael's and Gabriel's saving grace of wit."

"Popinjay," said Luke.

"My case rests," said the Beau. "How distressing to think that Luke is my nearest relative since my father died; I really will have to make a will. The thought of him inheriting anything but my ill-will quite gives me a spasm."

"You should get married, Beau," said Flora. "I would feel I was letting dear Henry down if I did not suggest that I was his choice as lady of this house."

"I think I can handle my own amatory affairs quite adequately without your aid, er, Flora," said the Beau. "I would dislike being married to you; and as I have quite rigid ideas about how a wife should behave, I fancy *you* would dislike being married to *me*."

Flora pouted.

"I have worked as hard as I may with dear Nessie's help," she said. "It will not be long before you will not be able to tell I was not born a lady."

"Alas, my fine Flora, it is no such thing – I must get

out of the habit of quoting songs – but the old fashioned idea I hold that a wife should be able to hold a household, order the meals, sort out squabbles between the servants, present a house that has an air of harmony, and, most important of all, be able to converse with me sensibly about current affairs" said the Beau.

"Why, I know all about current affaires!" declared Flora. "I knew before it was an on-dit all around town that Lady Bellington was having not one affaire, but two, one with Lord Astleigh and another with a fellow who acts at Drury Lane with Keane!"

A pained look passed over the Beau's face and Flora looked puzzled as Luke laughed sardonically and the twins uproariously.

"Flora," said the Beau, with heavy patience, "when most educated people speak of current affairs, they mean politics. Not the sexual acrobatics of the more incontinent of the *haut ton*'s members. You betray yourself again."

"Be fair, Daventry; most society women might make the same mistake," said Luke. "It's a hilariously precious idea, you wed to Miss d'Ambrose."

"Thank you Luke: your observations about society women are, alas, only too likely to be correct, but I fear that marrying to oblige you with hilarity is not my idea of a good choice of nuptial endeavour," said the Beau, "and as, alas, I know all too much about the fair Flora's origins, even were she as ladylike as my own mother was, I must feel unable to enter into such a notion. Uncle Henry was, I fear, naïve."

Flora cast him a look of dislike.

"You nosy torchecul!" she said. "if you were a man you'd not turn me down!"

Luke laughed again.

"Well, that's a revealing insult – more revealing on the insulter's origins than on any predilections of poor Daventry – though I fear he's too nice to understand your meaning."

"Oh my facility with languages has taken me into contact with some of the coarser cant," said the Beau, equably. "Inaccurate, Flora; and foolish to make such comments," he went on quietly, and Jane had to strain to hear, as he added, "hitherto I have considered you with mild contempt but a degree of disinterest. You would not wish me to decide that my contempt was enough to discuss what I know with Lionel Avery; you have told enough lies that I fancy the settlement could be broken as being obtained under false pretensions. You were better to play least in sight if you expect to be even tolerated by Henry Popham's relatives."

Flora looked angry; but she turned away and walked out.

"*What* did that word mean that dreadful female used?" demanded Mrs Kemp.

"I have no idea" said her husband. "However as Luke plainly knows, I expect it was low."

Luke gave a coarse laugh.

"*Very* low, dear Cousin Egbert" he said. "I trust there will be some luncheon available; after so busy a morning I believe I am in more need of fortifying myself than usual."

Caleb and Jane emerged as the family drifted out of the library.

"Dear me, a particularly distressing reading of the will" said Mr Avery. "I fear I cannot like all of poor Henry's relatives very much."

"Caleb, did that word mean much what I think it meant?" asked Jane.

"It is specific to being, as it were, on the receiving end," said Caleb. "That young female has riper language than many a footpad from Soho; I am sorry you were exposed to it, my dear."

"The Beau threatened her – softly, quietly and without any to-do about it – that if she did not play least in sight he would inform Mr Avery of all he knew about her, as likely to break the settlement as having been made on her under false pretences. Is that possible?"

Avery frowned.

"A very difficult business now that Henry is dead and cannot testify that he believed whatever she told him," he said. "I do not know that it could be broken, but if she believes that it can, then perhaps she will be less strident. If only I did not fear that she would insist on returning with poor Miss Fanshawe and hanging on her sleeve in the Hampstead residence."

"If you ask me, staying in the quiet rural fastness of Hampstead when she had the chance to be lady of this pleasant house and a fine fortune was one thing; to do so for the sake of it will not suit a romping doxy like that," said Caleb. "She will pine for the bright lights and excitement of the world of the theatre; and she is one who does not like to be without a protector. She will use the settlement first to cover herself in what she considers finery and then if there is any left, or if she can touch only the income, she will use it to supplement what she can get by returning to being an actress or an opera dancer. I fear she is one who cannot learn to be a lady; you were right about that, Mr Avery!"

"She is a repellent piece," said Avery, "and I apologise all the more, Mrs Armitage, for mistaking you for one moment for her."

"I suppose meeting a woman you did not know in this house meant that your assumption was understandable, since you were tired from having ridden from London, and with no idea what was toward," said Jane, dropping a little curtsey. "I was somewhat out of charity with you at first, but I have revised my opinion. You were, I think, a good friend to Mr Henry Popham; and he needs friends to uncover who might have killed him."

"Have you formulated any theory as yet?" asked Avery, eagerly.

Caleb grimaced.

"I have not yet questioned the men," he said. "I do

not want to suspect the Beau, but he is a cool hand; cool enough to just walk into a study, kill a man, and walk out as though nothing had happened. The poignard had a fairly large guard, the blood might spurt but would probably catch against the guard not do more than stain the cuff of the murderer at most, unless the person who stabbed him was unlucky. By leaving the knife in the wound he or she ensured that the blood would not spurt wildly as happens with wounds in that part of the throat."

"Or she? You think one of the women might have done it?" asked Avery.

"I do not think Nessie likely to have done it; it does not seem likely that she would have sent for me had she done so, she knows I never was fooled by her air of helplessness," said Jane. "Emma Kemp is, I believe, too young and vulnerable to manage to not only commit the deed but to get away with it afterwards. If it was a woman it would have to be either Mrs Kemp, whom I have not yet questioned, and who is capable of killing kittens without appearing in any wise disturbed; or Flora herself. And as she had every chance of a most respectable position as Mrs Popham, lady of this house and a respectable fortune, I find it hard to see that *she* might have any motive."

"Of course she did believe the will was in her favour" said Caleb, judiciously "But there is still a world of difference between inheriting all of this, when you are not married, and any relative might reasonably be expected to contest such a will and be likely to have judgement found in his favour, and being a wealthy wife. If she was going to kill him, you'd expect her to wait to be a wealthy widow."

"Indeed," said Avery. "So you did not think the reading of the will revealed quite a lot?"

"You mean did I think that Luke expected a lot more and was not expecting any condition?" said Caleb. "It did cross my mind. It also crossed my mind that if

Mr Kemp were angry enough about something, he might forget his aversion to blood. He was most unhappy about the bequest to the hospital; as I recall in glancing through the unsigned will, that clause remained unchanged?"

"Even so" nodded the solicitor. "Insults and all. If Henry taxed him about that letter from the Colonel, a quarrel might have sprung up; the Reverend Kemp is not the most stable of men; such insults, and too, the leaving of the majority of the estate to a, er, scarlet woman, or one he would undoubtedly see as such, might lead him to thinking he was the, er, sword of Gideon as you might say."

"By Jove, yes!" agreed Caleb. "I've heard preachers like him, their favourite word seems to be 'smite' and they always get on to 'whom the Lord loveth he chastiseth' which I've always thought a damned tactless text on a Sunday before a judicial flogging."

"Well, gentlemen," said Jane, "The sooner we discuss luncheon, the sooner we might question the men; and not discounting either the concept that Simmy and Henry might bring us news of neighbours or tenants who held grudge enough to come visiting. "

"Ah, indeed!" said Avery.

"I've no quarrel with that immediate plan!" said Caleb.

Chapter 15

The Reverend and Mrs Kemp, Luke Popham and Flora seemed less than welcoming as Jane and Caleb came to sit down for luncheon, but the twins and Emma were more concerned with their viands than with any atmosphere, Nessie was fussily accommodating and the Beau all that was affable.

The light midday meal was one of cold meats and salad; a leg of ham vied for the attention with Melton Mowbray pie, giblet pie and potato pie. The salad was really a species of salamagundy, a beautiful thing of many layers with sliced hard boiled eggs, anchovies, veal, and a selection of vegetables each layer on layer, topped with curled parsley. Another dish held another version of salamagundy, a row of hard boiled eggs cut in half with the yolk removed and the hollow filled with a variety of things, anchovies, beetroot, red pickled cabbage, grated tongue and ham, and a sprig of parsley between each.

"Blood on white skin," said Michael, ghoulishly, indicating the oozing beetroot. Flora gave a little cry.

The Reverend Kemp paled.

"Really Michael! That remark was a very poor jest indeed!" he declared.

"Go to your room, Michael; you may miss luncheon" said Mrs Kemp.

"And you may discuss the matter with me later," said the Reverend Kemp. Michael paled slightly but got up, bowed, and left the room. Gabriel looked upset. Jane knew the look in Michael's eyes. It was the look she had seen in the mirror when Frank had smiling said that they would discuss some matter more when they were at home. It was the look which expected a beating.

"Boys are so fond of melodrama, are they not?" said Jane. "Really, though it was foolish, I am sure none of

us refine much upon it; it is not as though Michael and
Gabriel knew their uncle well enough to grieve in the same way that a sister might. I am sure none of us would wish him to be in to deep trouble for this."

"Whom the Lord loveth, he chastiseth," said the Reverend Kemp.

"I hope you have the skin off the back of the nasty brat," said Flora vindictively.

Jane was looking at Mrs Kemp

The boys might be her angels but not apparently enough so to save them from their father's wrath. A complex family and not a very pleasant one. Emma was almost crying.

"Really, Miss d'Ambrose," said Jane, lightly, "a *gentleman* does not chastise his son in such a way as you describe; it is the sign that a man is quite inadequate if he needs to beat his children any more harshly than a slipper across the backside when they are very small; certainly one does not beat a young man of Michael's age! It would be a laughable idea were it not so pathetic."

"You – you do not approve of the doctrine to spare the rod and spoil the child?" asked Mrs Kemp. Jane forced herself to laugh.

"Well you have to admit, that quotation is most antiquated," she said. "I understand that beatings are common in schools, in the army and in the navy; but one cannot expect such institutions that deal with young men in quantity to be able to instil the level of respect as may be instilled within a family without resorting to such practises. And of course in the military there are men from all walks of life, some of whom know nothing but violence and so are unable to respect anything else; and there is little time to teach them that there are other ways."

"Beating spoils a good man and makes a bad one worse; it's an adage of Cochrane's, and as an army man I may have a friendly rivalry with the navy, but it's true enough," said Caleb. "What a subject for a meal! No reasonable person would expect to beat a boy for a foolishly fatuous comment, Miss d'Ambrose."

Kemp glowered at him; but turned back to his meal.

Gabriel touched Jane's sleeve as she was sat next to him.

"Thank you," he said softly. She smiled at him.

"I'll ask the housekeeper to put aside some food for him," she replied. "If he's banned from dinner as well he'll be glad of it, whatever else happens."

Gabriel smiled, and Jane was reminded of a puppy asking for caresses.

"I'll interview all the men after the meal," said Caleb. "Oh, and I believe, Mrs Kemp, you have not been asked any questions; perhaps you and the Reverend would like to be the first, so that you may then take a post-prandial nap if such is your custom at all."

"I really do not see why I need to answer any questions," said Mrs Kemp. "How can I tell you anything about murder?"

"Oh everyone is questioned; in case they know something vital without realising it," said Jane, pleasantly. "An incident on the morning in question that has slipped your mind might well return when we discuss the matter."

"I want to speak to my son," said the Reverend Kemp.

"Oh it will wait," said Caleb, airily, "after I have spoken with you, I will see Gabriel, which will give you ten minutes or so to tell Michael that he has no manners – which none of us find any surprise in a stripling – and send him down to me for his interview. Hopefully if we can clear the Kemp family of any involvement and find out anything you might collectively know, you might then depart for your own home and not be held perforce here."

This was not entirely what the Reverend would have

liked to have heard since the table set at Amberfield Abbey was naturally much superior to his own board in the vicarage; but he could scarcely say so. Caleb maliciously thought that the man was also thwarted in his desire to take a belt to Michael for making him feel nauseous; and whether that was because he was genuinely affected or because as the killer, the thought of blood on white flesh upset him all the more, Caleb preferred not to think. Being unequal in general to facing the sight of blood did not stop the man being prepared to beat his sons badly enough to make them fear it. And that meant that he was capable of violence.

"Pray come into the music room, Mrs Kemp" said Jane. "I'm sure you will not mind if my husband remains so I do not have to go through everything again."

"Would it make any difference if I did mind ?" asked Mrs Kemp.

"I would note your objection" said Jane.

"You are unkind – subjecting us to all this!" cried Mrs Kemp.

"Mrs Kemp, you should bear in mind that the one who has subjected you to all this is whoever killed Mr Popham; we, my husband and I, are merely here to find that out – after all, it may be that other members of his family might be at risk," said Jane, crisply. She was not about to let this hysterical woman work herself up by turning the blame onto herself and Caleb. "I ask my husband to be present partly as an impartial witness since I do not personally like you, for reason of your comments yesterday; which I have not shared with him, and to be certain that he remains impartial I will not share with him at least until we leave here. If you prefer your husband to remain with you, we can question you together."

That would keep them both out of the way as Jane had nodded to Gabriel to take some food up to his brother while their parents were questioned.

The Reverend Kemp hovered with protective pomposity.

"I have to ask you," said Jane, once seated, "whether you had any reason to kill your brother."

Mrs Kemp gave a little cry.

"What a question to ask her! Of course she did not!" said the Reverend Kemp.

"Mr Kemp," said Jane, levelly, "I am asking your wife the questions; you will have your turn to answer. If you
cannot refrain from interruption, my husband will take you elsewhere. Now pray be silent! Mrs Kemp, please answer my question."

"No, I had no reason to kill Henry," said Mrs Kemp, "how could you suppose I could kill anyone?"

"Because you dispose of kittens" said Jane.

"Why, such has to be done; it is not like killing a person!" said Mrs Kemp.

"I would not be too sure about that," said Jane, "for are they not God's creatures? I concede that there are too many kittens born and to kill them quickly is better than leaving them to die of starvation, but to do so does argue that one might also be able to see certain people as inconvenient as kittens are, and therefore to deal with them."

The reverend was actually gagging. Caleb shook his head in amazement that a man who could have such sensibility over even hypothetical kittens could also cruelly beat his own children. The reverend was an odd creature indeed.

"I hate doing it, but Egbert cannot," said Mrs Kemp, sobbing. "He makes me do it; I dare not refuse. He would punish me if I did not."

"Oh, I had already realised he was a coward, ready to hurt those smaller than himself, and rant about the crippled, and to expect others to do what he is too afraid to do," said Jane. "I suppose as you are both here, one of the things we need to determine is whether he might be enraged enough to perform a violent act upon your brother with what he perceived as the Sword of Gideon for something he said."

"You blaspheme," said Kemp.

"No, sir; whoever killed your brother-in-law did that," said Jane, "but you had been called to book in a letter to Mr Popham; if you felt yourself righteous you might have
been angered and acted without consideration for the sanctity of life."

"What nonsense does this woman speak?" Kemp turned to Caleb.

"Scarcely nonsense, Mr Kemp, since Colonel Murray Wilson made a legitimate complaint to Mr Popham, asking that he revoke your living on grounds of what may be unravelled to allege unorthodox and indeed Unchristian preaching and questionable understanding of Theology" said Caleb.

"Nonsense! That old fool Wilson doesn't know what he's talking about, pandering to ruffians who would be better left begging if they can't stir themselves to get jobs, of which most are perfectly capable or they'd not manage the makework that is provided for them! And his ideas of pandering to the sick, who are nothing but lazy and their ills nothing but the product of sinning and lack of faith! I've never had a day's illness in my life!"

"How lucky for you," said Caleb, dryly, "that you do not count your extreme aversion to blood as a sickness of the brain and therefore lay snug at home while others fought to be sure that Bonaparte never overran England as he overran most of the other countries on the continent. I count myself lucky that *my* wound has not wholly incapacitated me; though I was told I would never walk again, I confess it was not faith in the Almighty that made me prove them wrong but determination that I would not be beat by a lugubrious sawbones who drank too much. I see you are confessed from you own mouth in this dubious theology; and since you hold to it so firmly I cannot but wonder if you have quarrelled with Mr Popham over the same and in the rage I see you working yourself into grabbed up the nearest weapon to stab him."

"He did not go to see Henry at all on the morning he was killed," said Mrs Kemp. "It being a fine autumnal day we stepped out into the garden; he wanted to write a sermon with the bright autumnal colours as an allegory of
the display of wealth and gaudy excess of a decadent modern society presaging the fall into the death that is winter."

"I would certainly consider that dubious theology too, but let us not concern ourselves with it," said Jane. "Then you have not spoken with Mr Popham regarding the letter from Colonel Wilson?"

"I have no idea what letter you mean," said Kemp. "By what right do you question my theology?"

"Oh, only as a clergyman's granddaughter, I admit," said Jane. "I cannot say that I have ever heard such an interpretation of the turning of the seasons in God's wonderful world in such an extraordinary allegory. However it is not your theology that is in question but the keeping of the Ten Commandments; we know you have broken at least one."

"It is not true!" howled the Reverend. "I never looked upon that scarlet woman in lust, but in disgust, and I have not laid a hand on her; it is she, the Jezebel, who put her hand on my arm in her encroaching manner and said that it would be more pleasant to be friends! She thought to cozen me, knowing my influence with the younger members of the family, and I was never taken in for one instant nor moved to thoughts of incontinence!"

"With this household's fondness for quotation, 'methinks the gentleman doth protest too much," said Jane, dryly.

"Besides," said Caleb, "I for one wasn't thinking of the prohibition on adultery; I was thinking of 'Thou shalt not steal' which as I recall lies some few points ahead of adultery, and therefore although not placed, making a good showing on the field."

"You are a wicked man, making reference to racing terms when speaking of the commandments," said Kemp "And I have never stolen!" he pointed a bony finger at Caleb, his sleeve rising up to display a long, angry scratch on his wrist.

"I'm afraid adultery comes between 'thou shalt not kill' and 'thou shalt not steal'" said Jane, "you are thinking of coveting."

"Aye, that'll be it," said Caleb. "He's just broken the bearing false witness one as well, because we have it on the testimony of Glossop and indeed the dying deposition of Henry Popham, by means of his last will and testament, that the Reverend Kemp pilfers brandy and other drink quite freely."

"It was due to me as a gift from my brother!" declared Kemp.

"Not according to him, and that's what counts in a court of law," said Caleb. "My, a cheerful picture we have of a clergyman, who steals, covets his brother-in-law's goods and bride to be, even if he never got as far as adultery in more than thought, bears false witness and is moreover uncharitable to the sick, halt and needy. Can you wonder that I also have to consider that I might back the failure to observe 'thou shalt not kill' to place? In other words, your brother-in-law knew you as a thief; may have observed the looks you gave his bride, smouldering equally in disapproval and lust, and when he heard of your observations on your parishioners, including those whom he wished to remember in his will, you can understand why I have to question you closely in case your wife is perjuring herself out of loyalty, and you left her in the garden with some small excuse to knock on Henry Popham's window, having recognised the handwriting of Colonel Wilson and knowing that he would be complaining of you, and killed him, rejoining your wife, and maybe making excuse that you caught your hand on something to explain any blood?" he pointed to the scratch on the reverend's wrist.

"He was not away above a minute!" cried Mrs Kemp "He – he wished to relieve himself! And he did catch his hand on a thorn, for I saw it, and it made him most ill!"

"But can you be certain there was no blood before he deliberately scratched himself to explain it?" asked Jane.

"He could never deliberately – oh *dear*" added Mrs Kemp as the parson passed out.

Chapter 16

"Strewth!" said Caleb. "I suppose brandy…"

"Water" said Jane. "He's less used to it; it will provide the necessary shock to the system that most people derive from the imbibing of brandy."

There was a carafe on the table, that Jane had bespoken beforehand, more for her own and Caleb's benefit in needing to refresh themselves with potentially long hours questioning potential suspects. Caleb loosened the man's shirt and held the crystal glass to induce him to drink.

The reverend coughed slightly on the water as his senses returned.

He groaned.

"I – this is intolerable!" he moaned. "I – I could not hurt Henry; I pray you, cease this!"

Jane wondered if any of his offspring ever found his beatings intolerable and begged him to cease. Had he swooned simply from the shock of being accused, the memory of blood from being scratched most nastily by a thorn, or from the horror of a terrible deed, she wondered. He was pale, and neither he nor his wife likely to manage any further testimony; though what they had produced already might be damning enough if interpreted that way. Caleb and Jane exchanged a look.

"You may both retire," said Caleb. "Perhaps you will ask Gabriel to come in next."

It was a most shaky reverend who left, his wife holding him solicitously by the arm.

"Papa looked really shaken," said Gabriel, nervously. "I really don't know anything that I might tell you that might help, you know."

"You might know more than you realise," said

Caleb. "For example, you might be able to tell me if you saw any of the household during the fateful morning; your brother, say, or your parents."

"I know what Michael did, he went to see Uncle Henry before he tried to go after Cousin Luke; but that's hearsay, isn't it?"

"That depends whether you would lie for your twin," said Caleb.

"I would, sir," said Gabriel. "We squabble about minor things – like what we like to wear – but we're twins. We'd do anything for each other."

"And you see, that's one reason I can't rule the both of you out," said Caleb, "because either one of you might have dressed in the other's clothes to make sure of being seen inside, or indeed outside, whilst being no such thing; and instead of Michael galloping off down a ride, he might have come quietly back, and two Gabriels might be in evidence."

"And it's not as if we haven't done that at school to get each other out of trouble," said Gabriel. "There's a room with a boarded up door and we managed to undo it so one of us could be both indoors in normal clothes writing lines and outdoors dressed for cricket. It takes some pretty sharp timing I can tell you! And both of us needing to get most of the lines done before and after all this so Michael could hare off down to the village and pay his debt to that thief of a bookie before he came dunning the bagwig about it, and I had to bag the position on the outfield and hope nobody whacked one my way while I was being Michael inside. But we didn't do anything like that. Neither of us has any grudge against Uncle Henry, least of all one big enough to even wish him dead, let alone do anything about killing him. It's a pretty low trick, sir, to stab a man who's sitting there expecting no harm."

"It is, lad," said Caleb, "and I have to say that your willingness to tell me about your use of your looks tends to make me predisposed towards believing the pair of you innocent – of murder, anyway. Of turning the hairs of your dominies quite grey I cannot acquit you."

Gabriel chuckled.

"I suppose now we're studying to go up to Oxford we should behave a bit better when we're back at school," he said. "We should have been back last week, but this invitation from Uncle Henry was a stay of execution," he paled suddenly, "And I say, sir, that wasn't meant how it sounded," he added.

Caleb nodded.

"We all use figures of speech without thinking twice about them – until they ring too unpleasantly against circumstance," he said. "Did you see your parents at all that morning?"

"Papa asked mama to take a turn about the garden with him as he wanted to try out some ideas for a sermon" said Gabriel. "Which means haranguing her like a congregation. By the time they came in he'd talked her into a headache; but he'd scratched himself and was looking most ghastly himself. He was bleeding you see…" he broke off and added "I say, sir, he may have had a little blood on his cuff but he really had scratched himself, I saw the wound. I can't have you taking me wrong."

"How much blood was on his cuff?" asked Caleb.

"Enough to show" said Gabriel "At least if he lifted his hand; it was all underneath where the cuff had lain against the cut. There was a line across it."

Caleb nodded.

"And you were wise to tell the whole truth about it," he said. "Too often the innocent may be suspected because others will not tell the whole truth and so when the matter comes to light, it sounds suspicious – and all facts might not be fathomed. That is all I have for you at the moment; please send your brother to me."

"Yes sir" said Gabriel. He turned to bow to Jane. "Thank you for helping me see he got something to eat" he said.

"I should not perhaps help young – what did Mr Avery call you? Demons of mischief, that was it – flout their parents' discipline, but it did seem a little harsh for a rather tasteless comment," said Jane. "Cut along do, lad; with luck your father may not feel like any more than a perfunctory word on the subject with your brother."

Gabriel left, having made another bow,

Michael entered and made his bow.

"I say, sir, ma'am, Gabe says it was you who talked papa out of wanting to beat me; thank you," he said.

"I don't hold with beating a child – or a youth – save for the odd chastisement of the rump when they're too young to understand much else," said Caleb. "A beating never constitutes a cogent argument for better behaviour. And the offence was trivial."

"I say, I really have to make an apology for resenting Mrs Armitage for making disparaging remarks about us too," said Michael.

"You were neither of you showing yourselves in a very good light," said Jane, "and my words were out of line as I was irritated with your mother. I, too, apologise."

"Have we all the niceties out of the way so we may get on?" demanded Caleb. "Good. You already told me that you followed Luke out and on the way to the stables knocked on your uncle's study window to ask him for a loan; concerning which he was somewhat negative, and you left, and he snibbed the window behind you. Correct?"

"By Jove, sir, what a memory you have! Yes, that's exactly what happened; and I went and saddled up and the groom did not remember which way Luke had gone, or he said he did not, but his grin said otherwise. I rode off on the ride that affords the best chance of good pace in the hopes of seeing Luke and maybe learning from watching him ride. I did not know then," he flushed, "how much of an embarrassment he found it being admired by a young cousin. I – I do not know quite what to think; he is an excellent horseman and he boxes and is an all round sportsman, and all that is admirable; but he was rather unkind in his way."

"Lad, just because a man is good at sport does not make him a good man," said Caleb. "There was a young officer in my unit who was a good sportsman, but he was also too fond of betting on results of sporting engagements, and good at sport he may have been, but judging horseflesh or other sporting contest he was less good at, and he was heavily in debt. It was with a very heavy heart that I overheard him with a lady – sometimes you overhear things you do not mean to, though I was glad that I had done so in the end – who was arranging to have his debts paid in return for telling her exciting stories that included our dispositions. So poor was his judgement that he was telling a female spy exactly where our men were to facilitate an attack."

"What did you do?" asked Michael.

"The only thing I could do; I reported the matter to my colonel together with my opinion that the young fool had no idea that he had just turned traitor and sold secrets. He should have been shot," added Caleb grimly, "as what he told her could have had the regiment cut to ribbons. As it was, forearmed, the Colonel changed the dispositions in a hurry, including ambushes for likely attacking forces, and sent him home in disgrace."

"That was pretty merciful," said Michael. "How stupid of him!"

"I've observed that some men who excel at sport have concentrated on that because they are not clever enough to concentrate on anything else," said Caleb. "There are, of course, those who are clever too, because they are the sort of men who excel at all they do. They are rarer. Luke Popham is quite clever, but by no means as clever as he thinks himself, and I would warn you that whilst I'm not going into details he has probably been guilty of some fairly despicable behaviour. "

"You mean he…er, believes in exercising *droit du seigneur*" said Michael.

"And as it's illegal in Britain, he's not exactly behaving well – even if he overwhelms a girl with his personality and position to make her act willingly," said Caleb. "Well, you know of his ungentlemanly conduct in that respect; do you really think him so admirable? What would you think of someone of higher estate – a duke say – who dazzled Emma into such a position and left her with child?"

"I'd want to kill him," said Michael.

"Precisely," said Caleb.

"He's rather unpleasant, really, isn't he?" said Michael. "I didn't see him at all, though, so I cannot say if he was abroad or not. When I returned it was time to change quickly for luncheon; and then of course we rather went off eating because we all crowded into the study when Glossop yelled in horror. And Flora said that Shakespeare thing about the old man having too much blood in him, and Cousin Nessie ticked her off, and papa had to be revived with brandy, and mama had hysterics, and Gabe, Emma and me shabbed off because it was pretty awful."

"A fair and full summation, I think," said Caleb. "Was Luke there?"

Michael thought, frowning.

"No sir; but he often did not come to luncheon, he reckoned it was a meal for women. I'd have liked to have been that indifferent, but to tell the truth I'm hungry most of the time."

"It's a complaint of the young" said Caleb. "Your body is still growing and demands the food to help it do so. Perfectly normal. I didn't stop feeling hungry all the time until I was over twenty-one; but then I had a lot of growing to do."

Michael looked admiringly at Caleb's tall, well built frame.

"I wager you could take on Luke and beat him without working up a sweat too," he said, "*and* you're devilish clever; I should think you'd be the sort of person any man ought to model himself after."

"Personally I'd be flattered to think any youngster would think so; and feel that it gives me a dreadful responsibility to be worthy of it," said Caleb, "but then, any good father feels the same; a need to be worthy to be respected by his children."

Michael looked thoughtfully at him, and gave a rather twisted smile.

"I pitied Simmy for his twisted face and withered arm and limp," he said, "but I was wrong. He's lucky. And I – I wish him well."

He bowed and left as Caleb nodded his dismissal.

Chapter 17

Luke Popham came into the music room with a swagger and an arrogant look to his face, and set a chair to sit backwards on it, arms folded on the back of the chair. Jane suppressed the giggle that almost arose at the thought that the mighty Corinthian evidently could not think if he were not sat on some semblance of a horse.

"By the way, *what* rank did you say you achieved in the army, Armitage?" he drawled.

"I didn't," said Caleb. "I don't use it; though I understand from my man that there's been wild and unfounded speculation in the servant's quarters which also involve a forlorn hope and the sort of desperate heroics that one usually only reads about in despatches and are usually either exaggerated or else the poor sap cast as a hero ended up in the situation more or less by accident. Unless they're just raving lunatics like Harry Smith of course," he added.

"Oh!" said Luke, shifting uncomfortably. Caleb smiled, blandly. The fellow had hoped to wrong foot him and put him in a position of having an unlikely story pointed out as such; having Caleb doing the refuting was not what Luke had expected. Caleb put him down as the sort of man who would probably happily accept any accolades and look as though he were trying to look modest. All squeak and no breeches, thought Caleb.

"Would you like a snaffle for that chair?" asked Jane, sweetly. "It looks as though it's trying to throw you."

Luke glared at her, got up, turned the chair around and sat on it properly, one leg cocked over the other and his arms folded.

"I wonder that one of your exalted birth is permitted to work as a Bow Street Runner" he sneered.

"We prefer the term 'Officer of Bow Street'" said Caleb. "Frankly, my birth is not at issue. I have very little contact with my family and in the case of my father's side, I like to keep it that way. I don't like any of my uncles. I consider them the greatest rogues unhung."

This happened to be true; Caleb had shed the taint of his father's brothers as soon as he could, since both worked for the Navy board in supplies and did well for themselves in cheating the King's sailors. His father had called them the scum of the earth, and one of Caleb's first lessons was that there were worse thieves than the relatively honest pickpocket. With the rumour, however, that his father was the Duke of York, this could be taken as a comment about the Prince Regent and the other Royal Dukes, and was a sufficiently common view not to be entirely surprising. Princess Charlotte was the only truly popular member of the Royal Family, especially with nationwide sympathy for her illness in her pregnancy, now almost to term.

"Well, I doubt I have anything much I can tell a Bow Street Officer," Luke made it a sneer. "I've told you where I was. I was hiding from the cub and then I went for a ride. Hardly giving me time to kill my cousin – and as the tiny amount he left me hardly amounts to enough to kill a man for, you don't need me any more, do you?" he stood up.

"Sit down," said Caleb.

"And if I choose not to?" said Luke.

"I'll sit you down," said Caleb, "and if need be I'll place you under arrest for obstructing an officer of the law. You won't get a prison sentence for it, but you'll get a telling off from a magistrate and you'll have had to have spent time in handcuffs and the embarrassment of being marched past your family in the same. There are a lot of things I want to talk to you about, Mr Luke Popham, none of which are to your credit, and we can do it here or we can do it in the holding cells at Bow

Street."

Luke sat down with a careless but angry laugh.

"Well I don't see what there is to talk about, but get on with it. I'd like time to dress to go out to a mill late this afternoon."

"Then the less time you waste posturing like the half flash, half foolish young ape that you are the better," said Caleb, equably.

"I don't have to take this!" Luke's face was livid.

"Actually, yes you do," said Caleb. He had very little real power unless he arrested Luke, but he was finding that the airs of a gentleman who assumed the right to command gave him a greater *de facto* if not *de jure* authority with other gentlemen; and where many an officer would find himself almost apologetic to be asking questions of a gentleman, treating them like a bunch of raw recruits caught out in trouble seemed to work quite well. He went on, "The motives for killing your cousin that you claim so negligible. Well, let us first consider the amount; two thousand pounds. Your own income must be considerable if you consider that to be negligible – ah, I see it is not" as Luke flushed. "Two thousand pounds might be small change to a high roller at White's who may drop that in a night's play, but it is enough for a single gentleman to live on in some comfort for ten years, even if not invested; or in considerable comfort for a couple of years; or to pay off a pressing debt that might otherwise embarrass him. Of course, even now, you might not inherit that, er, paltry sum."

"I wager it's not paltry to a man on your pay," said Luke.

"My pay, as you probably know very well, is around eighty pounds a year," said Caleb, "which a man and his family and a servant or two might live on with care, and as I also have some private means, my income is not to the point. You don't think I could afford to have my coats from Scotts if I did not have other means did you?"

"I wondered if you took bribes," said Luke.

"Well I will put you right in your wondering; I do not," said Caleb, "and moreover I should arrest anyone who tried it. You are warned" and he smiled grimly as Luke looked shifty. He went on, "The post brought three letters to your cousin which were directly concerned with
you, and which might well have caused him some irritation, leading to a quarrel in which you might have killed him."

"I really cannot see what these letters might be about," said Luke sulkily, "and I have told you, I hid from the cub, and then I went for a ride."

"Easy enough – for I have checked – to go out of the second door of the tack room where you said you hid, double back and be hiding from the cub by having knocked on your cousin's study window" said Caleb. "Or indeed to have gone for a ride, and once out of sight, double back, leave the horse out of sight in the paddock again, and quietly make your way to his window later in the day. Indeed, I suggest that you did return early because of certain looks directed your way at the breakfast table that you wanted to speak about with your cousin. You were seen, even though the witness will not swear to who he saw" added Caleb mendaciously having seen a slight rigidity to Luke's posture as he postulated this theory.

"All right; I returned. But I did not go in. He had Flora with him; and they were having an argument" said Luke.

"Indeed? And what was this argument about?" asked Caleb.

Luke shrugged.

"I couldn't hear; the window fits tightly. He was banging his hand on some document on his desk. I presume she'd incurred a bill beyond what he was prepared to pay and he was giving her chapter and verse about it. I went away."

"And did not return?" Caleb was sceptical.

"No I did not return," said Luke. "I planned to, and I rode for a bit, and I was not thinking carefully and I took a toss. A careless piece of work. Alcippe cut her leg on a flint where she stumbled and I had to lead her back after I'd checked it and so I was late for luncheon."

"So you, too, have good reason to have blood on your cuffs if the servants mention it?" put in Jane.

Luke glowered.

"If you stoop to questioning the servants, yes, Harman-mort."

"A little less insulting than your previous forays into cant," said Jane. "I cannot, however, claim to be officially associated with Bow Street. I merely aid my husband to the best of my abilities."

"I'm sure he appreciates all your abilities," said Luke. He made the comment insulting.

"I'm not allowed to call suspects out, you know," said Caleb, conversationally, "but then I wouldn't wish to be accused of murdering the afflicted if I did."

"You and I might however meet when this is over," growled Luke. "So! What was in these letters?" Luke was beside himself with curiosity to know what lay against him and it warred with his desire to enact violence upon Caleb. That curiosity won was due in some considerable part to the uncomfortable feeling that this atypical Runner could best him, and would not feel the least compunction in so doing.

"One is a letter; the other two pieces of correspondence are by way of being bills" said Caleb.

Luke frowned.

"Bills? Don't be ridiculous. My bills come to me."

"Yes, Mr Popham; but not the bills for the repair of a groom's boot and the physicking of his leg caused by what appears to be known as your Ill-tempered bay."

"Alcippe is a little playful with people who are not used to her that is all," said Luke, angrily.

"Playful enough to break the ankle of a man not used to her; and whatever you may think of the care of dependents, depriving your cousin of a groom until he was healed and meaning that he would have unnecessary expense that a friendly warning or a ribband in her tail could have rendered unnecessary," said Caleb sternly.

Luke looked angry. Caleb recognised it as the anger of a man who knew himself to be at fault and who would not admit to it.

"Well he should have been careful," said Luke, "and the other letter?"

"The letter of a man who has a daughter known as Sukey whom you got with child," said Caleb.

"What? The father of that little lightskirt could write?" Luke sounded surprised.

"Well, I'm not a relative of yours to express my opinion of a man who gets girls who are his social inferiors in the family way, but as I understand it, and considering the clause in the will, your Cousin Henry would have been likely to have words with you regarding it," said Caleb.

"Well, he did not" said Luke.

"No; he died before he could make an issue of your issue as you might say," said Caleb.

Jane hid a smile; it was a serious matter for the poor girl involved, but Caleb's way with words had been what had first attracted her to him.

"If the girl is pregnant she has nobody to blame but herself; and who's to say it's not the child of someone else?" blustered Luke.

"I rather fancy that the will might be read that if there was just a chance of it being yours, you had the legacy revoked" said Caleb.

"DAMN you" said Luke. "That's preposterous – an untenable clause!"

Caleb shrugged.

"I imagine it's something for Mr Avery and the

Beau to determine," he said. "Well, I don't think I'm going to get any further with you; you may ask the Beau to step in."

Luke growled something unintelligible and hurled himself out.

"Must check if his horse has a cut hock," said Caleb.

"The problem of course is, as with the Reverend Kemp," said Jane, "he could have seen blood on his cuff and decided to cut the horse to cover his tracks. He might value his horse, but Mr Luke Popham values his own skin more. Except that I do wonder whether it would even occur to him that the servants might remark upon a bloody cuff; he seems remarkably arrogant regarding anyone he sees as beneath him."

"Yes; I wanted to shake the puppy," said Caleb.

"Fortunately I think he realises that you could, and is not about to take the chance that you might," said Jane. "You have him off-balance and uncertain about you. Which is just as well. What a very truly unsatisfactory young man he is, to be sure."

Caleb laughed.

"Unsatisfactory!" he said. "Well, that is a ladylike way of putting it, Jane-girl."

There was a tap on the door and Daventry Popham came in.

"Thought you might like a list that's been compiled by your man Fowler that he and Mrs Armatage's dresser put together," he said, "as it covers all those people with any kind of blood or other red stain on them that day. I'm afraid it includes me, though I hadn't thought a word about it; as I knocked over a glass of claret."

"Early in the day for claret wasn't it?" said Caleb.

"No, no, you mistake; this was before breakfast by some considerable margin, it was late, and I hadn't by then gone to bed." said the Beau, "only they were making a list of all laundry recovered that day, and there was my shirt mentioned too. And if I had killed Uncle Henry, I'd be almost bound to say it was no blood stain

but a claret stain from the night before, wouldn't I? Though frankly, if I were going to stab anyone, I fancy I might have the sense to wrap my hand and arm in something first if I wanted to keep the whole affair secret. Not sure what I'd do with it;
burn it maybe, or stuff it into one of the hideous but valuable Chinese vases Uncle Henry keeps – kept – outside his study.   I advanced this theory to Fowler who gave me a deucedly fishy stare – saving your presence, Mrs Armitage, though I dare say you've heard worse – and told me that if I was suggesting such a thing that would normally be the last place anyone would look if considering me a suspect but that he intended to do so anyway in case I had either hit on some truth or was trying to use some double bluff. He's no idiot," the Beau admitted.

"I certainly value Fowler very much," said Caleb, "shall we get on with your testimony now?"

Chapter 18

"Sounds infernally like a court of law when you put it that way," said the Beau. "My testimony. Well I understand that some of this hinges on breakfast; and having sat up late with the claret the night before – reading, if you were wondering what might keep me up in a place untouched by the more debauched gaieties of society – I was feeling a trifle delicate and preferred to keep my own company for breakfast. Not so much the delicacy that eschews any but the lightest of comestibles, but the delicacy that could not quite face the Kemp twins being normal hearty sixteen year old boys. I consumed a pot of tea, two lightly coddled eggs with bread and butter, after which I felt strong enough for some coffee, beef and pickles, toast and jam and a few macaroons. A good breakfast, if eaten slowly and peacefully enough sets one up for the day whatever the excesses of the night before."

"Aye, I'm inclined to agree there," said Caleb, "having the courage to set to is often the hardest part, though; but drinking plenty of tea or small beer will usually bring you about with something light to keep it from feeling too liquid as you might say."

"Military experience?" laughed the Beau.

"Yes," said Caleb. "The Black Brunswickers are good soldiers, but their drinking contests! If battles were settled in ale houses, all Europe would fly the flag of Brunswick. I was the only one who had a hope of outlasting them, being as big as I am so I was hastily promoted for a night to Major, and my colonel told me that the honour of the regiment was at stake and if I lost I'd be lucky to be a drummer boy in the morning because he, personally, would see that I would be a pretty drummer girl."

"What happened?" asked Jane. "You have not told me this story."

"To tell the truth it had slipped my mind," said Caleb, "you know how I feel about boring people with military reminiscences."

"All very well, Armitage, but what happened?" asked the Beau.

"He passed out first," said Caleb. "Like the Old Nosey – the Duke of Wellington, I mean – said after Waterloo, though, it was a damned close run thing. I think I registered that he had fallen to the table before I lost my own senses. However, what really won our reputation with the Brunswickers was my habit of breakfasting; they had to take away my erstwhile opponent and revive him all over again."

Jane and the Beau both laughed.

"Well, aside from the fact that we share similar ideas about breakfast, a sense of humour and have nothing in common over dress, I suppose I had better move back into being the suspect being questioned," said the Beau.

"Believe me, Mr Popham, I dislike questioning the people I like a very great deal," said Caleb. "I dislike arresting them even more."

"Ever had to?" asked the Beau.

"Only once" said Caleb. "A most engaging jewel thief; he operated by scraping the acquaintance of someone with some pretensions to society, talking himself into being invited to a ball, and he was, by the way, an exquisite dancer, which usually had him invited to another ball or two. He had his scruples; he would never rob the person with whom he had scraped the acquaintance. Didn't think it was fair. Anyway, he then proceeded to take the necklaces off the necks of the ladies he danced with as he escorted them off the floor, and hid them in full chamber pots. He would do a quick change and, looking every inch a footman, take them to empty, and never be seen by that group of people again. Left a string of dented, if not broken, hearts as well. If he hadn't hit a real footman, who fell and split his head open, he might still be getting away with it. Wonderful fund of funny stories. However he was sentenced to hang – but enough of the ladies whom he had enchanted sent letters begging for a reprieve that he was transported instead. I was glad of that; he was a resourceful man and should do well once he's served his fourteen years. However, that's getting us no further, you cozening stories out of me."

"I was enjoying them too," said Jane, "but he's right, Mr Popham; when did you come downstairs?"

"Just after that bl – er, wretched, woman had left Uncle Henry," said the Beau, "she pushed past me on the stairs, looking a bit wild eyed and distinctly dishevelled. I did wonder whether Henry had been a trifle, er, premature with her, but dismissed that immediately. She would have looked as though she was the cat who had got the cream had he misbehaved. I wondered then if she had done something to irritate him and he had lost his temper and given her a good shaking. Hearing later that he was rather irritable over breakfast, I wondered whether he had discovered a bill of hers that shocked him. Somewhat on the parsimonious side, Uncle Henry, when he didn't see a reason for a high bill; believed in paying for the best, which is why he was less than happy about the set of young Michael's coat, distinctly inferior tailoring, but never saw the point of paying for the name of one's tailor – or modiste, I suppose. And I have to say that when I heard her bemoaning a bonnet he would not buy her for two hundred guineas I can see why; milliners are having a joke at the expense of their clients when they become fashionable. Any competent young lady could make the same bonnet for no more than a dozen guineas, if that."

"This competent young lady does," said Jane. "Female accoutrements are ridiculously expensive; men must have the tailoring performed by an expert. Women do most of their fine tailoring with pins."

"And a very good chaperone, too, is a well tailored

lady's garment," said the Beau.

"No bill was found in the study – none belonging to her, anyway," said Caleb.

"Well I imagine she took it with her," said the Beau, "I didn't notice; she was holding her spencer all crumpled up – I can't imagine the creases that must have put in it – and
holding herself awkwardly. Anyway, I went down and into the billiard room, and knocked a few balls around. One of the footmen brought me some coffee in there. I drink too much, but not until after noon. If I was her I'd want to possess myself of the evidence; if you ask me she fled his wrath."

"There is some evidence that she quarrelled with him," said Caleb.

"That'll be it then," said the Beau, "however, if you want to ask me who went in and out of the study, I am afraid I have no idea. The sound of the balls kissing was what I chiefly heard, the door was shut, and yes, I could have done it myself quite easily as the billiard room is next to the study. I could have either slipped out of one door into the other, or let myself out onto the terrace and knocked on the window. I didn't do either."

"How many windows open onto the terrace?" asked Jane.

"Enough to make it entirely too easy," said the Beau, "except for one thing. I swear I would have noticed anyone going along to his window. When I wasn't facing the window, I fancy the shadow of anyone passing would have put me off my shot; there's a mirror too, to increase the light in there, a Venetian one of the Renaissance, terrible mirror but it would show movement."

"I thought Venetian glass was supposed to be rather good," said Caleb.

"The fault is in the age of it," said the Beau. "The backing has been damaged too often and it's a bit flyblown as you might say. Poor frames if you ask me but it isn't mine so..." an odd look crossed his face. "Actually it is mine," he said softly. "Well, perhaps I'll have to consider having someone in to look at it. In any case, the point is that it reflects, albeit badly."

Caleb nodded.

"Could you see anyone approach the study window from the direction of the stables?" he asked.

"No," said the Beau, "nor in any direction bar along the terrace. There's too much decorative stonework that hides the angle, and anyone coming from the gardens would come up the steps hidden by the unkempt monstrosities that the gardener refers to as topiary and which I consider somewhat less worthy of the name. Below the terrace the ground drops away. Anyone could come up the steps, or round the corner from the stables, I'm sorry."

"Well that leaves the Reverend still in the running as well as Luke," said Caleb. "Well, thank you, Beau; I can't think of anything else to ask you right now. Is it almost time for afternoon tea?"

"It is," said the Beau, "or in my case, my customary ratafia. Which I do not think anyone else here likes, but if either of you wishes to join me, I would be more than happy."

"I'll stay with tea, thank you," said Caleb.

"I also prefer it," said Jane. "I dislike the strong flavour of bitter almonds in such as ratafia and even less in orgeat where it is sweetened too much.."

The Beau bowed beautifully and withdrew.

"I think I know why Flora may have been holding herself oddly, and why she was more volatile," said Jane, looking up from the list Fowler and Ella had compiled. "She has bloody garments for the best reason any woman might, and has a bloody sleeve because she bundled her clothes all together with the diaper cloths, Ella thinks, having extracted the bundle from the laundry maid. She may have been in a hurry because things were... uncomfortable and she needed to refresh herself."

"Especially if he did shake her," said Caleb. "Who else has a stained sleeve?"

"The Beau; Luke; the Reverend" said Jane.

"Who all have good and valid reasons to be thus stained" said Caleb. "And as the Beau – who is quite as unwholesomely clever as Fowler – pointed out, a clever man, or woman, might cover their hand with something."

"Or take off their jacket and turn their sleeves back," said Jane, "like a man playing billiards."

"Indeed," said Caleb, grimly. "I had not considered that. He had only to say, however, that he saw a shadowy figure in the mirror and took no notice of it. As for what can be seen, a clever man like the Beau is not going to tell anything but the truth, for it is easy to check. Either the Beau is very clever indeed, or he is innocent. And the trouble is, I cannot declare him innocent because he is very clever indeed."

"Let us stop worrying our heads and take tea," said Jane. "I am in need of refreshment."

Caleb sighed.

"So too am I" he said.

There was sudden uproar outside the salon where tea was to be served as the footman holding the tray with the Beau's ratafia on it gasped for breath, and crumpled at the knees, the tray crashing to the floor.

Caleb rushed to him, ripping off his cravat and opening his shirt to allow easier passage of air as the poor man gasped for air, pink in the face with effort. Caleb sat him up and worked his arms back and forth.

The women were, it seemed, all collectively shrieking. Except Jane, of course, who never shrieked. There were too many people.

"Beau, get these damned guests of yours out of the way and come bear me a hand," growled Caleb.

The Beau's exquisite elegance and firmness of

purpose soon dispersed everyone into the salon where the Beau ordered that tea be sent.

"What's toward?" his voice lost its languid drawl and became incisive as he knelt down.

"Cyanide" said Caleb. "The smell of bitter almonds is too strong. This drink was meant for you and this poor fool sampled it. Unless you knew he was inclined to sample it, and prepared it with a dose low enough you hoped would not be fatal, to remove suspicion from yourself without running any risk yourself."

Chapter 19

"Now suggesting that I'd risk a servant is a hit in the belly, Armitage," said the Beau. "Acquit me: if I was going to do that, I'd run the risk for myself, you know."

Caleb regarded him.

"You know, I'm inclined to believe you," he said. "Now, somehow, I do not think it very likely that two people in one household should suddenly develop murderous tendencies; which does tend to make it more likely that I can suspect you less."

"You have to, I suppose," said the Beau, soberly, "consider that I prepared this for myself and did not know that Perkins would imbibe. As it happens, I did not know. Is there any chance he will live?"

"I think so" said Caleb. "I think he filled the glass too full and drank some to make the level easier to carry. I suppose the decanter of your ratafia is easy to get to and in plain sight?"

"Yes," said the Beau, "anyone could top it up with a solution of cyanide quite easily; and might have done at any time since yesterday afternoon."

"I think it more pertinent to consider it from any time since luncheon today," said Caleb, "after the will was read. As you are now the owner of this house."

"And Luke is my heir," said the Beau, softly, "but somehow this use of poison does not seem in keeping with his character."

"He may be a desperate man; as he will lose the two thousand over the girl he has impregnated," said Jane.

"That is so… I cannot like Luke but to consider this? To consider being a target for anyone wishful of killing me is most uncomfortable," said the Beau.

"What we have to wonder is where anyone might get cyanide; it's a little exotic and not easy to make," said Caleb, grimly.

"Oh that is easy too," said Beau Popham. "You see,

the gardener has been distilling laurel leaves to make the stuff to exterminate the wasps in a nest in the greenhouse. It's been stored in there in an earthenware jar. He warned all of us, by addressing Uncle Henry while we were all gathered together, to stay out of the greenhouses while he made his murderous assault on the wasps, and informed us that if it had not killed all of them he would need to make a second attempt, and had enough poison to do so. He made a joke with Uncle Henry that the ladies should not go mistaking it for Ratafia for its smell of bitter almonds."

He was, meanwhile, holding the man Perkins while Caleb continued to work his arms, in the hopes of increasing the amount of air going into his lungs. Perkins groaned.

"Good man," said Caleb. "You're going to make it; you'll be devilishly sick, but you are going to make it. Here, you, what's your name?" he demanded of another footman, hovering, uncertainly.

"Jamieson, sir," said the man.

"Very well, Jamieson, have a girl see to putting a hot brick in Perkins' bed, and have a boy to sit with him all the time in case he takes a turn for the worse; and when you've done, you can fetch me the chief gardener into the salon, and then you can get someone to help you carry Perkins to bed and make him comfortable. See that the Utensil is where he can cast up his accounts into it if need be" he added. "And have the chief gardener check the level of his wasp killing solution too!"

"Yes sir!" said Jamieson, heading off with alacrity now that he had orders to undertake. Caleb looked up as a door banged, but it was Henry and Simmy back from their excursion.

"That looks, on *prima facia* evidence to be a possible problem," said Henry.

"Has he croaked?" asked Simmy, more prosaically.

"Someone was trying to poison the Beau," said Jane. "No, Simmy, your father has every expectation that Perkins will survive the experience. We'll look forward to your report soon."

Simmy and Henry looked at each other and said together,

"*Cui bono?*"

"Lud, one Cicero apparently was enough for the Romans, I'm not sure I can cope with two of you," said Caleb. "Well only his immediate heir on the face of it, but of course someone might be working through all the Pophams; or someone might think the Beau knows something about the first death and has panicked into this action. Someone who perhaps was on the terrace and saw you, Mr Popham, but whom you failed to detect."

"That's possible" admitted the Beau. "Ah, Smedley; Mr Armitage wishes to speak with you" he added as a most uncomfortable-looking old man shambled in, in company with Jamieson, looking most out of place in an old frieze coat and disreputable trousers, held beneath the knees with twine.

"That's right, Smedley, I'd like you to come into the Salon while Jamieson and, er, the other footman help Perkins to bed," said Caleb, pleasantly. "I would like to corroborate – check – what you told Mr Henry Popham and his guests."

"Arrrr, been muckin' with my wasp poison, have 'ee?" Smedley jerked a thumb at Perkins.

"Well it appears somebody may have," said Caleb. He ushered the gardener into the salon.

"Look here, Armitage, what's going on?" Luke was first with the question.

"Herded into here like cattle, after that man made such a fuss and passed out!" cried Flora.

"You owe us an explanation!" cried the Reverend.

"Please, Mr Armitage, is poor Perkins dead?" asked Nessie.

Caleb smiled at her and shook his head slightly while waiting for the hubbub to die down. It did not.

137

"Beau," said Caleb, "Are any of those porcelain figures over the mantel anything that you value particularly?"

"I like the way you think," said the Beau, "personally I think them all hideous but I believe Emma likes the Doulton shepherdess and as it has some value, I'm minded to give it to her. Pray do what you will with any of the rest."

Caleb strolled over to the fireplace, picked the most hideous figure, and dropped it, deliberately in the fireplace.

The hubbub instantly subsided into a shocked silence.

"Got your attention now, have I?" said Caleb, genially. "Good; I have answers and questions and I'm not about to compete with the sort of row usually only heard at Billingsgate at the fish market. Perkins imbibed a quantity of the ratafia intended for the Beau. Fortunately he did not drink enough to kill him. He is, however, fairly sick. This means we have either had someone cheeky enough to sneak into the house – which pending the report from my son and factotum I do not necessarily rule out – or, as seems more likely, one of you attempted to poison the Beau."

"Or he did it himself knowing that the man tippled," said Luke.

Caleb bowed punctiliously.

"A valid conclusion as far as it goes, though from what I have seen of the Beau, more likely to have poisoned it himself to discover its bitter taste. It would have tasted unpleasant to the connoisseur of ratafia and he would be likely to notice it first sip," said Caleb. "No, Mr Popham, I have not been able to rule the Beau out by this, but fortunately he takes my ruminations in good part. Now I daresay you all recognise Smedley here."

"Why would one recognise any of the lower orders?" demanded Flora.

"Let me amend Mr Armitage's comment; anyone with any claims to intellect and breeding doubtless recognises Smedley here," said the Beau, "as the last time we all saw him was but a few days ago when he was warning us all about the poison in the greenhouses."

"Oh to kill the wasps!" said Emma. "He said the ladies might mistake the smell for ratafia; why would not the gentlemen do so? Do gentlemen not smell things in the same way? If not, why do ladies and gentlemen both like perfume?"

"Emma," said her mother, "You are pert to speak out so."

"It's an interesting comment though," said Caleb. "Smedley, why did you warn the ladies specifically?"

Smedley stared.

"Well, stand to reason, don't it, sir? gentlemen don't maudle themselves with stuff like ratafia, and ladies don't have no more sense than to drink what they finds wherever they finds it, account o' not having proper brains."

The Beau murmured to Jane,

"He appears to have a prejudice against both of us, Mrs Armitage; I fancy Mr Armitage may have a hard time preventing another murder if he continues to express himself so freely."

Jane gave a wry smile. She always found it galling when men held firmly to the opinion that women, by reason of their sex, were mentally incapable.

"I fancy the housekeeper might set him right if he expresses such an opinion to her," she replied.

Caleb merely sighed.

"I wondered if I was likely to pick up some interesting clew there, but if it's only a matter of prejudice, let us pass on," he said. "Smedley, has the level in your jar of poison gone down since your first attempts at wasp killing?"

"Arrrr" said Smedley, nodding vigorously to emphasise the idiom of his affirmative. "Powerful lot that have gone down; enough to kill the whole household, I'd say," he added gloomily.

"How do you kill wasps?" asked Jane.

"Well ma'am, I squirt that stuff into the nest and they falls out dead," said Smedley.

"Don't you risk being stung? Would it not be more sensible to mix it with sugar to attract them to drink it?" asked Jane.

"Bless you missus, that wouldn't do much good!" said the old man. "Mixing it with sugar seem to make it less effective, see?"

"Oh!" said Flora opening her pansy brown eyes wide "So if it's bitter enough for anyone drinking it to tell and someone mixed sugar in to make it taste less bad it might mean it wouldn't work?"

"Well, miss, it might or it mightn't," said Smedley, "depending on how fit they was or how infirm. It weren't my fault that stuff got in the house and nobody can't say as how it were," he added firmly. "I warned them, I did; and I never brung it inside at all. Can I go now, sir?"

"You may go," said Caleb. "Very well. I now need everyone to cast their minds back over this afternoon to where they were between luncheon and now. I think that is the period in which it must have been done; since it appears likely to have been done since the reading of the will."

"You seem to know a lot about the contents of the will," said Luke.

"Naturally," said Caleb, "since Mr Avery wished me to hear its contents. I sat quite discreetly in the library, however, so as not to be an embarrassment to the family."

"Oh! How demeaning!" cried Flora. "Where were you? I can't *bear* to think you might have overheard any private conversations!"

"I was behind the bookcase at Mr Avery's back, if it makes any difference," said Caleb. "I rather thought that most of what was said by the family aired opinions in a way that should have been private conversations but somehow failed to be so."

"Preposterous!" spluttered the Reverend.

"What is preposterous, Mr Kemp," said Caleb, "Is that a man lies seriously ill, and might have been dead for the want of a more efficient poisoner. And I am beginning to run out of patience. My wife and I will retire after tea for a consultation over possible external sources of the harm done to this unhappy family, and then we shall re-question everyone with this new development in mind. Miss Fanshawe, if you will be good enough to serve us tea and macaroons, I am as dry as a bone and I will risk any cyanide."

Chapter 20

Henry and Simmy, having changed out of riding clothes, came in to drink tea with the rest of the company. Jane gave Mrs Kemp a look that offered some unspecified retribution if she commented on Simmy, who was going out of his way to be a perfect little gentleman in handing round the light refreshments that accompanied the tea.

"Did you find out anything interesting?" Jane asked.

"Not hugely," said Henry. "Of all of Mr Popham's tenants, the only one with anything close to a grudge was the one with the daughter in the family way, and he had every expectation that Mr Popham would arrange matters satisfactorily; indeed he was mightily put out that Mr Popham was dead, and fearing who might be his heir."

"I'll ride over tomorrow and see him and let him know that his girl has two hundred pounds coming to her under Uncle Henry's will," said the Beau. "Well he is one who would have the very opposite of a motive to kill Uncle Henry."

"Indeed," said Henry. "So far as we were able to ascertain through a reticence regarding speaking to the gentry that bordered on the bovine in its loquacity, or rather the lack thereof, the tenants are satisfied, feel well treated and even the most cussed one only lowed a bit about the matter of a barn that needed repair."

"Henry, you are a bad boy to take the bovine simile as far as lowing" said Jane.

"You didn't hear him," said Henry with feeling.

"And the neighbours are mostly in charity with Mr Popham too," said Simmy. "Henry told them that we were helping out by seeing if they knew anyone who might have a grudge as there had been some trouble, which I thought was very clever to not come right out and say that he was murdered, and apart from Colonel

Wilson spending some time laying down law about when caring for indigent relatives is right and proper and when they become an embarrassment they were all unable to say much."

Kemp glowered at him.

"That Colonel Wilson certainly is a rattle once he gets going!" agreed Henry, unaware of the fulminating glare aimed at his back. "He has a pretty odd way of judging a man in some respects – after all being able to take a fence flying is not the principle attribute I'd be looking for to define a gentleman – but he cares for his men, indeed for any of the men hurt in the war. And as Mr Popham contributed regularly to the hospital, none of them would be likely to have any reason to wish him dead."

"Moreover, those as weren't too halt to walk up to the Abbey would be short an arm to do the deed," said Simmy, ignoring the little moan from Mrs Kemp. "And actually, pa, would Mr Popham have been likely to let any of them in and relax back anyway?"

Caleb looked at the Beau, who shook his head.

"Let in, possibly; relaxed, no," he said, "it has to have been one of the neighbours or one of us. And apart from Colonel Wilson, who might duel him, but would never strike a foul blow, there is Mr Beeston, an elderly gentleman whose hand shakes from a combination of palsied eld and a lifelong fondness for strong liquor, Mr Corston, who would never have the decisiveness nor resolve to stab anyone, and Mr Partridge, who is as fat as a flawn and the idea of him skulking stealthily up the steps of the terrace and in the window is too full of comic imagery to take seriously."

"We should have asked you, rather than finding all this out for ourselves," said Henry.

"By no means, my dear boy; I am, after all, numbered amongst the suspects and your observations, should they tally with mine, are what I believe you scholars of the law would call corroborative evidence," said the Beau.

"I must say, Daventry, you take it very coolly that you are numbered as a suspect!" declared the Reverend.

"What other way is there to take it?" asked the Beau. "Is anyone cleared, by the way?"

"Emma and Nessie," said Jane, "and probably the twins who owned up to pranks that might have been likely to look black for them if withheld. Moreover they have no real reason to kill their uncle; they might guess that any legacy to a minor would be held in trust at least until his majority, so unless they plan to work their way through all who stand between them and this house, I should consider this highly unlikely."

"They'd have to be pretty hardened to do that; I think the twins stand in the clear," said the Beau. "Mr Armitage? I thought perhaps dismissing all who were cleared so we could examine who might have caused this harm to Perkins."

"No I cannot do that," said Caleb, "because even if innocent, any of the young people or Miss Fanshawe might have seen something without realising what they were seeing that becomes of more importance; someone loitering around the table where the decanters stand."

"Oh, seeming perhaps to admire the flowers Flora carried there after luncheon?" asked Nessie. "They are wilting rather already though, which is a shame."

"I did not notice anyone loitering while I did the flowers," said Flora.

"Was the level in the ratafia decanter the same as it had been earlier?" asked Caleb.

Flora shrugged.

"How would I know? I didn't look. I don't like it much," she said.

"And she only does the flowers because it is her idea of genteel ladylike occupation too," said Emma, in scorn. "I don't suppose she even knows why having Davenport fowls for dinner is in any wise related to salamagundy for luncheon."

Flora stared.

"You are making that up, you stupid pert brat to pretend knowledge!"

Mrs Kemp had opened her mouth to reprove Emma for a pert comment but instead rounded on Flora.

"You dare to accuse my daughter of lying? You vulgar piece, I fail to see what my poor brother saw in you! For your information, as you are so ignorant, the whites of the hard boiled eggs served stuffed with other salad in the salamagundy are those whose yolks have been used as part of the stuffing of the Davenport fowls. Even a wealthy household is not profligate in its use of food, you know!"

Flora stared.

"But that's the job of the servants!" she said.

"Foolish creature," said Mrs Kemp with scorn, plainly now all the sister of a wealthy man more than the downtrodden wife of an erratic parson, "any woman who is unable to order the household and understand domestic economy in order to oversee the servants is unworthy of the name of woman and is certainly no lady. Cousin Agnes, if, as I understand, your task was to oversee turning this young person into a lady, I fear you have failed signally."

Nessie burst into tears.

"It is true; I have let cousin Henry down!" she sobbed.

"He didn't give you much time before he wanted to display his acquisition to the family though," said Jane. "Why it is but a few months, less than three, since you wrote to me of this fortunate position. It takes a girl a lifetime of watching her mother or other mother-figure to learn how to hold an economy and how to be the perfect hostess to a household. I would not think it possible to learn all the ways to pass even superficially in less than half a year, and a need to continue studying for some years to come, watching others and following the lead of those whose social style and tone is admirable. However, I believe you have been handicapped in having a pupil more concerned with the outward trappings and display, and who believes that it is a case of acting a part, to be put on and off with the costume."

Flora glared at her.

"Easy for you to criticise, born to wealth and position!" she said, "and ready to increase that by grabbing someone of royal blood, even ready to put up with his ugly, deformed brat to get that position!"

Jane had slapped someone once before for being insulting about her relationship with Caleb, and had regretted having lost her *savoire faire* merely because she had been both disturbed over Frank's death and doubtless affected by the fact that she was carrying his child; this time she counted to ten within her own thoughts and kept her hands firmly at her sides.

"I think you have a very false idea of my birth, marriage, and relationship with my stepson," she said. "Most important of all is that I love Simmy as well as if he were my own child, and his deformities are something that do not trouble me beyond the fact that they cause him some difficulty at times. I am the daughter of a lowly lieutenant, orphaned in my infancy and reared by my aunt, a daughter of the manse, hardly born to wealth and position. I was, however, reared as a lady, which is not dependant on wealth but on understanding the subtleties that make up being one that are hard to teach if they do not come naturally. Being a lady I will not even comment on the vulgar comments on my second marriage. I do not consider them worthy of notice."

Flora flushed.

"Flora, for shame!" cried Nessie. "When Jane and Mr Armitage have put themselves out to try to find out who has killed poor Cousin Henry your attitude is filled with ingratitude!"

"I still don't see why they think it was one of the

household," said Flora, sulkily. "The window was open, wasn't it?"

"Oh Flora, I explained that!" said Nessie. "Cousin Henry would not have stayed sat in his chair if he had not known the person who killed him. Someone might have come through the window, along the terrace, but they must have been someone with whom he was comfortable to be seated."

"And actually, unless the Beau killed him, the window is likely to have been opened from the inside by the killer to suggest a false idea that the killer came from outside," said Jane crisply, "because the Beau was in the billiards room and could see out onto the terrace directly or in the mirror on the wall. It is possible, of course, that the Beau was looking the other way, distracted by something, and someone slipped past him, which could be the reason that this poison was administered – in case he did see someone and has not had a chance to speak to us yet about it. He has spoken of what he has seen and what he has not seen. It is, of course, further proof that the murderer is one of the household as nobody else could really have had the chance to find out about the gardener's cyanide and obtain it and place some in the decanter. Flora, if you think that a killer came from the outside, I'm afraid you are displaying a singular lack of thought and intellect."

Flora gave Jane a poisonous look; Jane had unconsciously moved from the polite usage of calling her Miss d'Ambrose to using her first name, showing that Jane had given up any fiction of treating her as a social equal.

"Although I have to consider the possibility that Mr Daventry Popham may have arranged to poison himself to hide his own involvement in murdering Mr Henry Popham," said Caleb, "I am inclined to think that he is as shocked by this as anyone might be. Of course he might be shocked by the sickness of his footman when he expected to risk nobody but himself; but I also have to look at the idea that someone made an attempt on his life quite seriously; which would be, so far as I can see, for one of two motives."

"One of two?" asked Nessie.

"Yes," said Caleb, "The obvious motive is of course inheritance; the immediate benefit being, as I understand, to Mr Luke Popham."

"Oh, I had not thought of inheritance" said Nessie.

"Trying to pin it on me, Armitage, because you don't like me?" sneered Luke.

"I'm not trying to 'pin' it on anyone," said Caleb, "but to pursue lines of reasoning. The initial line of *cui bono* is you; and if you should die providentially falling at a bullfinch because your horse has a burr under the saddle, who then?"

"My father," said Luke.

"And then?" asked Caleb. Luke considered.

"Probably Cousin Hester here," Luke indicated Mrs Kemp. "Somehow the idea of her stabbing my cousin and poisoning Daventry and arranging an accident to me and then my father seems a little far fetched."

Caleb shrugged.

"But the ones who benefit from her inheritance are her husband and children. Unlikely? Possibly. Impossible? No, I cannot say so. However, there is the other reason that the Beau might have been targeted; which is to prevent him telling something he might know."

"Why what might he know? that's ridiculous!" said Flora with a titter.

"You are a fool, Flora" said Michael. "You don't even listen; Mr Armitage already made it clear that someone might believe that the Beau saw them through the window of the Billiards Room, and decided to try to silence him before he was able to talk about it, just in case he was looking, not perhaps racking up the balls when I defy any man to be looking out."

"Oh, yes, of course" said Flora. "I can't see that

anyone but the Beau was going to benefit though; he's the one who's been left everything, contrary to dear Henry's true wishes. He understood about signing things and killed poor Henry to stop him leaving me well provided for!" she added, bursting into tears.

"'Her tears will pierce into a marble heart'" murmured the Beau.

"Not much sign of you being a tiger that 'will be mild whiles she doth mourn', coz" said Luke.

"Well, when you think about it, Luke, as she's just outright accused me of murder, I can't say I feel mild" said the Beau. "However, I leave it all in the capable hands of Mr Armitage who doubtless knows his onions well enough to recognise stage tears, even without the provocation of that useful vegetable."

"Oh, I can see beyond the end of my nose," said Caleb grimly, "and I'd like to get on."

Chapter 21

"The problem lies in the fact that we've all been in and out and around since luncheon," said Beau Popham, "and as I was last to be questioned, in theory I had the longest time to prepare the whole business."

"Pa," said Simmy, "is there any reason to suppose that the getting of the poison and the putting it in the decanter happened immediately one after the other?"

"You mean, might someone have abstracted some of the cyanide the instant they knew of its existence in order to have a means of dealing with the Beau? Wouldn't that mean foreknowledge either of the will or expectation that he might be a witness?" asked Caleb.

"If he's in the habit of playing billiards then the possibility that he would be a witness might have occurred to the killer" said Simmy.

"I think," said Jane, "that whilst that's within the realms of possibility, it might be that the killing of Mr Henry Popham was a premeditated matter, and that the poison may have been extracted to that end, the stiletto he used as a page cutter presenting itself as a better choice at the last minute, or perhaps when taxed with some wrongdoing."

"There's something to look into in both thoughts," said Caleb. "Though the crime has a very impulsive feel to it; I am wondering whether someone took some poison equally impulsively as something to use at need; as you might say, a form of insuring his safety. Of course if the Beau did the killing, he might well have had poisoning himself in mind to demonstrate innocence from the moment of killing Mr Henry Popham; it's not more than a step from the study window to the greenhouse. But it's a good point, that it may have been collected beforehand, as going to the greenhouse after lunch and bringing it back and getting it into the decanter is cutting things a little fine."

"And moreover I was in the greenhouse with Flora immediately after luncheon," said Nessie, "we would surely have seen anyone lurking!"

"Well I wasn't looking for other people," said Flora,"I was looking for the best blooms for the hall table; the vase had been knocked over and they needed replacing. Henry grew beautiful flowers in his greenhouse and if I was at one end cutting flowers with Nessie, we might not have noticed anyone slip in."

"Wouldn't you feel a draught if the door was opened?" asked Caleb.

"Oh *no*!" declared Nessie. "Why, that would be bad for the plants; there is a second door, like a porch, so that one might come in, shut the outer door, and only then go into the greenhouse. However, I doubt we were there more than twenty minutes, choosing the blooms, Flora wanted to make sure they matched the vase so she brought it with us, and I went straight away because I knew there were some wonderful double Georginas that Cousin Henry had brought from Belgium as well as the normal ones, and the most wonderful mix of hues! And not so *scraggy* as chrysanthemums, which is about all there is outside, and a few late Michaelmas daisies, but past their best of course, only the greenhouse really provides good flowers for displays indoors! The Nerines are so pretty too, and we needed to choose those Georgina types that toned well with them and with the vase, you know, because Nerines only come in pale pink, and there were some Laurestinus in early flower too, with their lovely dark shiny foliage to set off the colours of the other flowers. It's such an *odd* selection of colours, it's an old Wedgewood agate ware vase and the marble patterns are in dark reds and almost puce and the white in it makes a range of pinks too, not like the fashionable Moonlight lustre shells we have in here," she came up for air, and nodded in pride at the pinkish lustre shells hung from the walls and filled with myrtle and laurestinus and lobelias, the warmth of the greenhouse ensuring that the latter continued flowering.

Jane controlled herself not to make some ejaculation of surprise that Mr Popham had been so wealthy a man as to cultivate Georginas – including new varieties from Belgium – and nerines. She had not been to see the greenhouse – which sounded more like a hot-house. No wonder his lobelias were so profuse, both red and blue varieties, neither of which entirely matched the shells; but perhaps it was Nessie who had arranged these and it was Flora whose artistic sensibilities were upset by flowers that did not match the vase. Jane reflected that a celadon jasperware vase was suitable for any flower as the green would at least not be out of place with any leaves.

"Is the greenhouse separate from the house, that you need to go outside?" Jane asked.

"Yes, indeed; it is on the southern side of the house, forward of the stables," said Nessie, "you must surely have observed it when you arrived, it is a large building, with much of each side being glass, and a dome in the centre to accommodate the lemon tree, though it is by no means tall enough yet to require the extra height," she added.

"Good grief!" said Jane, taken aback. "I had not realised that so extensive a structure was the greenhouse; why I quite thought it to be a ballroom when first I glanced across. And I have not really had much time to explore," she added.

"It's a bene place," said Simmy, "And Miss d'Ambrose is quite right that anyone could lurk there and hide from anyone else; why you can readily lose sight of someone you know is in there, amongst all the bushes and flowers and things. It's got a boiler to keep it warm, just for plants!" he added. Jane knew he was thinking that the heating for this structure would be enough to keep many a London beggar child warm.

"Oh there is no question of 'just' for plants, Simon, dear!" said Nessie. "Why it means that Cousin Henry was able to provide vegetables that are not normally in season which means it benefits his guests too; as well as the preponderance of beautiful flowers we are able to enjoy.

And for luncheon we were able to have cowcumbers though it is autumn, and have them and other salad vegetables all year round, is that not wonderful?"

Simmy, who disliked cucumber, smiled vaguely and Jane was relieved that he held his tongue on any opinion thereof. She had wondered at the variety in the salamagundy, but had been too preoccupied with her thoughts about the reading of the will to consider the food deeply. She frowned in thought. There had been a conversation during that morning which might have a bearing on what had subsequently happened.

Caleb tapped on the tea table.

"I think we have exhausted the argument that someone might have, er lurked in the greenhouse, either being before Miss Fanshawe and, er, Flora, or who came in subsequent to their arrival and hid to avoid being seen on realising that he was not alone in there," he said. "It is possible, hurried though their actions would have been, for someone to have entered after they had left. I am assuming here that the collection of the poison was a sudden impulse. It's a clever theory, Simmy lad, and if I'm wrong I will eat humble pie, but the whole business has a hurried feel to it that I cannot reconcile with planning over several days. Several hours I will grant you. Flora, my girl, you said the flowers had been knocked over; have you any idea when that might have happened? Because they may have been knocked by someone careless, placing the poison into the decanter earlier; which would argue that they believed the Beau to have important information."

Flora looked vague.

"They were perfectly healthy when we went into the library for the reading of the will," said Nessie, eagerly. "I fear I did not notice afterwards, I was so insensate with amazement that Cousin Henry had arranged an annuity for me and the continued use of the house at Hampstead. So *kind* of him!"

"So they were not disturbed until the contents of the will was known," Caleb frowned. "Was anyone late in to luncheon?"

"Only you and your wife and Avery," said Luke. "Of course if you'd chosen to murder the Beau for his irritating ways and poor dress sense, I doubt anyone here would blame you, but I reluctantly have to concede that Mr Avery's collusion seems remarkably unlikely."

Mr Avery spluttered.

"Luke, you are taking a joke too far!" he exclaimed.

"Was I joking? If you say so," said Luke, coolly.

"Young man, I find your remarks in severely bad taste," said Mr Avery, sternly.

Luke raised a teacup in a mock toast.

"So too did Daventry find his ratafia," he said.

Mr Avery went purple with anger at such flippancy in the face of a potential second death but the Beau laid a hand on his arm.

"Lionel, Luke's comments do not hurt me; it is his loss that he has been so ill bred as to make jokes at the expense of poor Perkins, who is at least likely to recover. Jove!" he exclaimed. "Armitage, my dear fellow! I did not know of Perkins' inclination to tipple from an overfilled glass but do you suppose someone else knew and that Perkins saw something that made him the target for this cowardly attack? That it would seem to be an attack on me would divert suspicion away!"

Caleb froze.

"Beau, that's a good point. I will need to safeguard Perkins' life by speaking to him as soon as possible."

"I'll go to him now, Caleb," offered Henry. "I may not be up to Mr Luke Popham's standards in boxing but I wager if any tried to attack Perkins I could make enough noise to bring someone running. When he's able to talk I'll question him."

"Thanks, Henry, lad," said Caleb.

"And I'll go and see if I cannot wheedle more cakes in the kitchen and see if Perkins spoke to anyone else," said Simmy, sliding out with alacrity. Jane suspected that the excuse to be useful would also give him better company and a more amusing time than the rest of them were having. She and Caleb however had a job to do and in this case timing might be imperative; she must ask more questions.

"How soon after luncheon did you notice that the flowers had been spilled and were wilting?" asked Jane, of Flora. Flora made a Gallic shrugging gesture which added to her air of the exotic and threatened to spill her bosom over the top of her low cut gown.

"Quite quickly, I think," she said. "It will have been a careless maid cleaning in the library after we left to eat, no doubt. There was the whole afternoon for someone to get poison and pour it into the decanter, and we were all in and out of the salon. It could have been anyone, though if you ask me, the Beau looks a dashed shady character, and probably knows enough to be ill without dying," she added.

"Stage directions should dictate that you should rise on that comment, give me a look of 'more in sorrow than in anger' and exit stage left" said the Beau.

Flora had drawn up her feet on the *chaise longue* on which she reclined in order to rise in just such a manner and she hastily straightened her legs and gave the Beau a speaking look.

"Very well, let us make the assumption that the flowers were knocked over during luncheon or shortly thereafter," said Caleb. "The ladies withdrew first to attend to their appearances and change, those who do, into afternoon gowns," his gaze dwelt briefly and with fond approval on Jane's afternoon gown, a soft brown merino trimmed with ribbons of blue, and with a high ruffled neck of muslin threaded round the throat with blue ribbon, the cashmere shawl worn elegantly draped over Jane's elbows.

Jane had rebelled against wearing even half mourning now she was married, though she was practical enough to continue to wear such lilac garments as took her fancy, for she looked as well in lilac as in blue. Caleb thought that even the rich merino could not match the rich lights in Jane's glossy brown hair. He drew his contemplation from his wife and went on, "And when you returned downstairs the vase was knocked over; providential that it did not break. I am surprised a maid did not pick it up and thrust the flowers back, hoping to hide her carelessness and hope – if she thought of it – to top it up with water later."

Flora performed her Gallic gyrations again, aimed strategically at Caleb, who kept his face bland, hiding the thought that he wished she had the taste to wear a high necked gown like the other ladies and not a dress gown which he had a sudden urge to describe to Jane as a mostly undressed gown.

"Menials are too stupid to think of such things," she said, sounding bored.

"Now that's where you're wrong, my girl," said Caleb. "Most servants want to make sure they are not about to lose their place, for it's a precarious position; and though Mr Popham seems to have been a kindly master, if the task of doing the flowers was something you had taken on, I've heard you have a wicked temper, my girl, and might be most unkind to some poor clumsy lass."

"And you would know about how servants think, then?" asked Luke in a drawl as Flora plainly contemplated whether to have a tantrum, flounce out, or take this remark with studied dignity.

"Why, yes, Mr Popham; it's my job to know how all kinds of people think," said Caleb. "I've questioned enough people that I am able to give a good overview of the outlook of many classes. In the same way as I am

able to tell *you* that you are not merely angered by not having acquired all you desired from your cousin's will but are also afraid; afraid that this whole matter will rebound
badly on yourself. I do not yet know if that is the fear of a guilty man or the fear of an innocent one caught up in a situation beyond his control. But I do know that you hide behind your façade of rudeness to conceal it."

Luke was white.

"*Damn* you, I – you are insolent!" cried Luke.

"Under the circumstances, I think the phrase you were looking for, coz, was 'the devil damn thee black, thou cream faced loon,'" put in the Beau.

Caleb chuckled.

"That would suit," he said. "I just want to know who has done 'this bloody thing' though; so perhaps we might just go through where everyone was from after luncheon?"

Chapter 22

"I did not change into an afternoon gown but went into the music room straight away," said Mrs Kemp firmly. "Where you and your wife proceeded to give my husband and myself a most unpleasant time."

Caleb bowed.

"Oh, believe me, madam, you must know that neither Jane nor I enjoyed the discussion any more than you did," he said.

This passed Mrs Kemp by entirely but elicited an ejaculation of,

"Upon my soul!" of indignation from the reverend. Jane resisted the temptation to catch Caleb's eye and refused to be drawn by the Beau's murmur,

"He didn't learn that level of subtle insult from any Royal Prince."

"I found Mrs Kemp in the salon when I returned from helping Flora, though Flora was still arranging the flowers," said Nessie, "and I believe Gabriel was already there when they came out."

"Yes, I had come to the salon to await a summons to be questioned," said Gabriel. "I arrived not long before my parents came out, and of course went in straight away."

"If you came into the salon, one might wonder where you were in the meantime," said Luke Popham maliciously.

"He came up to see me after I had been sent to my room, Cousin Luke, risking annoying papa, to assure me that Mr and Mrs Armitage at least did not consider my hasty words unduly improper," said Michael, "so you may cease your nasty imprecations that it is a suggestion of guilt, for he must have had to hurry to get down again. You might be feeling yellow about this business but I'll not have you try to put anything onto my twin."

"And what's more, Cousin Luke, before you start, I

had not been down long enough before my parents emerged and papa went up to talk to Michael for him to have sneaked around getting poison and putting it in decanters and so on," said Gabriel, "before you start laying any insinuations on him."

Luke Popham laughed nastily.

"Oh, of course each of you will back the other up" he said.

"There will have been servants above stairs to corroborate that a young volcano went up and down the stairs at the time Gabriel says he did," said Caleb. "Boys, being boys, are constitutionally incapable of performing any action quietly, especially if it involves stairs. I've known enough raw subalterns their age to know *that*."

"One should be pleased, I suppose, that they do not try riding horses up stairs," murmured the Beau.

"Oh that would be nothing new," said Caleb. "I know of a certain young lieutenant and the Marquesa of… perhaps that's not a good story to recount."

"Probably not," said the Beau, regretfully. "Over a brandy after dinner perhaps?"

"Well, I'll consider it," said Caleb. "Well the boys are fairly well accounted for. Mr Luke Popham! It is not in your nature to sit about waiting with patience, I think, for your turn to be questioned. How did you spend your time, where, and can anyone verify it?"

"I went out to the stables to curry my mare," said Luke. "Michael can tell you; he came out to tell me you wanted me next."

"Suppose after your insinuations about Gabe and me I find I've forgotten?" said Michael.

"Lad," said Caleb, "When someone has behaved childishly towards you, the bigger man is not childish back. This is about a murderer. If you shield a murderer, that's almost as bad as killing for yourself. And failing to speak up over who may be cleared is almost as bad as shielding a murderer. Only by knowing all that happened can I be certain to reach the truth."

Michael flushed.

"My apologies, sir," he said. "I did indeed go to the stables to find my cousin as I thought he'd likely be there. He was currying Alcippe so hard she was not enjoying it; but she appeared to have been done pretty much all over, so I should imagine that he had been there some time."

"Unless of course he took over currying her from the groom," said Gabe.

"That can be ascertained readily enough from the groom," said Caleb. "Gabe, go and extract my son from the kitchen and instruct him to go and ask questions."

"Yes sir," said Gabriel. "I could ask questions instead," he added.

"No, you're too close to it," said Caleb, "and it might be prejudicial. Simmy is impartial."

Gabriel nodded and went off, a coltishness to his gait that highlighted how young he still was.

Luke scowled, but volunteered no further comment.

"And I," said the Beau, "was in the library, writing a letter that I dispatched by one of the stable boys, having been confirmed as the one whose responsibility it is, requesting the services of a vicar in Nether Amberfield to conduct a funeral service for Uncle Henry as soon as possible, and to make arrangement for burial to take place in the family crypt in Amberfield itself at St Michael and All the Angels."

Mr Kemp stirred himself.

"How dare you take that upon yourself? I am the incumbent of St Michael and All the Angels, and I forbid that any other vicar should take a service for my brother-in-law!"

Daventry Popham regarded him coldly.

"Uncle Henry felt himself unequal to removing the living from the husband of his sister, Kemp, but do not rely on me being so sentimental. I did not feel it appropriate for the obsequies to be in the hands of not only a close relative but one not yet cleared of murder, and thought that an outside party would fit the bill far better. Moreover I have always been very fond of Uncle Henry and I dislike you intensely. I do not want my memory of him marred by your brand of hell-fire hypocrisy; I want him laid to rest in the family crypt not in some whited sepulchre of your oratory. You will comply with my wishes or I will write to the Bishop requesting that he send me some deserving incumbent."

Kemp went white.

"I – you cannot do that!" he cried.

"I beg your pardon, Kemp, but I can; the avowdsen is in my hands now I am lord of the manor," said the Beau coldly.

"The lord of the manor giveth; and the lord of the manor taketh away, blessed be the name of the lord of the manor," said Luke.

"Inappropriate, but for once actually quite funny, coz," said the Beau.

"Blasphemer!" said Kemp.

"Hadn't you realised that yet?" said Luke.

"Beau, is your family always this puerile, or is it just the strain of the circumstances?" asked Caleb.

"We're always this puerile," said the Beau.

"They are childish in the extreme!" declared Kemp.

"Oh, were you under the impression I was excluding you?" said Caleb. "I wasn't. Well, I think that covers most people, and pending Mr Luke Popham being covered for the period by the groom's testimony we're no further forward; here, Flora, my girl, how long were you out there, messing with those flowers? Who did you see come in and out of the salon?"

"I'm not going to answer any questions if you don't address me properly, Armitage," said Flora, sulkily.

"Is that so?" said Caleb. "Well if you're absolutely certain of that, there's no help for it. Jane, what did you say the wench's real name was?"

Flora gave a little screech of horror.

"NO! she's telling lies! I am Miss d'Ambrose and you should call me that!"

"But Flora dear," said Nessie, "You asked Mr Armitage to address you properly; and if he assumes you want to be known by your real name, you really cannot blame him for understanding that such is what you meant, can you?"

"That female doesn't know! she cannot! I – my real name is Floradora d'Ambrose!" cried Flora in a panic.

"Really, Flora!" said Jane, "We are all aware that you are an actress and that you use that as a stage name; it helps when applying for parts to be something a little more distinguished sounding than Jemima Harris, but it hardly matters here when you have no need to act any more since you are likely to have to make do with the generous settlement Mr Popham already made; and where you have not gone out of your way to make any of the family feel sufficiently warm towards you to see you more comfortable."

Flora started as Jane said her name.

"But – but how can you know? HE told you! The Beau!" she cried, glaring at him.

"Not me" said the Beau.

"Why Flora, dear, I told dear Jane a long while ago!" said Nessie.

Flora stared at her.

"Nessie! How could you? You have been prying into my private things, poking around like a thief! Have you stolen from me, as well?"

Nessie jerked back as though slapped.

"Flora! What a wicked thing to say!" she said. "You should know I would not pry through anything private – it is most unladylike, and no lady would even consider such a thing!"

Jane reflected that this was the difference between a lady and a lady who was married to an investigating officer as she was now wondering what there might be in Flora's private possessions that might reveal more about her – if indeed it were relevant.

"I do not see how you might have heard that name otherwise," said Flora.

"Why Flora! It is the name on the letters you get every month or so from your friend in Holborn, the one who calls herself Esmeralda de Vere on stage" said Nessie.

The Beau gave a sardonic laugh.

"For all your careful planning, my dear Flora, you are 'hoist by your own petard' in having clung to a friend from the old way of life who knows your name and uses it. And to think I thought I was being quite clever to find out more about you."

"*YOU*!" Flora howled. "I *HATE* you!"

The Beau laughed.

"I'm not terribly fond of you, Flora," he said, "but I suppose I am sorry enough for you not to want to queer your pitch too much. I think, you know, you are only going to damage your outlook more by saying anything much more. Why not preserve a ladylike silence?"

"Is that baggage an imposter and an *actress*?" demanded Kemp.

"Imposter? not precisely," said Daventry Popham. "She has a stage name that she prefers, and I am presuming that Uncle Henry was aware of that; if not, I believe the phrase is *caveat emptor*. She is certainly an actress, but not a very good one."

"*Jezebel*!" declared Kemp, pointing a bony finger at Flora.

"Let's not confuse matters with even more soubriquets," said Caleb.

Kemp glowered at him, and then declared,

"I demand that she is put out of this house immediately; she is not the kind to associate with my family."

"My house; my decision," said the Beau, "And I fancy Mr Armitage would have a thing or two to say about that as well as she's part of his investigation, so no need to cite the hoary old 'either she goes or I do' chestnut, for I imagine he'd forbid it."

"I will," said Caleb.

A footman entered the room at that moment with a salver on which lay a letter; he took it to the Beau who opened it.

"Ah, good," he said, "the funeral will be tomorrow at ten."

Chapter 23

"Beau, what do you want Jane and me to do?" asked Caleb, quietly, drawing the Beau into the relative seclusion of a bay window. "We'll gladly attend to show respect, but if you feel that we'd be *de trop* we'll stay away."

The Beau regarded him thoughtfully.

"You're the soul of tact, where it counts, Armitage; even if you can call someone down with the level of exquisite rudery I've rarely heard outside of the peerage. I think if it's all the same to you, this should be a family affair. And Flora. She may not be mourning Uncle Henry half so well as she sincerely mourns the loss of this house, but she will give every appearance of mourning for the sake of the servants. I'll have Cousin Agnes see that she turns up in black, not merely a white muslin trimmed with a few black ribbons designed more to enhance her attributes than declare her grief. People generally behave as they are supposed to at funerals so I doubt you'll see much on faces to mark out a guilty party."

"That's what I thought" said Caleb. "Is there time to make her a black dress?"

"I wrote another letter as well as the one to the vicar of Nether Amberfield, addressed to an acquaintance of mine whose sisters are just out of mourning for his brother, and they will send me gowns sufficiently up to date to suit even the fair Flora," said the Beau. "I am sure Cousin Agnes will be up to adjusting sizes."

"Jane will aid her, I'm sure," said Caleb. "I still need to find out from the wretched woman if she saw anyone enter or leave the salon while she was doing the flowers, who might have loitered, or gone to loiter elsewhere until she was finished."

"Unless they drew attention to themselves by

praising her for her womanly virtues, I think it highly unlikely that Flora will remember a lot more than that she was presenting a most attractive picture of the lady of the
manor" said the Beau, dryly. "Here, Flora! How about answering Mr Armitage's questions that got interrupted by the letter arriving?"

Flora frowned.

"I don't suppose I know anything," she said, tossing her head.

"Who's that, Desdemona or Cleopatra?" said the Beau, unimpressed.

"Shab off, Popham" said Caleb.

The Beau laughed.

"Now I know we're friends, Armitage; you feel easy being bluntly rude to me. I'm glad I've done nothing to alter that," he said, moving away and leaving the privacy to Caleb and Flora.

"I don't understand," frowned Flora. "How can being so rude to him show that you are friends, Armitage?"

"Mr Armitage to you, young woman" said Caleb. "I don't intend to pry but I fancy if I looked under your real name, I might find an indictment or two for one thing or another. However as you might yet be wishful to learn how to be a lady, I'll explain; men who like each other can be infernally rude to each other without taking or giving offence. In the same way that they might call each other just by the surname or nickname, as a stage before using a given name, without bothering with any honorific. A lady only uses a name without honorific if she's speaking to a peer of the realm when, if she knows him well enough, she may address him as his title. Lesson over; now pray cast your mind back to when you were arranging the flowers and see if you can't recall who came in and out of the salon."

Flora opened her magnificent eyes wide and let her eyelashes flutter. Caleb was almost certain her lashes were enhanced by artifice.

"Oh dear, that is so *difficult*!" she exclaimed, clasping her hands together girlishly. "One is so deeply involved in the task that one scarcely *notices* anything else!"

"Don't overdo the ingénue," said Caleb, "if you didn't notice, just say so; I'm more likely to believe you than if you playact. It don't do you any favours."

"Much you care" pouted Flora.

"Frankly, if you want to move up in the world and can manage to achieve it, I've nothing against it," said Caleb, "but I do take exception to you running the gamut of stage emotions. Did you notice anyone or not?"

Flora flushed .

"We got back as that boy Gabriel came thundering down the stairs like a runaway chaise and four," she said. "I told Nessie that I didn't need her – I think that that horrid old parson had come out of the door by then. But then I was very busy and people came and went, but I didn't pay much attention to them. No, I don't recall."

Caleb nodded.

"Thank you" he said.

She looked surprised at the courtesy, and Caleb smiled at her; she had been through a few shocks after all.

It was a mistake. Her own smile became quickly calculating and she laid a hand on his arm in an intimate little gesture, gazing up at him with her melting brown eyes.

"Oh Mr Armitage! I wanted to be a lady for poor Henry, but I want so much to go back to the nice little house in Hampstead, don't you think you might permit me to go? You could always ride over to question me there alone if you needed to know any more" she added breathily.

"Madam, if your tone is telling me more than your words, may I remind you that I am married" said Caleb frostily.

"Oh but such a little colourless thing, Mr Armitage, a man of affairs needs a real woman as a mistress, even when he has affection for his wife!"

"Good heavens!" said Caleb revolted. "Any man scarce come from his honeymoon is not a man if he chooses to roll with a lightskirt, however expensive she may be!"

Flora was taken aback.

"But – but you and your wife have children; how can you be scarce from your honeymoon?"

"Because, you silly chit, we have both brought children to our marriage; and with such a woman as my Jane, why, I have no doubt that I shall still feel as though I am on honeymoon in a dozen years and a quiverful more of hopeful offspring," said Caleb. "I might have half considered sending you and Miss Fanshawe off but now I'm more determined to keep you under my eye where I can see what you might be up to."

"You are unkind," tears welled up onto the long lashes.

"Yes" said Caleb.

Flora achieved a flounce and stormed off.

"Who won the honours there?" asked the Beau, moving back beside Caleb.

"I did," said Caleb. "What a little trollop she is to be sure!"

"Solicited you, did she? Well she should think herself lucky not to be taken in charge," said the Beau. "Every time I try to be sorry for her she does something that makes me want to put something across her rump and throw her out."

"You too, eh?" said Caleb. "Ah!" he added as Simmy and Gabriel came back into the room.

Simmy came over and sketched a bow.

"The groom isn't prepared to swear how long Mr Luke was currying the prad, pa; seemingly when he's in one of his tempers, he curries so fast that it ain't

scarcely fair on the mare; and all he knows is that Mr Luke was fetched by Mr Michael and threw the curry comb at him – at the groom that is – and told him to dandy her and finish the
grooming. I can't rightly say he wouldn't have had enough time, because he's bold and would be a fast and efficient planner, I think."

"Am I supposed to feel grateful for that backhanded compliment, young shaver?" demanded Luke, who had come over to hear what Simmy had to say. Simmy bowed to him punctiliously.

"No sir," he said, "it wasn't meant as a compliment but as an assessment. I like your mare; she never tried to kick me, but then, horses don't. If you killed Mr Popham and need to raise the dibs for a defence can I put in an offer for her?"

Luke gaped.

"Well, I - good Gad, you insolent infant! I have never heard – you quite take the wind out of my sails you young prodigy you! It's not going to happen for I didn't kill him, but 'fore Gad, I like you the better for that style of impudence."

Simmy chuckled; being with adults most of the time he was rapidly acquiring an air of assurance few schoolboys his age managed.

"Well, sir, I think I like *you* the better for having the honesty to say so," he said.

"Well, I do not like that I am back under your father's scrutiny," said Luke. "I had been quite certain that when you returned I would be shown to have been unable to have poisoned Daventry, however tempting it might sometimes be. I suppose I might have acquired the poison, set myself to be seen currying Alcippe and added the, er, cyanide to the decanter after having been under question?"

"A man as bold as yourself might even fetch the poison and do the deed in the time we were speaking with the Beau, though it would be a fine matter" said

Caleb.

"I would hope that any of the others foregathering here would recall that I left the salon for the briefest time," said Luke.

"He did not go for long," said Nessie, "and I assumed he wished to refresh himself."

Luke made her a half mocking leg.

"A delightful euphemism," he murmured.

"However you might have got the poison earlier," said Caleb.

"A question, Mr Armitage," said Luke, "which is to say, what form does this poison take? Is it a powder or what?"

"It's a distillation of laurel leaves," said Caleb. "It's in liquid form. I see what you mean, Mr Popham; carrying a liquid about the house is not so easy as carrying a powder which might be placed in a snuff box, say."

"I'd carry it in a common utensil that one averts one's eyes from expected to hold liquid if I were doing it," said Jane, meditatively. "Though there are enough footmen here to empty such utensils that I suppose for one of the guests to do so would be remarkable."

Caleb laughed.

"Yes, that's so," he said, "but it goes to show why I'm glad you've never turned to crime, my love; you would be formidably good at it with such a pragmatic streak."

"So, what you want to know, then, is if any of us were seen carrying anything that might hold a liquid," said Luke.

"It is a line of enquiry we need to pursue," said Caleb. He exchanged a look with Jane; this was a line of enquiry to pursue with the aid of the invaluable Fowler and indomitable Ella as he was wont to describe them to his wife. The sight of Jane, so fresh and wholesome after the encroachingly exotic personality of Flora, made his blood run hot, and he added, "personally, I intend to retire to dress for dinner; if anyone has anything further to tell me, I will speak to you this evening, but in the meanwhile I have other avenues of enquiry to pursue and will leave you all alone until after the funeral."

Caleb offered his arm to Jane, and they went upstairs, where he proceeded to kiss Jane very thoroughly.

"Caleb, I shall be mussed before even changing for dinner," she said, "and I thought you were hungry?"

"I am" said Caleb.

Jane gave up further argument in satisfying her husband's appetites.

Chapter 24

Caleb reflected that it was as well that someone like Beau Popham would not think it strange to take an hour or more to dress for dinner; Fowler and Ella had anticipated the needs of the Armitages and had brought hot water to bathe quickly. Once in their undergarments, Caleb instructed Fowler to open the connecting door in order to discuss what was required and succinctly explained the events of the afternoon to their servants.

"I tell you one thing, Mr Caleb, and that's about the parson o' prigging," said Fowler, who paused for a moment wondering if he was pleased with the alliteration despite having to choose cant to find it. "Vicar of Venery and Vinery is better," he added.

"Fowler, I'm uncommon fond of you, but I wish you'd get to the point and stop tasting those words like a connoisseur of fine brandy," said Caleb.

Fowler chuckled.

"My apologies, sir; your own appreciation of words is infectious. He was not long with that boy Michael; because he was straightway down and into the cellar, and he was wandering about in the hall with bottles of best brandy – or at least bottles. Which you might draw an inference from, sir, or you might not."

"I might indeed," said Caleb, "although I am inclined to think that this is merely more of his ongoing peculation. Still, being known to engage in the same would mean that the bold thief might readily carry a bottle containing something less innocent than brandy and nobody would think anything of it save the usual mild contempt for him."

"Fowler, did you see him?" Jane's voice came through.

"Yes, Mrs Jane, I did," said Fowler.

"Did you happen to notice if the bottles were sealed,

or if one might have been opened?" Jane asked.

Fowler froze.

"Gawd help me for a nodcock!" he declared. "Mrs Jane, I confess, I didn't notice. I assumed – just like Mr Caleb said anyone would – that it was more of the same of his theft. I – I think he had his hands held over the tops, it would be hard to see, but I could have done if I'd only thought of it."

"When you saw him, I doubt anyone might have guessed that there was to be a poisoning, Fowler," said Caleb mildly. "When you've finished seeing to me, by the way, I wish you will relieve young Henry, who's sitting with poor Perkins."

"Yes Mr Caleb" said Fowler. "Perkins will more likely spill his budget to me anywise; not being as in awe of me as he is of a gentry-cove, but being sufficiently in awe of a London Gentleman's gentleman as to do as he's bid."

"I'll arrange a tray for you and him both," said Ella. "It will give me the opportunity to find out if any vessels went missing from the kitchen and if anyone else was seen carrying something that could hold liquid."

"Good girl," approved Caleb. "If there's anything to be extracted from the servants, I wager you'll have it faster than a tooth-drawer."

"Caleb," said Jane, "are we stood too close to the problem and overlooking the obvious?"

"I have wondered," said Caleb, "but I'm puzzled about a motive in either case. The killing of Henry Popham could not be advantageous; and why try to kill the Beau?"

"I think that the burned letter might hold more of the key to the first question than anything else," said Jane, "though what it might mean, and in what respect it is significant I cannot begin to guess."

"It is a puzzle" admitted Caleb.

"There was also a conversation that the Beau had which might lead someone to wish him dead to avoid potential loss of security," said Jane. "It is not impossible that an attempt on him was not for inheritance but to ensure tenure of the *status quo*."

"A different form of *cui bono* as you might say," said Caleb, chuckled softly and added, "as our budding attorney at law almost certainly will say."

"Simmy has the ability to make people forget the slight twist that remains to his face," said Jane.

"He's also been stretching it in the mirror and filling his mouth with Fowler's round pebbles" said Caleb. "With the determined exercise he's doing to get as much motion out of his arm as possible, and with the built up sole, I wouldn't mind wagering that by the time he's grown, most people won't look at him twice."

"I hope so," said Jane, "though on the whole he's able to hold his own against the rudeness of people."

"That boy has come on a treat, Mrs Jane," said Ella. "Don't you fret about him; he's one that can make people like him, unless they're too plain nasty for anyone to find being liked by them desirable."

Caleb and Jane said simultaneously,

"Mrs Kemp!" and laughed.

"Her!" said Ella. "The servants call her 'Mrs Too-much-trouble' because she whines about surely such and such isn't too much trouble to do. Usually at the most inconvenient moment. *He* hits her about and she passes that on to servants."

"A nice harmonious Christian family," said Caleb dryly.

"Nobody has any real objection to the youngsters," said Ella, quickly. "They had most of their upbringing by a nanny provided by Mr Popham; he's been generous to his sister. None of the servants think it at all unfair that she's not been left much, because she had anything she wanted while he was alive. Well, that's to say," amended Ella with a sniff, "anything money could buy, being that she was born discontent and wanting being more an avocation for her than enjoying what she had."

"Goodness, Ella, she really is not popular!" said Jane.

"No, not hardly," said Ella. "And Mr Popham was a well-loved master; the servant's hall is keen to find out who killed him, they're ready to tell us anything and pleased that you are good enough to let us talk so they don't have to have official questions. You and Mr Caleb are much liked for it."

"And the footmen have a book on who did it of course," said Fowler.

"I'm not sure I want to know about that," said Caleb, "or on second thoughts, maybe I do. Servants are often pretty shrewd."

"Well the clear favourite is the Reverend, but I fancy it's got as much to do with wishful thinking as anything else," said Fowler. "The joint second favourites are Mr Luke and Miss d'Ambrose, then Mrs Kemp, with one outside bet on Miss Fanshawe and several agreed that it must have been an outsider. None for the Beau; he's a popular successor."

"I'll feel even worse, then, if I end up taking him in charge," groaned Caleb. "In effect, it's about who is liked and who is not, rather than who they feel might have genuinely done it?"

Fowler hesitated.

"Not entirely," he said, "since it's been discussed; the servants' hall reckon that the reverend has the mad ruthlessness to do the deed – his fear of blood has been brushed aside – and so have Mr Luke and Miss d'Ambrose got the stomach to do something drastic; the ones the servants apostrophise as 'pushing', those who take what they want without asking. Mrs Kemp just whines until someone gives her what she's asking for in order to keep her quiet. The couple of people who have a penny on her mostly get shouted down by the rest who feel that she's more likely to threaten to kill herself messily to get her own way than kill someone."

"Why Nessie?" asked Jane.

"Oh that's the laundress; Miss Fanshawe ticked her off for improper removal of smuts from a garment, and she's
sore about it," said Ella contemptuously, "said she wasn't expecting smoke stains on a cuff and could hardly be held accountable. Silly chit; one of those as knows everything and knows nothing. She's obviously never washed for the educated before that will trim wicks to read better without taking account of their garments!"

Jane flushed.

"I'm sorry I put you to extra trouble, Ella," she said.

"Oh well, you and the master are less trouble than some, no doubt," said Ella tolerantly, "and those of us who know how to use soda and white vinegar to deal with the greasy nature of smoke don't have any real trouble."

"I expect the laundress does know how and merely did not notice the stain; and is defensive because she knows that she should have done," said Jane.

"Oh I have no doubt that you are right, Mrs Jane," said Ella, "and besides, she was concerned with getting out the blood that had spread from those cloths one does not generally discuss in front of men," she added severely.

"I'm a married man and used to such matters," said Caleb cheerfully. "Here, Fowler, if your ears are too delicate and innocent, you'd better not listen."

"I'm sure I'm no more delicate than you are, Mr Caleb," said Fowler, severely. "However, now you're respectable to go and eat, I'll be away to relieve young Mr Henry and see what I can't get out of Perkins. Dare say he'll be feeling well enough for a game of picquet," he added thoughtfully.

"Don't you go ruining the poor lad," said Caleb.

"Why, Mr Caleb!" Fowler sounded injured, "I had thought to play for snippets of scandal about our respective families as the stakes."

"Do we have any scandal for you to recount if you lose?" asked Jane.

"No, Mrs Jane; but I have a remarkably good imagination. *If* I should happen to lose, which is highly unlikely. for I've picked up far too many tips watching people fleece Mr Churchill while I served them drinks," he
added.

"Fowler, at times you come close to going too far," said Jane.

"Yes, madam; I beg your pardon. I was out of line to remind you of those days," said Fowler, in contrition.

"Forgiven," said Jane.

Fowler left to send Henry to dress quickly for dinner, and Ella took herself off to the kitchen to make up a tray.

Caleb came into Jane's room and regarded her with approval. Though the sad death of the host precluded too low a décolletage as indecent – which fact had not stopped Flora from wearing her gowns cut low morning, noon and night – Jane's white shoulders and upper chest emerged from a froth of blonde lace that trimmed the top of her evening gown, a sheer muslin embroidered with bugles and stitchery, worn over a new jonquil satin slip, her Mameluke sleeves caught at intervals with silk ribbon the same colour as the slip and bodice of the gown.

He drew her into his arms.

Jane laughed.

"Now here is a piece of work, not to crumple my gown and disarrange my hair without Ella to put me back together!" she said, putting up her face for his kisses.

"Mrs Armitage, if you will persist in looking so delectable, you should not complain about your husband wanting to muss you," said Caleb.

They managed an embrace as decorous as might be managed by two people much in love, enjoying the spice of needing to avoid too much evidence of dissipation being wrought to Jane's appearance.

A few pins sorted out the slight damage to her hair, and some twitches and smoothing, helped willingly by Caleb, put to rights anything that might be noticed by any but the most discerning. Then Jane and Caleb went down
to dinner with Jane looking as demure as she possibly could.

Caleb promised himself that the gown might be mussed more efficiently later.

Chapter 25

Dinner was a sombre meal; the air of suspicion and fear had permeated through the company with the attempted use of poison. Henry had managed a quick word with Caleb to report that Perkins could not think of any knowledge he might have which could have made him the real target of the poisoning; and Caleb was philosophical. If Perkins knew anything, Fowler would find it out. Meanwhile conversation at the table did not so much flag, as never started in the first instance.

Nessie Fanshawe managed to speak the thoughts many were thinking.

"Well at least we may be comfortable in knowing that if that poison tastes of bitter almonds we may all avoid ratafia, orgeat and anything flavoured with ratafia," she said.

"Not that cyanide is the only poison in that greenhouse," said Caleb. Nessie gave a little cry.

"Why, Mr Armitage, I have not heard that the gardener was killing anything but wasps!" she cried.

"Oh, I don't suppose he is," said Caleb, "but there's enough poisonous plants in any gentleman's greenhouse to murder a regiment. I'm not an expert on poisons of course, but I've seen plants outside and in that could be deadly in skilled enough hands. It's quite fortunate that the household poisoner is something of an amateur to all appearances, or wholesale death from apparent accident might yet ensue. I've issued orders regarding the feeding of the children, to safeguard them, and my nursery staff carry pistols of course," he added mendaciously. The desperate and not entirely logical mind that had wrought so far was yet unlikely to perform any action that would be a personal risk; and Caleb decided to take a calculated risk in bringing Fanny and Joseph to the thoughts of those assembled in order to make clear that any attack on them would be looked for and countered, just in case the killer hit upon an idea to distract him and Jane.

"Surely nobody would be so depraved as to attack your children?" asked Nessie, shocked.

"There are some people depraved enough to hurt children, Miss Fanshawe," said Caleb.

"There wouldn't be any point for any killer to do so because they aren't his children so anyone who threatened them isn't going to get his attention anyhow," said Flora.

There was a stunned silence.

"Miss d'Ambrose, there is such a thing as slander in suggesting that Mrs Armitage has played her husband false," said Mr Avery.

"Fanny and Joseph are my first husband's children," said Jane. "Joseph was a posthumous child. Flora, I fear you must have had a very unfortunate upbringing if you think in that fashion. Dear me! And you also as good as accused me of not loving my stepson; one can only hope that you do not manage to bedazzle a widower with young children if your concept of an enlarged household is such as to consider stepchildren with such a lack of favour."

"Catch me taking on someone else's brats!" said Flora. "Not without a fortune a lot more than Henry had, anyway. Why are you all staring at me?"

"Flora, dear, I think you might wish to listen more, and speak less," opined Nessie, "as you are not impressing anyone with your attitude."

"Well I don't see how…" began Flora

"Hush!" said Nessie, firmly.

Flora actually broke off and sulkily turned her attention back to her fricassee of fowl. The meal proceeded in silence, the well-prepared and attractively served dishes given sparse attention by the older members of the gathering, though the three Kemp youngsters, Simmy, Henry and Jane and Caleb did justice to the viands set before them.

Simmy murmured something to Henry who had a coughing fit and had to leave the table briefly. Simmy sat looking so angelic that Jane eavesdropped shamelessly
when Gabriel drew him aside after the meal to ask what he had said.

"Oh," said Simmy, "I merely remarked with such fine chandeliers and the lowering looks around the table, above all was light and 'below there was nothing but darkness and the gnashing of teeth'"

Gabriel cuffed him for so aptly managing a Biblical quote and stealing a march on a vicar's son by so doing. Simmy grinned, accepting that as a just rebuke.

Caleb and Jane escaped from the rest of the company to devote the evening to playing with Fanny and Joseph. They needed time away from the rest of this sorry family in order to relax, and put their thoughts in order.

"Early night?" asked Caleb, hopefully, when the little ones were kissed and put to bed.

"We should see whether Fowler managed to obtain anything more from Perkins," said Jane, "and what Ella may have about missing vessels suitable to hold poison."

"There is that," said Caleb, "and then an early night?"

"Unless something else calls for our attention," said Jane, blushing in pleasurable anticipation. They called their servants to report.

Fowler shrugged annoyance.

"If Perkins knows anything at all, he has refined so little upon it as to make it disappear from his memory," he said, "for he is quite certain he has not seen anything germane to the killing of Henry Popham at all. Indeed he was busy in the kitchen lifting and carrying for the cook the whole morning. I think that the original surmise, that his poisoning was accidental, is indeed the correct one, for he told me that he was not in the habit of tippling, it really had been a case of having filled the glass too full; he wanted to make it easier to carry."

"There have been no vessels that disappeared from the kitchen, Mrs Jane, dear," said Ella. "Of course, many men possess hip flasks; and though they would need to wash them thoroughly after storing poison in them, it is the obvious way to carry a liquid unnoticed, I would think."

"A good point, Ella!" said Jane. "I also have an idea of what may have been used, that would have been utterly overlooked. Indeed, I believe I know who the killer is, but I am still puzzled as to why. The attempt on Beau Popham I can explain, but I cannot see what might have led to the killing of Mr Popham in the first instance."

"We shall talk this through while the rest of the company is at the funeral; and look again at the remains of the letter" said Caleb.

"And in the meantime, we shall sleep on it" said Jane.

"I wasn't planning on doing a lot of *sleeping* for a while" said Caleb.

Jane flushed prettily.

"I believe, Ella, Fowler, we will take our breakfast in bed tomorrow morning; and no earlier than eight of the clock if you please" she said.

Like good servants, Fowler and Ella bowed and curtseyed without so much as a flicker of the eyes. Jane appreciated it.

It may be understood that no further conversation with regards to murder, attempted murder, poison or any other such unpleasantness occurred that night, nor indeed a great deal of conversation regarding any subject; but it should not in any wise be supposed that Jane and Caleb suffered from boredom for this lack of stimulating discourse.

Caleb and Jane managed to avoid seeing anything of the family in the morning; carriages took the mourners to the funeral, with the encoffined body of Mr Henry Popham solemnly preceding them in the ornately appointed carriage got up as a hearse for the purpose. The Beau had permitted the servants to have the morning off to attend the funeral, and the house was virtually empty. Caleb and Jane stood at the window to watch the cavalcade depart, the hearse leading, its four horses bedecked with black feathers, black velvet drapes and the hooves muffled. The
hearse was covered with black velvet and more feathers adorned its roof; evidently the Beau had arranged all that was proper to be sent from the nearest town. The servants were lined up to follow the hearse and other carriages all the way to the church. The mourning gowns Beau Popham had asked to borrow had evidently arrived and had been shared amongst the ladies; and Jane was relieved to see that Flora was at least decently covered, and had apparently decided to perform in tragic role.

"Melpomene hoping to upstage even Mrs Jordan" said Jane.

"Put your claws away and forget her for a few hours" said Caleb. "Muse of tragedy she may be; at least that means she isn't likely to be an embarrassment to the Beau. Let us leave them to get on with it."

"Let us take the children into the greenhouse to see the pretty flowers and see if there is anything within that enlightens us," said Jane. "It will be like a walk in the park but without the unpleasant intervention of weather if it is indeed heated; it should be a most excellent time with them."

"It seems a good plan to me," said Caleb, "since Fanny is not yet sufficiently able to be likely to accidentally discover any poison."

"Annie must be careful though, not to let her touch anything," said Jane, "for there are, as you yourself pointed out, poisonous leaves and berries about, and too some plants like Mezereon which can cause a nasty rash. What a shame it is that our murderer did not try to use that, as the berries are also very poisonous; a rash would have been something of an indication!"

"Our murderer is not sufficiently well versed in plant lore to know what plants are deadly and what are not," said Caleb, "for this is a most unplanned series of events I feel sure. It begins with a letter that caused Mr Popham to wax irritable, and the killer grabbed up the page-separator and by sheer blind luck has not managed to spray the whole of the room with blood, for the size of the hilt of the knife. Covering up why there is some blood took some ingenuity, I grant that. Then the conversation you heard at the reading of the will leads the Beau to be a danger; and so again a hasty, clumsy solution, recalling that poison had been mentioned by the gardener, and formulating a bold but hasty plan to abstract some, recalling the gardener's comment about ratafia and that it is the Beau's favourite afternoon tipple. This time our villain had less luck – not only did the wrong person drink enough to cause some symptoms, but the sweetened drink may cause it to be less effective, if the gardener is correct in his belief about that. What's important is that it failed, and I cannot help wondering if there will be another attempt."

"I cannot think that poison will be tried again," said Jane, "for it is altogether too risky save when the one that you wish to poison partakes of a particular comestible or drink not commonly partaken of by the others. We should warn him perhaps to be on his guard."

"He is aware," said Caleb, "and too I ventured to drop him a hint after dinner last night. He resolved to lock his door and open to none save myself. "

"He has gone to the funeral by carriage which should be a safer matter than if he rode," said Jane.

"Yes; it occurred to me, too, that if he rode, a burr

under the saddle might be enough to cause him hurt if not death, and a wounded man is easier to kill. However as the obsequies are to be attended to with full ceremony, and the Beau will travel with Luke, Nessie and Flora in one carriage while the Kemps go in another, even our singularly foolish killer is not going to want to risk killing the wrong person. The servants would be there to bear a hand in the event of any mishap, and are well disposed to the Beau as he gave permission for them to make their own best way on foot save those who wished to follow the cavalcade. As this appears to me to be all of them, I'd say
it says something for a man when his servants prefer to show respect in walking the long way round by road rather than cutting across fields. But that the Beau was prepared to permit this means they are likely well disposed towards him too."

The children held out their arms to Caleb and Jane; for Jane was insistent that she and her husband should spend as much time as was practicable with Fanny and Joseph, so that their parents were not distant figures to be held in awe. Fanny was not quite a year old, and though she stood quite firmly was still finding walking something of a mystery. She was learning how to express a need for the call of nature, which when she could manage every time would obviate some of the bulkier garments that made walking less easy. Her speech was becoming plainer and she could manage 'ba-ba' to signify Caleb and 'ma-ma' for Jane now. Unfortunately it was hard to tell when she said 'ba-ba' for papa and when it meant 'baby', speaking about herself – Fanny declined to notice Joseph as yet – and the little girl could get frustrated if her meaning was not immediately understood. The children were both well wrapped in shawls to cross the short distance from the side door to the greenhouse.

"It would have been more sensible to have either built it against the house or joined it to the house with a passageway" said Jane.

"It wasn't thought through properly," said Caleb, "for the horses are led through here to be brought to the front of the house. It would have been much more sensible, why in high winds you risk damaging any tender blooms to be brought in."

"And the most delicate bloom – at least in her own estimation – is Flora," laughed Jane. "Ah, yes, I see the arrangement, one goes into an antechamber so that the draught does not get in, shutting the outer door before the inner."

Caleb held the inner door when all were in the antechamber, and Jane gasped at the heat, and at the riot of colour and profusion of plants. To the right, down the length of the greenhouse, it was like looking upon an exotic garden, and it was quite easy to see how anyone might hide behind this shrub or that cascade of flowers. To the left was a door, standing open, into what looked to be a work area, where empty pots were stored and benches stood ready to work at. The big jar labelled in a semi-literate hand 'pizen' stood on one of the benches.

"And if the door were closed, nobody in the rest of the greenhouse would notice someone lurking here," said Jane. "And they might decant the poison in privacy. Flora and Nessie did not tell us this."

"Overwhelmed by obviousness, no doubt," said Caleb. "Or put it down to 'just an area the lower orders use'. Well, now we see how it might easily have been done even with someone else in here. That explains a lot that had bothered me, for one could not guarantee that another party might not look around a shrub at an inconvenient moment."

Chapter 26

Jane had always liked flowers, without having had much opportunity to do much gardening in the tiny cottage where her grandmother and Aunt Hetty lived, nor when she was at school. She knew that the numbers of new blooms that had been introduced over the last decade were quite amazing, however, and caught her breath as she took Frances down towards the other end of the greenhouse to see the Georginas. She recalled reading something about Lady Holland's experiments in cross breeding the earlier varieties with those she had sent home herself, but much of the information had been during the dark days with Frank, and it had been hard to concentrate much on anything. Nothing Nessie had said prepared her for quite a wide range of colours, yellow, orange, red, subdued oranges that were a rich peach, and reddish purples. One of these was the famous double Georgina, no doubt, from Belgium, sporting a second layer of petals around it. No wonder Nessie had been captivated!

Jane turned to look back towards the end where they had entered, and indeed from this point it would have been quite impossible to see anyone using either the outer door, or indeed the door into the working area. The clumps of Camellias and Azaleas made it quite impractical as their heavy, evergreen foliage blocked the view down the artfully serpentine path through the planting areas. Fanny was shouting about something and Jane turned to give her attention to whatever had attracted the little girl. The ornate fountain's plashing cascade had been caught by a low, thin sunbeam and turned into a curtain of myriad colours richer than those that might be achieved by the best crystal chandelier. The romantic side of Jane drank in the beauty, and she leaned back against her husband as he caught up and put his arms around her and little Fanny, in time to share the

magical beauty of the scene. The practical side of Jane noted that the sound of the flowing water would be sufficient to mask any slight noises made
by anyone at the other end of the greenhouse.

The sun slipped behind a cloud; and the moment was gone. Water still cascaded tinkling over the stones from the ornate piece of statuary that might, or might not, have represented a nereid or other watery nymph.

"Loud enough to drown out half a dozen murders being done," commented Caleb. "Oh, I'm sorry, I spoiled the moment."

"No, it had passed of its own accord; to be remembered and savoured," said Jane, "but not to intrude on our work. I had been thinking the same thing, my dear. Anyone choosing flowers down here could neither see nor hear anything at the other end. And that made it easy."

"Well now we know for certain, don't we?" said Caleb.

"I'd still like to look over that letter again," said Jane.

"This hot atmosphere is getting to me, and it can't be good for the children; now Fan's had a chance to look at the pretty flowers, let's get back into the house," said Caleb.

Jane and Caleb looked at the sheet on which Henry had transcribed the words of the burned letter.

> "ralda
> elf ridiculous
> thoroughly
> ssed garters
> will tell you all about it later"

"I'm guessing that the second line would be

'himself' or possibly 'herself' ridiculous," said Caleb, "possibly someone writing to apprise Mr Popham that one of his guests is behaving in a less than acceptable fashion?"

"I – I am wondering whether it is a missive he has read by mistake," said Jane, thoughtfully. "You see, I am thinking of a reference made to a Shakespearian character for whom the fourth line might have been made."

"You're right, Jane," said Caleb, "as you so often are. You think maybe our murderer had been writing a letter and left it lying about and Mr Popham found it? but then there is the fact that he was so furious when he read the mail that morning,"

"Any one of the mails he got in the morning might have been enough to infuriate him without necessarily being the cause of his death to maintain silence," said Jane, "and therefore it might be incidental and not connected with taxing anyone with such peccadilloes. We have not got all the facts in our possession. Are there enough to make an arrest?"

Caleb scratched his head in thought.

"It's still all a little circumstantial," he said, "and though we see the chain of inference quite clearly, it might not be clear to a jury, especially without a clear and apparent motive."

"I am worried that the Beau might be in danger," said Jane, "for though he is something of a quiz in his dress, I confess to liking him very well indeed."

"Me too" admitted Caleb. "I've a fancy that his mode of dress is a habit acquired as a means to be discounted and disregarded by much of society as having no mind above his dress, for having surmised that he worked in the foreign office covertly during the war possibly even decoding ciphers, it is my belief that he still acts covertly to uncover potential trouble within society."

"He is a spy on his own kind?" asked Jane.

Caleb looked uncomfortable.

"I should say, rather, he probably watches for those who are about to betray their family and birth with such behaviour as... those induced to be foolish," he said.

"You mean he would be someone who might see higher born men than Frank but of the same stamp, and perhaps be able to avert their fall into moral turpitude?" asked Jane.

"I believe that is the way he may operate," said Caleb, "Which being so, it is possible that he and I might find ourselves colleagues in the future if my ability to pass as a gentleman means I am used more in crimes of the gentry."

"I will not mind him as a colleague; he is clever as well as being apt to use his tongue wittily and not always kindly," said Jane.

Caleb looked at her with sudden fear in his eyes.

"Jane-girl – are you attracted to him, one who really *is* of the same class as yourself, not counterfeit-coin such as I?" he asked.

Jane got up and walked around the desk where they were sat, and wrapped her arms about his shoulders.

"Caleb Armitage, I like the Beau very well indeed. I love you; I adore you; and I want no other man to be my dear husband than you," she said. "What foolish maggot is this in your head?"

He looked sheepish, taking her hand and kissing each finger in turn.

"A maggot that always wonders how so wonderful a woman as you should choose such a man as I," he said.

"And I often wonder that so wonderful, astute, clever, and compassionate a man as yourself should come to have chosen a poor little dab of a woman such as I am," said Jane.

"Poor little dab? Never!" exclaimed Caleb. "It is true that when I first knew you, you were somewhat cowed and had been hurt, but I marvelled at the strength of your character that came through the trials I gradually learned had been yours to bear, to show the strong, determined woman that you are; and that you showed that my admiration was not repulsive to you, but that you found yourself drawn to me, as I to you, was the most wonderful thing that had ever happened to me!"

"Oh Caleb, don't you realise that it was your admiration that gave me the strength to learn who Jane Fairfax was, so that she might forget being Jane Churchill and walk with eager steps into the arms of the name Jane Armitage?" said Jane.

"Woman," said Caleb, "This is no suitable place to be having this kind of conversation."

"Then, Mr Armitage, I suggest we remove to a more suitable location" said Jane.

They proceeded to do so.

By the time the funeral cavalcade had returned, Caleb and Jane were ready to meet them in the salon. It was plain that there was something of an atmosphere of tension and disquiet between the mourners; and the servants who hastily brought drinks were plainly trying to stay least in sight and quite emanated disapproval. Both the Kemps and Flora were served as quickly as possible and with a manner as close to insolence as might be managed without being close enough to be called upon for bad behaviour.

"What happened?" Jane murmured to Nessie.

"Oh Jane, it was quite terrible!" declared Nessie. "First of all Mr Kemp made a scene because the other reverend gentleman – I didn't catch his name – had moved things in Mr Kemp's church, and he used the wrong words in the funeral service, or so Mr Kemp said. Something about him using an older prayer book that was a step too close to Popery. I didn't think it mattered much as long as Cousin Henry was buried properly and I told Mr Kemp that as Cousin Henry was now in Heaven he probably knew more theology than Mr Kemp or the other Reverend, and I thought Mr Kemp was going to have an apoplexy," she looked round quickly and whispered, "and despite being grieved for Cousin Henry, you know it was rather entertaining and *quite funny!*"

"Dear me, I can see that it must have been so," said Jane, picturing the scene. Mr Kemp was too volatile to make a very good pastor to a rural community; the concept of him objecting to any deviations from the 1662 book of common prayer was almost inevitable; and perhaps if this other pastor was using, for some reason known best to himself, the book of 1552, it might indeed be seen to be containing practices since abandoned by the Anglican church. Jane wondered idly whether Mr Kemp would have been more, or less incensed had the service been taken by a Wesleyan, and firmly told herself that to ask would be an unnecessary frivolity and unlikely to serve any useful purpose.

She sighed. It might have been entertaining.

"There is a lot of ill will in the air to be accounted for just by that nasty little man's outburst" she ventured to Nessie.

"Oh, it was not only his outburst that has caused such tensions," said Nessie, "nor even the Beau telling him that as soon as you and Mr Armitage permitted it, he might return to his manse to pack up, bag and baggage, and be out of the village within three days of leaving Amberfield Abbey!"

"He was warned," said Jane, "and can hardly complain after being so rude as to interrupt a funeral. Very well, Nessie, what did Flora do?"

"How did you know it was Flora?" asked Nessie.

"The fact that the servants are giving her as much of a cold shoulder as they might," said Jane. "I'm assuming that Mrs Kemp also made an exhibition of herself."

Nessie pulled a discreet grimace.

"Oh Cousin Hester had hysterics when Cousin Daventry told her husband he might go; she was plainly mourning the loss of the living far more deeply than she mourned poor Cousin Henry" said Nessie, with a touch of spite. "And then Flora started, wailing that they were profaning the memory of her darling Henry and in one breath accused the Kemps of being mercenary and in the next bemoaned that her dear Henry's last wishes regarding her own financial situation were not being adhered to. Daventry threatened to throw the lot of them in the horse trough," added Nessie, with evident regret that this had not come about.

"There is perhaps something to be said for the custom of not taking women to a funeral," sighed Jane, "for we, the weaker sex with regard to control over our emotions, may find it hard not to succumb to a fit of the vapours and hence perhaps, too, say those things which we might later wish had been left unsaid. However, I would myself hate to be excluded from a chance to say farewell."

"But then, dear Jane, nobody could ever accuse you of hysteria," said Nessie, "for indeed you are the most self-contained of people, and the mood you present is ever one of well-bred coolness."

"Thank you, Nessie; I do indeed attempt to present such a front," said Jane, "and has the Beau made any threat to Flora?"

Nessie shook her head.

"No; he was much overcome and I fancy was fighting unmanly tears himself for he commanded the vicar quite *harshly* to get on with it. I told Flora that if she did not bring herself to silence I would slap her," she added. "It seemed about the best thing to do."

Chapter 27

Flora had made sure to display her grief to everyone, and Jane wondered if it were second nature for an actress to make everyone else feel as though they were the audience.

"She reminds me of stories I have heard of that fellow 'Romeo' Coates'," Jane said, *soto voce* to Caleb.

"Even I've heard of the fellow – but he's rich enough to fund his over-acting and foolish antics on stage as I understand, and if he wants to make a fool of himself, I suppose it's his money to waste," said Caleb.

"I would object less if his wealth was not made on the backs of the poor slaves of his father's plantation," said Jane, "Though I fancy fair Flora would also be one who would care more for the opportunity to show her thespian histrionics than be remembered in the prayers of any she emancipated. I suppose one's own views cannot be visited upon others."

"No, but it does no harm to make people uncomfortable by mentioning them from time to time," said Caleb.

Jane brightened.

"That is true; like refusing to serve or drink coffee and making sure to only purchase sugar from any source but cane. Oh dear, I do wish Flora were less taken with the histrionic."

Flora had been told bluntly by Luke to stop making such a cake of herself when nobody wanted to listen, and shrieked and started tearing at her breast.

The Beau grabbed her wrists.

"That won't do, my girl; those clothes are borrowed and if you tear them, you'll pay to have them mended," he said grimly.

"Oh, I am sure I could make a neat mend, Cousin Daventry," said Nessie.

"I'm sure you can, Cousin Agnes; but why should

you have to do so?" demanded the Beau. "Don't you dare to make a fool of me to my friends when I have promised faithfully to care for their property, Flora; nobody believes that you're so filled with grief as all that, so stop this. I note you're not so upset as to tear at your face, for that would be an assault upon your own looks, not upon clothes that do not belong to you. I even wonder if you would so readily rend your own gowns. I suggest you take yourself to your room and adjust your attire," he added in disgust, for Flora's manipulations had revealed far more than was tasteful.

Flora flounced out with a bang of the door.

The Beau sighed.

"Armitage, will you be done with us soon?" he asked. "Whilst I hate to sound inhospitable, I will be most pleased when you are on your way, for it will signify that you have solved this sordid murder and taken away whoever it is who is a risk to the rest of us. And the likes of Flora and that ghastly vicar of Satan will be gone too," he glowered at Kemp.

"I believe that I have almost all the threads of this in my hands," said Caleb, quietly, "and once I can add one or two small pieces that are required to show motive, I will have a case to answer."

"Are you saying you know who it is? Armitage, you are as good as inviting this killer to make an attempt on you!" cried Daventry Popham.

Caleb smiled, enigmatically.

"Well if that occurs, assaulting an officer of Bow Street would be an added charge," he said, "and I would be making a very speedy arrest. However, I don't think anyone is going to try. I have my reasons for that supposition."

"You play a bold game," said the Beau. "I will like to have the chance to know you better when I am not one of your suspects; it's an uncomfortable position to be in."

Caleb smiled again.

"I imagine it must be, and quite a change to you," he said, "And perhaps as such a situation that may help you."

"You are what they call a peevy cove, Armitage," said the Beau, "and it will indeed give me some valuable insights – especially into how there is an overwhelming urge to prevaricate or lie, even when innocent. I can't say I'm enjoying the experience though," he added.

"I'm not sure that anyone does," said Caleb, dryly. "However I am fairly certain that tomorrow I shall be making an arrest."

"Moonshine," said Luke Popham, scornfully. "I don't believe you have the slightest idea; and if you ask me, you're only making such an intimation in the hopes that it will frighten someone into attacking you."

"Ah, an intimation for intimidation you mean, Mr Popham?" said Caleb. "You know, it's not a method I would despise to use were there no other means at my disposal. But I pray you, do take my intimation as you see fit!"

"I shall," said Luke.

"You have no manners, Luke," said the Beau.

"Excuse me, you say that I have no manners? I was not the one threatening to throw others into the horse trough – one at least of whom was a lady," said Luke.

"Neither female showed any signs of it," said the Beau, "and I wager the only reason you did not cause further disruption was because you could not think how."

"Is that what you think?" demanded Luke. His face took an ugly expression.

"I know you rarely pass up a chance to make trouble" said the Beau, his own face hard.

Jane thought they looked like a pair of tom cats waiting for an opportunity to scratch and bite. Caleb cleared his throat.

"Well, I for one am going to take advantage of the cold collation that I believe the servants laid out under dishes for luncheon for whenever you all returned," said Caleb, loudly, "since although there has been ample time to poison the dishes, I assure you that neither my wife nor I succumbed to the temptation."

"Oh very good, Armitage!" approved the Beau. "I quite concede your strength of mind, and your cleverness."

Daventry Popham forced himself back to his suave self and bowed his thanks to Caleb.

It took a little longer for the cutting comment to penetrate the understanding of the rest of the company, and the ensuing offended silence was broken by Nessie who gave a watery smile and said,

"Why, Mr Armitage, you are quite a wit; I fear we are not, as a family, really in the mood to *appreciate* it fully, but I assure you that I will eat without fear!"

Caleb bowed.

"Miss Fanshawe, nobody could possibly ever wish to poison you!" he said gallantly.

"I should think not!" said Mr Avery, taking Nessie's arm to lead her in to luncheon. "An ill timed jest, Mr Armitage."

"Do you really think so?" said Caleb. "I rather thought it diverted the Beau sufficiently that he and Mr Luke Popham were not about to be at daggers drawn; and in such a tense atmosphere it would not have surprised me had blades actually featured in further discussion."

Avery considered.

"I – yes, I suppose you are correct. Thank you, Mr Armitage."

"Mr Avery!" Luke spoke up as they ate. "The terms of the will deprive me of my inheritance if I get any dependant of my cousin's with child. What is the situation if I make an honest woman of the wench?"

Mr Avery looked startled.

"I – why I do not know. The terms of the will were

that you should not be found to have caused the pregnancy of any tenant or servant; but I suppose if you intended marriage…" he broke off.

"I didn't; but I'm happy to marry a complaisant wife if it gets me the funds," said Luke. "She can at least read and write and keep household accounts too I dare say; and she'd need less entertaining than some society wench."

"Ah, the very substance of a romantic novel!" said Jane, brightly. Luke glowered at her; he had learned enough about Jane to recognise that she was more likely to employ irony than to genuinely make such a fatuous comment.

"What if she won't have you, coz?" asked the Beau, with interest glinting maliciously in his eyes. "You never know; you might be tolerable enough for an *affaire* but she may feel that as a husband you would fail to measure up."

"She'd have nothing to complain of," said Luke. "I *need* that two thousand; I'm in debt. It was a debt of honour," he added. "I was going to borrow from Cousin Henry. I was nervous when he cast me those lowering looks at breakfast, which is why I wanted to talk to him and why I lurked at the window observing him with the fair Flora as Daventry dubs her. I was hoping to get over whatever problem had arisen – of course, as Sukey can write, I should have realised her father might do so too. She never seemed discontented with the arrangement that we had; he had to get greedy of course."

"Luke," said the Beau, "if you promise to maintain the child, I'll loan you the two thousand, or three thousand if need be. There's no need to make the poor girl miserable in being leg-shackled to you; you'd lead her a merry dance, I wager."

Luke regarded him curiously.

"Why?" he asked.

"Because you just spoke out from the heart without

sneering; and because it's a debt of honour; and because this miserable family has had enough of murder and I do not wish to see you kill the girl in a rage because she's not of your class. It really does not work, to marry out of your class, unless both partners are quite exceptional people and are prepared to compromise."

Jane shot the Beau a quizzical look. Did he know?

He met her eyes blandly.

"Well, I can't say that I would refuse, Daventry," said Luke. "I hate to be overwhelmed by your generosity though."

"Blame whoever has killed Uncle Henry for making it me that you have to be beholden to, not him," said the Beau, "and if that was you, well then, I'll settle the debt of honour for the sake of the family name in any case."

"I didn't kill him," said Luke, sulkily.

"Then Lionel Avery shall draw us up an agreement," said the Beau, "and as soon as the estate can forward the money it shall be yours to use. Make sure you do use it to pay that debt though," he added, a steely note in his voice.

"I shall," said Luke, "I'm not such a fool as to think I can recoup losses by playing more; oh very well, if you would have it, I was gulled! Taken for a flat!"

"It's a man who can admit it," said the Beau.

"Gambling is a sin and an abomination...." began Kemp.

Both Luke and the Beau turned to glare at him. Kemp subsided, and Jane hid an involuntary chuckle at how much the cousins looked alike with that moment of solidarity.

"Let us not get to a point of quarrelling in the same way as our cousins, Gabe," said Michael, suddenly, having also marked the similarity.

"We ain't so stupid," said Gabe simply, earning himself a hard stare from Luke and a chuckle from the Beau.

Caleb waited for the Beau as the company broke up.

"Have you been enquiring into my origins, Mr Popham?" he asked.

"No, Mr Armitage; though I might for my own satisfaction," said the Beau, "you are very nearly perfect. I presume you have not deceived your wife?"

"My wife knows all there is to know about me," said Caleb.

"I fancied that she would," said the Beau, "a shrewd lady. You make the very occasional slip with the accent and hesitate slightly with some social usage. A clever way that you misdirect without telling any lies; masterly. Frankly, I think you more a gentleman than many born to it and I admire the way you have done what fair Flora could not do in a whole lifetime."

"But then she was doing it for money; I did it for love" said Caleb, simply.

"I knew I liked you," said the Beau. "I do, you know; and I'll value your friendship when all this is past. Are you any closer?"

"Ask me tomorrow," said Caleb. "I have a theory that I am wishful to test out, but it means riding out to question a servant about certain mail sent out. And I am not wishful to make a long ride when it will be dark before my return; I was planning to go first thing in the morning."

"Then I wish you a good journey if you should leave before I am abroad," said the Beau.

Chapter 28

Luke, the Beau and Mr Avery took themselves into the library for a long and legal discussion involving money; Luke half sneering again, hating the idea of having to be grateful to his cousin, and knowing that he had little choice in the matter seemed half reluctant; the Beau looked happier about his relationship with his cousin than he had done since Jane and Caleb had arrived; and Mr Avery was distinctly disapproving that the Beau should be lending money to someone the solicitor plainly considered a wastrel.

Simmy and Henry appeared from somewhere in the grounds somewhat muddy and looking very pleased with themselves having applied to the Beau for permission to hunt. .

"Game pie for dinner," said Henry, happily. "I thought we might as well make ourselves scarce during the funeral so we took ourselves bread, beef and cheese and a couple of flagons of ale and went shooting. Bagged a brace of partridge, a heap of fat pigeons, and a rabbit that we thought was a grouse until it moved."

"Henry is that clever, he figured out a way to tie the fowling-piece in a kind of sling to help support it so I had enough strength in my arm to hold it and fire!" said Simmy, eagerly. "Them – those – exercises I've been doing meant I didn't need much help either!"

"Henry is a clever lad," said Caleb. "I hope he showed you how to clean and check the piece, and make sure there was nothing loaded in the second barrel?"

"I sorted him a single-barrelled fowling piece; less weight to it," said Henry, "though it's a lesson to learn, young Simon! Always make sure your piece is empty before putting it away, carelessness kills. And of course cleaning out the unburned powder and oiling your piece means it stays in tip-top condition."

"And one day I will be able to clean out and reload

for myself without feeling that I have not enough hands," said Simmy. "Henry had to help me. But Pa, he is an excellent shot, and he took down the partridges even though we were using five-shot because we were after pigeons!"

"Luck," said Henry, modestly, "that and the excellent Manton fowling pieces Mr Popham keeps in his gun-room."

"Strewth!" said Caleb, "I hope our killer doesn't go getting guns out to try to finish off the Beau!"

"Not a chance," said Henry, "Glossop holds the keys and I told him not to give them to anyone but one of our family until such time as the culprit is caught. He's quite happy to be vague about who might have them, which young Simmy suggested."

"Nice work, both of you," said Caleb. He cursed himself for having forgotten that a gentleman like Mr Henry Popham would certainly have a gun room. "Are all the guns locked away all the time?"

"Yes; Glossop said that Mr Popham was insistent upon that in case the Kemp twins took any without asking and managed to accidentally shoot each other or anyone else," said Henry. "Glossop says he wouldn't give the keys out to anyone without permission from the master; fortunately I'd had the foresight to ask the Beau yesterday and he had spoken to Glossop."

"I really cannot think that the one we suspect would consider using a sporting gun," said Jane, "it seems out of character."

Caleb considered.

"It is rather stretching credulity; you are right, Jane-girl. Nonetheless, I think I'll have a quiet word with Glossop."

He proceeded to find the butler and asked to view the guns and ascertain that to the knowledge of Glossop, as keeper of the keys, that all the guns were in place and that none were missing.

Glossop looked startled.

"It had not occurred to me to check them all as the keys were in my possession, and the other set in Mr Popham's desk," he said.

"Glossop, if someone did not hesitate to kill your master, do you think they would hesitate to break into his desk?" asked Caleb.

"Gawd!" said Glossop. "I mean, of course, that had not occurred to me, Mr Armitage. Perhaps you would be good enough, having checked the guns, to ascertain the presence of the keys and take them into your own keeping?"

"Just what I was about to suggest," said Caleb. "I have reason to believe that the killer would not use a firearm by choice, but as Mr Daventry Popham may still be in some danger, I'd rather not force anyone into that choice."

"You know who done it?" demanded Glossop.

"I've a shrewd idea," said Caleb, "and no, I ain't about to share that! I might be wrong – though I don't think I am, as my wife came to the same conclusion independently – but I want enough evidence to make sure our party doesn't cheat the hangman. Mr Popham was killed from a position of trust, and that poor man Perkins might have died, not to mention the Beau. I intend to take every effort to make sure the Beau is kept safe, and if anyone tries to kill him, well then, being caught red handed is one way of having enough evidence. Now you list the guns out loud, and I'll write them down and check as you reel them off," he added as they came to the gun room.

All the guns were in their proper places; none were missing, and Caleb signed the list he had made and gave it to Glossop to countersign.

The keys to the guns were discreetly tucked away in a drawer in the desk in the study; Caleb strongly suspected that the killer might not have even recognised what they were. Nevertheless he checked them minutely and stiffened.

"Sir?" said Glossop.

"I feel wax," said Caleb, "and that means that someone has taken a duplicate of this key. Which cabinet does it open?"

"That is the cabinet in which the Manton fowling pieces are kept," said Glossop. "The same ones your son and his tutor used."

"I see," Caleb frowned. "There has not been time for anyone to send to a locksmith to make a copy; very well, Glossop, I am taking charge of these keys. Please pass on to the servants, indoor and outdoor, that if any of them made a copy of these keys in order to do a little quiet poaching, I'm not interested in that so long as they might show that the copy has not been made recently. Indeed I will be contented to have you approach me and tell me that the matter is solved, no names needed."

"Yes, sir," said Glossop, "though I'll have a few things to say myself."

"Better for any man who has done this to receive your opprobrium and any discipline you enact than to risk transportation for poaching," said Caleb, dryly, "which crime frankly interests me not at all, though it's a betrayal of trust to your late master."

"That was my thought, too, sir" said Glossop. He bowed, and exited, ready to enact wrath if this impudence had been enacted by any of the servants. Caleb did not think that it was the servants; but he had his own ideas.

He returned to the salon, frowning, and was pleased to note that most people still huddled listlessly there. Flora, never one to be away from an audience for long, had returned, having changed out of the mourning gown she had been loaned into a gown of the most vivid deep purple, a nod perhaps to mourning had not the extravagance of the mix of dyes to achieve the colour and the sheen of the silken threads not contradicted any

such implied obsequy. A heavy gold cross on a chain declared
her to be playing the role of some martyred queen; and Caleb reflected that white muslin and an attempt to be Joan of Arc might have been a more sympathetic role than what seemed to him to be more a semblance of Ann Boleyn, or was it Katharine Parr, whichever of Henry VIII's queens had been found to be playing him false. He doubted she would have managed to be faithful to Henry Popham. However, that was neither here nor there, he told himself.

Caleb held up the keys.

"These are Henry Popham's keys to the cabinets in the gun room," he said, "and somebody has used wax to take a copy of one of them."

He looked about the faces to see if there was a guilty look.

There were two guilty looks.

"Michael; Gabriel. Perhaps you can explain this," said Caleb icily.

The boys sprang to their feet, and it occurred to Caleb that they were standing before him in the same attitudes as they might do when confronted by their headmaster for some wrongdoing.

"It was my idea, sir," said Michael.

"But I did it," said Gabriel. "It was before anyone killed Uncle Henry; it's why that candle guttered so horribly the other day, we took wax from it."

"We just wanted to go fowling, and Glossop wouldn't let us have the guns," said Michael.

"There's an ugly word for that, you know, Masters Kemp," said Caleb. "It's called stealing."

The boys went red.

"I – we hadn't thought of it like that," said Michael.

"Oh my boys, my angel boys, that you should be so tempted and fall!" cried Mrs Kemp. "Assuredly your father will have to beat you for this, I cannot intercede!"

"But mama, it's only taking our dues, like papa does

with the brandy!" said Gabriel. "You said that Uncle Henry owed us a good life because he is your brother!"

"Well, the sons of a thief can hardly expect to know any better, as is shown by that comment," said Caleb, "and I suggest you keep your tongue in your mouth, Mr Kemp, and your hands to yourself. *You* have taught these boys to steal; though they at least display some contrition" he added as the reverend spluttered. "Have you lads yet had a chance to visit a locksmith with the facsimile?" Caleb asked.

"No sir," said Gabriel.

"Then you should be grateful; any honest locksmith seeing a wax copy of a key would almost certainly turn you in to the nearest magistrate for fear of being accused of dishonesty himself," said Caleb. "Go and get it; and hand it into my care now, and never do anything so untrustworthy, underhanded and low ever again and I'll say no more about it."

"Yes sir," it was a dual comment.

"Are those little demons planning on shooting us all?" demanded Flora. "Are there GUNS kept in this house? Oh, I can't *BEAR* it, I must leave! I cannot sleep under the same roof as such horrid things as guns!"

"Stubble it," said Caleb, "and don't act like a ninnyhammer. Every gentleman keeps guns for shooting; where do you think the game you have eaten so happily has been coming from? These idiot boys are, I grant you, more likely to be a danger to each other than to innocent birds, but nobody is planning on shooting anyone."

"Please, sir, we are very sorry," said Michael, much chastened.

"We had not thought of it as underhanded and low," said Gabriel, shooting his father a look of dislike.

"Well now you do know," said Caleb. "Go get the wax."

Gabriel shot out of the room, leaving the door open; which enabled those in the salon to hear both his feet on the stairs, and from above a crash and a cry, and some rather muffled expletives in Simmy's voice.

Chapter 29

Caleb took the stairs two at a time, passing a stunned Gabriel who declared,

"It wasn't me, sir! I haven't done anything!"

"Well if you had any sense you might have done something to see what was wrong!" said Caleb acerbically as he passed the boy. Jane was hurrying behind as fast as she might up the stairs in heavy winter skirts.

The door to Beau Popham's bedroom was open and Simmy was sprawled. He rolled half over, revealing blood on his face.

"Keep back, Pa! there's a trip-rope!" he cried shrilly.

Caleb looked down hastily and knowing what he was looking for was able to discern a fine line of some black material. Carefully he stepped over it.

"Son, how badly are you hurt?" he asked in a terrible voice as he knelt down by the child.

"Not bad, Pa; I thought I was killed at first, but if I had been a full grown man, I would have been," he pointed up.

At a distance from the door approximately Simmy's height in length, and at the bottom of the bed, stood an ornate candlestick, a figure in bronze of some Greek character who was not immediately apparent to Caleb, holding a whole branch of candle holders and with a central spike. The spike was adorned with something dark and sticky, as was the side of one of the candle holders that might be presumed to be Simmy's blood. Caleb took out his handkerchief and wiped away the blood from his son's head. The wound was by way of being a scrape more than any deep, penetrating wound, and Caleb gave thanks. Had Simmy been much taller he might have lost an eye at least, if not his life. A man? a man would probably have taken the spike in his throat.

"The trip rope is made of silk," Jane was saying behind him. "Embroidery silk I would judge; a whole skein."

"What is this?" the Beau had followed quickly. "Why has that candle sconce been moved? It should be by the fireplace – Good G-d!" as he saw the blood on Simmy's head.

"Beau, have you, Luke and Avery been in the library all this time?" asked Caleb.

"Yes; Luke insisted on a proper agreement," said the Beau.

"You have been in my sight since all returned from the funeral. Unless this was set up before you left I think we might safely say that Luke is cleared of complicity," said Caleb, "I can't say that the evidence clears you Beau, no matter what I think, for it doesn't; as you might have set it up before leaving, as a trap you could avoid by falling sideways and still look to be in danger. I happen to think that you did not; but you understand I have to speak for the evidence."

"Oh, quite so," said the Beau. "An infernally clever plan; I saw Mrs Armitage removing a rope of some kind; one trips, unable to save oneself is impaled like a butterfly by one of those butterfly collectors like Sir Joseph Banks. I know there are those who consider my sartorial taste like unto the gaudy excess of a butterfly, but I consider this a rather harsh way of pointing it out! I am also angry since it would not be like to be me who was caught by this trap, but my man, who would come to await me and lay out fresh cravats for my necessary endeavours in dressing for dinner. Why is young Simon here?"

"I was wondering the same thing myself," said Caleb, "but I was more interested in who may have left the salon while I was investigating the gun room with Glossop," at which he scowled at Flora who was clinging to Nessie giving little cries of horror since the whole of the family had seen fit to come to see what the commotion was about.

"I believe everyone left for a shorter or longer period during that time," said Jane. "One had, after all, to make oneself comfortable. The twins did not leave, so far as I am aware, though I myself did pass through to the usual offices at one point. Boys of their age have less pressing needs than women, or older men."

"I wager it was a trick from those boys, like stealing the key," said Flora. "We know they're always playing tricks!"

"Well we didn't do this!" said Michael.

"And who's to say you aren't lying?" demanded Flora.

Michael went brick red.

"We do *not* lie when we are caught, even to stay out of trouble!" he said. "And no *LADY* would doubt a gentleman's word!"

"But it is unkind of a gentleman to point that out, Michael dear" said Nessie. "Why is Simmy in here?"

Simmy looked uncomfortable.

"I wanted to borrow the Beau's hair brush," he said.

"But my dear boy, why? Don't you have an adequate one of your own?" asked the Beau.

Simmy scrambled to his feet and glanced up at the Beau with half a grin.

"But mine was already in Michael's bed and I know you have a very prickly one and I wanted it for Mr Kemp's bed," he said.

"Well upon my word!" cried the Beau. "You small demon! And this wretched murdering creature has spoiled your fun; for now everyone knows to look out for hairbrushes in their beds!"

"Made in apple-pie wise," said Simmy. "I wasn't going to do yours, sir, because I like you. Henry told me that when he was at school, he and another boy did them for Henry's brother's class and never even got caught for they used the victims' own hair brushes, but Michael's brush is such a poor thing I used mine because Michael and Gabriel are fine enough really and I shouldn't mind them drubbing me for it, only I couldn't resist."

"Small monkey!" said Michael. "Gabe, we must look into the construction of these apple-pie beds and make it our last trick against all the masters!"

"Oh yes!" agreed Gabriel with fervent eagerness. "Why is it called apple-pie, small brat?" he asked Simmy.

"Well, Henry says it might be because the top sheet is folded back on itself after the fashion of country-style apple turnovers, or it might be from the French, *nappe pliée,* meaning folded sheet, mangled by schoolboys. Which seems a little far fetched to me."

"Jove, I'll say so!" agreed Gabriel, "even Flora could not mangle French that much!"

"Well I've spent more time on Latin than French," said Simmy. "All the French I know is soldier's French and not fit to repeat where there are people present, pa says, as I've picked it up from the ex soldiers who work for him sometimes."

"And it shocks me," said Caleb virtuously. "You'd better go and dismantle your beds, young shaver; Michael and Gabriel may help you to understand the mechanics of it, so long as I get that wax impression first."

Gabriel recalled why he was going to his room in the first instance, flushed, and dashed off. He returned soon with the wax impression of the key. Caleb glanced at it and laughed.

"Well, your instincts for larceny are fortunately poorly developed, you twins; a locksmith would be hard put to make a decent key from this. I am glad to see it."

"Will we learn how to do it properly if we enter Bow Street?" asked Michael. "You have given me, at least, an enthusiasm to try my hand at the business of catching real villains!"

"Lad, most of the work is thief taking and means

long, thankless hours on watch in sleet, rain, fog or broiling heat, or whatever other unpleasant weather the Good Lord sees fit to bestow upon the land, with a lot of danger and precious few thanks" said Caleb. "The pay, if you don't have independent means, is about the same as that of a
legal clerk; well enough, but don't expect Scott or Weston to make your coats, though if you can save up to have your boots by Hoby it's an investment. If you take care of your feet, your feet will take care of you, same as in the army."

"I don't care about the pay; I'm not exactly used to being wealthy," said Michael. "If I apply, will you put in a word for me, sir? how old should I be?"

"Michael, I think you should complete university if you can," said Caleb, "and perhaps the Beau will see you and Gabriel through university for the sake of the ties of blood."

"Only if they work hard and there are no stupid incidents; being rusticated isn't something I'd look on with favour, though I'd listen to their reasons," said the Beau. "Are you any closer to the killer?"

"I think we now have a silken strand to hang someone with," said Caleb, grimly.

"That's ridiculous" said Kemp. "Silken rope is only used to hang peers of the realm; nobody here has a title at all. You speak in riddles, Armitage as well as trying to persuade my son into a low profession like being a Bow Street Runner."

Caleb turned on him.

"Your son, sir, has conceived this idea without any prompting from me; and if you ask me, it is an admirable thing for a young man to wish to serve the rule of law rather than take after his tippling, hypocritical, canting thief of a father! You have ignored the wellbeing of your children in flouting the wishes of the chief mourner by making a poltroon of yourself at your brother-in-law's funeral and costing yourself a

cosy if not lucrative living; well, I would expect any thief to object to his offspring following the law, so I should not be surprised. I suggest that you might wish to say less and try at least to think more, before I consider taking you in charge if Mr Popham is wishful to press charges of theft; you were seen carrying
brandy a little before the attempt was made to poison Mr Popham, you know, but the Beau has had weightier things on his mind than your peculations! I like your sons or I'd say more; pray do not tempt me to lose my temper, sir!"

Kemp ground his teeth.

"Daventry knows that it was no theft, just a little thirst slaking whilst under his hospitality," he said.

"Actually, Kemp, I know nothing of the kind," said the Beau, "and if you continue to be annoying, I might well press charges. Your name isn't Popham, after all; so I shouldn't be dragging my name or Uncle Henry's name through the mud."

Kemp paled and subsided.

Somewhere downstairs the doorbell clanged mournfully, and several people jumped.

"Armitage, did I hear you right, that I'm cleared?" Luke came forward.

"Yes; you can't have set this contraption," said Caleb, "for the Beau's valet would have been tidying in this room until it was time to leave for the funeral, and there would have been no time to do it all."

Luke took his hand and shook it vigorously.

"I thought you were guessing in the dark and ready to make a scapegoat of me, because as things stand I am Daventry's heir," he said, "but you are using reasoning… I have been rude, I'm sorry. You were right," he clenched his teeth to make the announcement, "I was afraid. Afraid of being made scapegoat for something I had not done."

Caleb nodded.

"I understand," he said, "And accept a man's

apology. I've known a few subalterns behave less than perfectly when in a tight place, especially when falsely accused of something. That's actually why I joined Bow Street when I was invalided out; when I was in the army I helped my Major to uncover the truth in a couple of matters that showed how an innocent man may act in a guilty fashion out of fear – especially as one of the matters involved a lad being set up to take the blame by another."

Luke nodded.

"I'm glad you were able to help them too" he said. "I – I feel almost sick with relief."

"There, lad, it'll pass; go sit down and ring for a brandy" said Caleb.

The loud, common voice floated up the stairs as more of a grating interruption than the bell.

"Look here, my man, I'm here to see my friend, what's going to be lady of this here manor; Miss Flora d'Ambrose her official name is. I am Miss Esmeralda de Vere. JemiMAAAA!" the voice rose in a cry that had Nessie wincing and Luke murmuring to the Beau,

"With that voice nobody would need a yard of tin at a toll gate!"

"With that voice, you could open the next two gates," replied the Beau.

Flora had a look of frozen horror on her face.

"You had better see her, dear," said Nessie.

The voice raised again and Jane glanced involuntarily towards the windows in case they might shatter.

"JeMIIIIIMA!"

Chapter 30

Flora ran out towards the stairs.

"Esmeralda! This is neither the time nor the place!" she cried, her voice breaking away from the deliberately cultured tones to betray a London twang.

"Jemima, *darling!*" cried Miss de Vere, "The *funniest* thing; why you have sent to me the letter you should have sent to your betrothed, wouldn't it have been just *hilarious* if you had sent my letter to him? I just *had* to post over to see you to share the joke, and see this place you're going to be mistress of; my, isn't it *FINE!* So which one of these men are you going to marry? There's only one old one but he looks more like King Lear than Malvolio, you know!" she looked at Mr Avery, who spluttered at being called old.

"Oh Flora!" cried Nessie in sudden horror.

"And that is precisely what I surmised," said Caleb, "the last part of Miss de Vere's name –alda near the top of what was written. Flora d'Ambrose, also known as Jemima Harris, was in the habit, was she not, Miss de Vere, of writing to you about her scorn for an older man who made himself ridiculous over her, likening him to Malvolio?"

"Well, yes" said Miss de Vere, giggling. "Who are you?"

"You big mouthed FOOL!" screeched Flora, launching herself towards Miss de Vere, now half way up the stairs.

Caleb and Jane both leaped to grab the incandescently furious woman before she should manage to push her friend down the staircase; Flora was swearing now, ugly, dirty words that made Jane wince and Nessie cry out in horror at the few she understood. Even Jane did not know them all, though Frank in his cups had enlarged her vocabulary as had her association with some of the lower elements of society, Caleb

preferring to explain words rather than leave her to use them innocently if he gave
more innocuous euphemisms.

"You didn't burn all the letter, Flora" said Jane, crisply. "There was the puzzling reference to crossed garters, which only began to make sense when you first referred to Mr Henry Popham as 'Malvolio'; what you had written I do not know precisely but I am prepared to guess that you suggested to Miss de Vere that you would persuade him to hold a ball with fancy dress and would see him 'dressed in yellow stockings and cross-gartered' to prove how much you had him in thrall."

"You were distracted by something and forgot which letter was which and addressed them wrongly; and left them for your maid to post," said Caleb, "in which task she was dilatory. I can of course have that checked; I had been planning to ride to question her about letters she had posted first thing on the morrow. But now there is no need."

"What's going on?" Miss de Vere was indignant at being attacked and sworn at by Flora and taken aback by Caleb being handed manacles by the imperturbable Fowler who had materialised with them in his hand with as much aplomb as a gentleman's gentleman might show in passing his master such essentials as a quizzing glass, or his cane.

"I am an officer of Bow Street" said Caleb.

"No! I thought you was a gentleman!" said Miss de Vere.

"Mr Armitage is a gentleman, er, Miss de Vere" said the Beau. "Armitage, might we confine the fair Flora somewhere or gag her? She offends me" he added as Flora made a few more choice remarks.

"Did she kill Henry then? I don't see how you worked it out" said Mrs Kemp.

"I think we might repair to the Salon and I'll explain" said Caleb. "Fowler, rustle up a couple of sturdy females from amongst the servants to watch this

she-devil, would you? I'm going to lock her in her room until the morning.
Perhaps you can find a village woman prepared to travel with her as a chaperone when I take her in, too; I'm not about to have Mrs Armitage's ears sullied by the creature's vocabulary."

"Oh, Mr Armitage! Ought I to go with her?" asked Nessie.

"Miss Fanshawe, you have more than discharged your duty to Mr Popham!" said Caleb. "And your ears ought even less to be sullied by the little besom. Jane knew the sort of low company I have to associate with when she married me; and the criminals too," he added, winking at the Beau.

Daventry Popham gave a wry smile.

"Your point, Armitage," he said.

With the aid of Jane and a sturdy chambermaid, Flora was manhandled to her room and locked in. She proceeded to screech and hurl herself against the door until she fell into sobs behind it. Caleb had every faith in Fowler being able to handle the sensibilities of any chamber maid who was, he thought he understood her to say to Fowler, volunteering the services of her mother as a female companion on the morrow. Caleb withdrew to the salon where Nessie had ordered tea, a piece of thoughtfulness that earned her a swift smile from him.

"Very well," said Caleb, "here is the evidence. Henry Popham was much angered by a letter in the post. There were letters that might have annoyed him, but not perhaps to such a degree. He asked to have Flora sent to him. She quarrelled with him – which Luke Popham observed through the window. Luke saw Henry Popham banging his hand on some document – which he assumed, not unreasonably, to be some extortionate bill. He slipped away; thereby missing Flora's next action, killing his cousin. Whether she realised that the large ornate hilt of the stiletto would protect her largely from spattering blood is, I fancy, a moot point; I really do not think she was even thinking, just reacting to the threat."

"But what was the threat?" asked Mrs Kemp. "Why should she kill Henry?"

Caleb sighed.

"Flora wrote two letters. One to her betrothed, in doubtless dulcet tones, yes, Miss de Vere?" he asked.

"I don't know about no dulcet tones but she was billing and cooing," said Miss de Vere.

"Dulcet tones," said Caleb firmly, "Whilst also writing to her friend, ridiculing Henry Popham. Was she in the habit of this?" he asked Miss de Vere.

"Strewth, I'd say so!" said Miss de Vere. "I mean, when an old gager gets himself all of a pother over a young woman, who wouldn't?"

"My cousin Henry was forty two, and Flora, *alias* Jemima Harris, convicted and serving a term of imprisonment for lewdness and immorality, was thirty two," said the Beau, dryly, "so not exactly an old man lusting after a young girl, Miss de Vere. She wore very well, I grant you, but she saw her opportunity and took it. She was not a, er, Cyprian as such, since that convinced her that seeking a protector was a safer course of action than outright, er, sale of her assets"

"Thirty two? She told me she was twenty-two!" said Miss de Vere, shocked. "You are saying she killed him then?"

"That's why I'm here," said Caleb, with patience, "as a personal favour to one of Mr Popham's cousins, to uncover his murderer. As I was saying, I don't think she was considering much beyond preventing Mr Popham from dissolving the settlement he had already made on her and tearing up his will in her favour – she had failed to understand that it was not yet signed and therefore invalid."

"Flora is rather intemperate and hasty when crossed," said Nessie, "and she slaps servants for doing things in the way she didn't want them done. I quite believe that she might have grabbed up the page-separator and stabbed Cousin Henry almost without thinking, or rather in a rage beyond thought. And then when I saw her looking mussed, it was from the fury of her actions, not as I thought from behaving improperly!"

"Well if stabbing someone to death isn't behaving improperly I don't quite know what is," said Caleb, unable to resist the comment. "And then of course she realised she had blood on her sleeve and took her spencer off – which also added to the idea you had of her kissing Mr Popham immoderately – and bundled it up under her arm to bear away with her. She used the fact of her, er, regular indisposition to disguise the blood; and indeed, I have noticed that these things might make a woman behave with less moderation than otherwise."

"Flora is not noticeably more temperate outside of such times," said Nessie, dryly. "May we move on from such indelicate subjects?"

"By all means," said Caleb, thankfully. "I have to say I think it unpremeditated in any case; and her quote 'who'd have thought the old man to have so much blood in him' was made in genuine shock at the blood. But then it was too late, and she had to cover up her deed."

"We had looked at all those with stained sleeves and their reasons for being stained," said Jane, "and as Mr Kemp's scratch and the damage to Alcippe's hock might have been deliberately inflicted to disguise the blood, and the Beau's claret stain likewise, we could not discount them."

"I would never hurt a horse deliberately," said Luke.

"But we didn't know you so well then," said Caleb, "and you were not going out of your way to be helpful. Any more than was Mr Kemp who is quite the most unholy parson I have ever known, not discounting the odd naval chaplain, and a greater set of rogues unhung you have to go a long way to find."

Mr Kemp had fallen in on himself since the Beau's threat to have him arrested and murmured only, a little resentfully,

"You go too far, sir!"

Caleb ignored him and continued,

"Anyway, the will was a shock to Flora, and she plainly was most disconcerted and mourned her portion far more deeply than she mourned poor old Henry Popham. At the reading of the will, Beau, you made certain remarks to her that revealed that you knew more about her than she wanted to have known – as you have just revealed, that she has been in gaol – and so she decided to kill you. At first the motive for the attempt on you was unclear; gain is the usual reason for murder, but there are more ways to gain than to attain a legacy; in Flora's case it was to avoid losing the competence she had had settled on her as part of a prenuptial agreement. You might be content to leave matters as they were, but she decided not to risk that. Having killed once in the heat of the moment, she decided to kill cold bloodedly and in a planned fashion. Albeit not very efficiently" he added.

"But how did she manage it?" asked Nessie, bewildered.

"She spilled the flowers when you went out to change and then 'noticed' it," said Jane. "Taking the vase to the greenhouse she directed you to help her find matching flowers, and slipped into the gardener's work room. Up by the Georginas, with that noisy fountain, you would not hear her, and you cannot see the door either. She used the vase as the vessel in which she carried the poison; no wonder the flowers quickly wilted! They had no water, just the residue of poison. She placed it into the decanter when seemingly occupied arranging them. And then this most recent attempt was effected using embroidery silk; Flora has an embroidery basket, I am sure, but I do not think she is a very diligent needlewoman. We shall find a skein of black to be missing I am sure. I expect that she planned to watch the Beau go to his room, and remove the thread quickly and hope it would be judged an accident; in many ways Flora has exhibited throughout a most extraordinary degree of optimism in expecting her schemes to work."

"They almost did," said the Beau, dryly, "had not you and Mr Armitage been clever enough to put together all the clues of her choice of quotes, her behaviour and finally the evidence about the letter. You already knew it was she, though?"

"Oh! Yes," said Jane, "it could not have been anyone else. Nobody else had seen Mr Popham alive after she had been to see him, which passed everyone by as we at first assumed someone slipped in after her interview. And nobody else had the clear opportunity in the greenhouse. Once we had ascertained that the letter was likely something that annoyed Mr Popham enough to reverse his decision to marry her – we thought, erroneously, at first, that he had found a draft letter she had written, ridiculing him, or been sent something she had written by a well-wisher – then the motive became plain. Especially as she clearly anticipated a will in her favour."

"*Cui bono!*" said Simmy.

"Exactly," said Caleb. "Well, Popham, you'll be rid of us in the morning; perhaps you'll see that Miss de Vere gets safely back to town, I doubt she'd like to ride with Flora under the circumstances. And mind you don't disappear, young lady," he added severely, "you're a material witness, and I'm going to get an order to possess the letter you received too!"

"It ain't got nothing juicy in it," said Miss de Vere. "I won't disappear; catching a rich gager that she laughs at is one thing, I ain't going to be any accessory to murder. Do I have to appear in court?" she added, hopefully. "Being a witness would help me be more famous, wouldn't you think?"

"I'm sure it can be arranged," said Caleb, dryly. This silly creature's artless babble would probably convict Flora more readily than any amount of evidence. "You shall furnish me with your address."

"Ooh, I take it back, you *are* a gent, 'furnish me with your address' he says!" said Miss de Vere, making eyes at Caleb.

"On second thoughts, you can give it to my wife" said Caleb, hastily. Miss de Vere looked disappointed.

"I am happy to extend hospitality to Mrs Armitage and her offspring while you sort out the formalities in London, Armitage," said the Beau. Caleb gave him a grateful look.

"If you would do so, I would be most pleased," he said.

"Nessie and I will have a lot to talk about, I am sure," said Jane. "Gentlemen, ladies; let us decide not to dress for dinner for once. The social amenities have been somewhat usurped; and moreover, Miss de Vere has doubtless not brought suitable evening attire and we should be discourteous to her in dressing when perforce she may not. Shall we retire to the dining room?"

"Gawd!" said Miss de Vere. "If you ain't a real lady! Ooh, my friends will be that jealous that I dined with real ladies and gents!"

"Madam," said the Beau, offering her his arm, "permit me."

Jane smiled to herself; it was a pinnacle of success for the little actress to be treated like a lady, and drinking in the whole way the ladies and gentlemen behaved. How ironic to think that she might have learned the lesson better than Flora, however much better spoken Flora might be!

But it was possible to learn; and her dear Caleb had done so.

And as she was to be without him for several days, Jane had plans for him that night too, now that the concern of having a murderer about the house was over!

Manufactured by Amazon.ca
Bolton, ON